Little shook his head. "I know who you are. You're Camp Houston and I ain't about to draw against you." Then, as if to make sure there was no misunderstanding, he clasped his hands together behind his back.

Houston continued to stare into Little's eyes. "You pretended to be John Calloway's friend for years," he said, "then by God you shot him in the back for no more than the money he was carrying. I'm giving you the chance you never gave him, Little; I'm gonna count to three then I'm gonna start shooting."

Little stood with his hands clasped behind his back, even as the count began. True to his word, when Camp reached the count of three, he drew his Colt and put two slugs in Little's chest. Only then did the man unclasp his hands. He grunted loudly, then fell on his face at the side of the road.

HOUSTON

★

DOUG BOWMAN

A TOM DOHERTY ASSOCIATES BOOK
NEW YORK

This is a work of fiction. All of the characters and events portrayed in this novel are either fictitious or are used fictitiously.

HOUSTON

A Forge Book
Published by Tom Doherty Associates, Inc.
175 Fifth Avenue
New York, NY 10010

Forge® is a registered trademark of Tom Doherty Associates, Inc.

ISBN: 0-812-59029-5
Library of Congress Card Catalog Number: 97-29859

First edition: March 1998
First mass market edition: January 1999

Printed in the United States of America

0 9 8 7 6 5 4 3 2 1

To my sisters: Edna, Nell, Dot, and Jean. And to my tireless literary agent, Robbie Robison, who took me on in 1992 when I was about ready to give up.

HOUSTON

I

The traveler, dressed in blue denim and riding a big strawberry roan, halted at the spring. He looked around cautiously for a few moments, then stepped down from the saddle, intent upon watering himself and his horse.

"Stand right where you are, fellow!" a deep voice commanded from behind the green willow saplings. "You're covered with three shotguns!"

The traveler stood still for a moment, then slowly raised his hands above his head.

"Drop that gun belt slow and easy," the voice continued, "then take off that coat. Shirt and pants, too."

The man complied, then stood in his underwear awaiting the next order.

"Take that rifle out of the scabbard and lay it on the ground, along with your saddlebags and bedroll. Then take off the saddle and bridle, and give that horse a whack across the rump."

A short while later, the horse, minus its saddle, galloped off into the woods.

"Now," the voice commanded, even louder now, "start walkin' and don't look back."

Looking toward the saplings, the traveler finally spoke: "I suppose you could say that I'm a tenderfoot. Do you mind if I put my boots back on?"

"Guess you can. You've got a long walk ahead of you. Put 'em on, and be quick about it."

With his boots on, the traveler spoke to the willows again. "Which direction?"

"East," was the response. "And if you look back, you're dead."

Wearing nothing but his underwear, boots and Stetson, the traveler moved away from the spring in short order. He did not look back.

A considerable length of time elapsed before Tom Baker stepped from the willows to review his booty. He decided quickly that he had made a fair haul. The purse he found in the inside coat pocket contained two hundred dollars. He threw the coat aside and picked up the pants. He tinkered with a fob for a moment, then pulled the chain, extracting an expensive-looking watch from a small pocket just below the belt loops. He searched the pockets thoroughly, but found nothing else of value. He discarded the pants.

When he found that the saddlebags contained only a few hard biscuits, and the bundle tied behind the cantle consisted of nothing more than a bedroll and a change of clothing, he discarded them also. He picked up the gun belt and the Henry rifle and trotted back to the willows, where he mounted his swift bay and headed west.

Though mounted on a speedster, Baker rode along at an easy trot. He never pushed the animal unless crowded. A man had to take care of his horse.

Tom Baker had been a thief all of his life, but only recently had he turned to such serious crimes as the robbery he had pulled off just now. His third within the past six months.

A native Texan, and the only offspring of a poor dirt farmer and his sickly wife, Baker was now twenty-four years old, stood a little less than six feet tall, and weighed about one-ninety. He had brown hair and eyes, and a ruddy complexion. Quite ordinary in appearance.

He had never worked at any one job for more than a few weeks at a time, and had done most of his eating at his mother's house. The frail woman had died the year before, and since then Baker had been living on whatever he could steal. He was a fair hand with guns, long or short, and had often imagined himself the leader of a band of tough outlaws. A dozen men. That's how many it would take to pull off some of the jobs he had in mind. And the newspaper writers would no doubt begin to call the outfit "Baker's Dozen" right from the start. He smiled at the thought, and chuckled softly.

He patted the two hundred dollars in his pocket. Easy money. The whole job had taken less than two hours. A hundred dollars an hour. He patted the money again. He had spotted the well-dressed traveler in the town of Leatherwood that morning, and had noticed his purse when he paid for his breakfast. After determining the man's direction of travel, it had been a simple matter to outdistance him and lie in wait at the spring. The man would surely stop to water his horse.

Nor could the traveler ever identify him, for the man had not seen Baker's face. In fact, the man had seen nothing. Baker would sell the traveler's Peacemaker, rifle and watch to someone at least fifty miles away, and never hear a word about the robbery. He would hole up at his dead mother's cabin for a while, then begin to scout around for something bigger. Something really big. Big enough to require the help of a dozen men.

As he rode into the yard and stepped from the saddle, he laughed aloud and began talking to himself. "I'll have to remember that shotgun trick, 'cause that joker sure bought it. Big as he was, he wasn't wantin' no truck with three shotguns. I could have claimed to have twenty and he'd have believed it, 'cause he sure couldn't see nothin'. Yessir, I'll be usin' that shotgun trick again."

He loosed his horse in the flimsy corral, then returned to the cabin, where he hung the traveler's rifle and gun belt on the bedroom wall. Then he took a seat in a kitchen chair, where he sat for a while admiring the watch he had stolen. Its case was made of solid silver, he decided, with lots of fancy tooling, and the large Roman numerals on its face appeared to contain a sprinkling of gold. Baker began to talk to himself again. "Purtiest watch I ever saw," he said softly. "Prob'ly made over in Europe somewhere. I'll bet they don't give these things away, and I won't be givin' it away either. No, sir, whoever gits it is gonna pay a right smart for it." He finally laid the watch on the small table beside his bed, then set about building a fire in the stove.

Half an hour later, he sat at the table eating warmed-over rabbit stew. The fact that the stew was thin and watery bothered him not, for very soon he would be eating considerably higher on the hog. He had cash money now, and would have even more after he turned over the guns and the watch. He would ride down to Menardville tomorrow and see what the market would bear. Selling the guns would be easy, but he might have to ride all the way to Fort McKavett to dispose of the watch. Any officer at the fort would be proud to show off such a fancy timepiece, and they all had money.

Baker loitered away the remainder of the day around the cabin, then went to bed at dusk without ever lighting a lamp. He slept soundly throughout the night, for he was a man without conscience.

He was on his feet at daybreak, eager to begin his busy day. He buckled on his gun belt, then stopped in the kitchen to eat a few bites of the leftover stew. He ate sparingly, for he intended to order up a large T-bone steak when he reached

Menardville. He dumped the remainder of the stew in the yard, then filled the pot with water. No more rabbit stew for him this week.

He took a few steps toward the barn, then changed his mind. He must make a trip to the outhouse first. He changed directions in midstride, taking the trail that led to the dilapidated, one-hole affair. The door squeaked on rusty hinges as he opened it and stepped inside. He hung his gun belt on a large nail that he had long ago driven into the wall for that purpose, then dropped his pants and began to make himself comfortable.

He had scarcely taken his seat when the door squeaked again, and he found himself staring into the business end of a .41-caliber, double-barreled derringer. Behind the deadly little weapon stood the traveler Baker had robbed at the spring. The man held the gun about twenty inches from Baker's nose. "Good morning," he said, smiling.

All color drained from Baker's face instantly. "Whatcha think you're doin', fellow? Whatcha—"

Baker never finished the question, for the traveler had squeezed the trigger. "Just wanted to hear that voice one more time," he said, as Baker's eyes turned to glass and his lifeless body slumped against the wall, "to make sure I had the right man." The traveler retrieved his purse from Baker's pocket and saw that his money was still intact. He stepped outside, and when he removed his hand, the rusty hinges squeaked again as the door closed on its own. Then he dropped the little Remington into his pocket, just standing there for a moment.

Baker's career as a holdup man had been short-lived, for yesterday, he had waylaid the wrong man. Of all the men in Texas that he could have chosen to rob, he had picked Camp Houston, a man who was feared, or at least respected, by every gunman in the West.

Houston had originally come from Arkansas, and had been in Texas off and on for the past ten years. He had been involved in three cattle drives from Texas to Kansas, and had walked the streets of Abilene, Ellsworth and Dodge City. He had been as far north as Montana Territory, and west to California, and had forgotten none of the things he had learned during his travels.

He had been raised on a farm a few miles west of Little Rock, the only child born to John and Rebecca Houston. He had been given the somewhat unusual first name "Campbell" because it had been his mother's maiden name. The name was shortened to "Camp" before the boy was knee-high.

Aside from the horses and cattle that were produced on the John Houston farm, hogs and chickens were sometimes butchered and, along with garden truck, peddled on the streets of Little Rock. Consequently, during his growing years young Camp learned not only how to farm and raise livestock, but how to market his merchandise as well.

Camp's had been a happy childhood, and he had already been about grown when his parents had their final argument. His mother moved out of the house the year he was fifteen, and remarried a year later. His father remarried a few months after Camp's seventeenth birthday. That was the day the youngster decided to leave Arkansas for good. He had no ill feeling toward his father's new wife; he simply believed that at six foot three and a hundred ninety-five pounds, he was big enough to be on his own. The very next day, carrying a thousand-dollar stake provided by his father, he loaded a pack mule, then caught up the best saddle horse on the premises. He shook his father's hand, then hugged his new stepmother, who was only six years older than he. Then he picked up the mule's lead rope and threw a leg over the big bay saddler. A few minutes later, he was out of sight. That had been ten years ago, and Camp had not been back to Arkansas since.

He found work on a ranch near Waco right away, and stayed there all summer. When the winter layoffs began, he was the first man to go. He had saved his money, however, and could very easily survive the winter without a job. Which is exactly what he did.

He took a job on a ranch near El Paso the following spring, worked till after the fall roundup, then drew his pay and headed north. It became his custom over the next few years to work hard and save his money through the spring and summer months, then loaf and travel all winter. It was a simple, uncomplicated life to which Camp Houston adapted quite easily, for he loved traveling and learning new things.

His life suddenly took a different turn shortly after his twenty-second birthday. That was the year he killed his first man. The shooting took place in the town of Brownsville, when a local gunslinger named Lew Thompson accused Houston of attempting to romance a saloon woman that Thompson considered his own. Houston's claim that he had never even met the woman went unheard as Thompson slapped him across the mouth and challenged him to a gunfight in the street.

One thing Camp Houston had never been short on was guts. He accepted the challenge immediately. He had practiced with his Colt for years, and was an expert marksman. And though he had never fired a shot at another human, he felt that he was fast enough to defend himself against any man. He was confident as he stepped out on the street to face the gunman.

There was no waiting around and no arguing. Nor did Houston wait for the gunslinger to call the draw. He simply drew his Colt and shot Thompson between the eyes. Thompson got off a shot as he fell, which went through his own foot.

The Cameron County sheriff arrested Houston within the hour, and kept him in jail overnight. He released Camp next morning, however, because one citizen after another, and sometimes several men at a time, came to his office complaining that young Houston was guilty of nothing more than executing his God-given right to defend himself; that he had been slapped and falsely accused, then challenged to a gun-fight. The saloon woman herself had provided the clinching testimony, saying that she had indeed never met Houston.

"Half the people in town are raising hell about me locking you up," the sheriff said as he unlocked the cell door. "Guess you ain't gonna be needing that lawyer you mentioned, 'cause there ain't gonna be no charges." He walked the few steps up the hall to his office, and Camp followed.

"Here's your hardware," the lawman said, handing over Houston's gun belt. "If I were you I'd damn sure strap it on, 'cause I've got a feeling you're gonna be needing it pretty often. Lew Thompson was known as a fast gun, and his rep-utation's on your back now." As Camp buckled on the gun belt, the sheriff stood by rolling a cigarette. He gave it a final twist, then touched it with a burning match. He blew a cloud of smoke, then began to nod very slowly. He pointed to the Colt on Camp's hip. "They'll be coming," he said. "You mark my words: they'll be coming."

The sheriff's prediction had been correct: they came. For the next three years they came on a regular basis, some a few years older than he, most younger. Would-be gunslingers had sought a reputation elsewhere of late, however. It had been two years now since anybody had insisted on testing Camp's hand, most likely because the word had gotten around that there were no survivors.

Now, standing outside Tom Baker's outhouse, Camp Houston opened the door again and took the dead man's Colt. Then he moved cautiously toward the cabin. After deciding that no one else was on the premises, he walked to the bed-room, where he immediately spotted his guns hanging on the wall. He dropped Baker's gun on the bed, checked the loads in his own Peacemaker, then strapped the gun belt around his middle.

He took his Henry off the wall and checked to see that it was still loaded. When he spotted his watch lying on the bed-side table, he picked it up and checked the time. Eight o'clock.

He returned it to his watch pocket and reattached the chain to his belt loop. He had bought the watch from a Mexican last year. Though the fancy workmanship was enough to make an unknowing person think it cost a lot of money, it was actually quite inexpensive. It had been made in Mexico, and sold new for about five dollars. Camp had bought it for a dollar, and it had proved to be a good conversation piece and a dependable timepiece as well.

He stepped into the yard, then walked to the barn. He opened the corral gate, freeing Baker's horse, then walked at a fast clip to the other side of the hill, where his own saddler was tied to a sapling. He shoved his rifle in the boot, then mounted and headed back to the spring at a canter. The big roan covered the distance in less than two hours.

As the animal drank from the spring's runoff, Camp sat in the saddle rethinking yesterday's event and shaking his head. The holdup man had not been very smart. When ordered to leave the spring in his underwear, Camp had walked no more than three hundred yards, then watched from concealment as the robber searched and discarded Houston's belongings and then rode away on a good-looking bay.

When Camp walked back to the spring and saw that the robber had taken only the money, the watch and the guns, he put on his clothes, picked up the bridle and began to track his horse. He had walked only about a mile when he came on the animal in a small meadow, munching grass. Catching the roan was easy, for he would stand if a man talked to him softly and approached slowly.

Mounting bareback, Houston rode back to the spring. He saddled the roan, retied his bundle behind the cantle, then remounted.

Having tender feet had not been Camp's only reason for asking the thief for permission to put on his boots, for high inside the leg of the left boot, in a special pocket sewn by an Austin bootmaker, rode the little Remington derringer. Camp had removed the weapon from his boot as soon as he reached the woods, and carried it in his hand. All the while, he was hoping that the robber did not decide to follow him, for the accurate shooting range of the little double-barrel was woefully short.

As he took up the trail, Camp could plainly see the bay's tracks, for the ground was soft here close to the spring. He rechecked the loads in the derringer, and shoved it into his pocket. Ever mindful of the fact that he could very easily be riding into an ambush, he continued west at a slow walk, one eye tracking the horse, the other on the terrain ahead.

He lost the trail more than once during the afternoon. At those times, he simply made a guess as to which way the rider would go. Each guess turned out to be correct, for he was soon reading the tracks again.

The day was almost over when he topped the hill above the run-down homestead. He dismounted and tied the roan, then crept as close to the cabin as he dared. He watched the place from behind a clump of bushes till full dark, but saw nothing resembling a human. Nevertheless, he believed that his man was in that cabin, and, even though the light of day was fading fast, he thought he recognized the bay in the corral.

He retraced his footsteps to the top of the hill, then led the roan partway down the other side. He picketed the animal on the best grass he could find in the dark, then made himself a bed under a bush. He would be back on the other side of the hill at first light, hoping the element of surprise might allow him to get the drop on the thief.

He was hidden in Baker's barn at dawn, with his eyes glued to the cabin door. The excellent condition of the bay told Camp that the animal had been eating grain on a regular basis, probably twice a day. In the West, even the lowest class of man was likely to take good care of his horse, for the animal was his only means of transportation. The man in the cabin would be no exception. When he awoke this morning, he would come to feed the bay. And Camp Houston would be waiting.

Half an hour later, Baker walked from the cabin, a gun belt buckled around his waist. Houston stood watching as the man walked a few steps toward the barn, then spun on his heel and headed for the outhouse. Camp was pleased, for he believed that the man would be completely unprepared for company. As soon as the man was inside and the door closed, Houston made his move. A few moments later, he jerked the door open, the little Remington in his fist.

Now, after watering the roan and slaking his own thirst, Houston remounted, and cast his eyes to the southwest. Those eyes were gray, and his hair was light brown. His complexion was dark, somewhat like well-oiled leather. He was a big man, standing six-foot-four in his socks, and his weight varied between two-twenty and two hundred thirty pounds. Square-jawed and thick-chested, he was broad at the shoulder and narrow at the hip, and a physical specimen that few women could resist giving a second look. He was at least as powerful as he looked, and more than a little handy with all kinds of weapons. Many men who had seen him draw claimed that he was the fastest gun Texas had ever known.

Houston was aware of the fact that many men would scorn the act of shooting a man off a toilet seat. He himself believed that it mattered little what a man was doing when he died. Camp had already made up his mind to kill the robber, so the man would have been just as dead even if he'd been someplace other than the outhouse. If the thief had had a gun in his hand, he would have died at precisely the same time. The no-good bastard had called the tune . . . and had paid the fiddler.

Houston rode away from the spring at a fast pace, for he was very hungry. He intended to order up a large T-bone steak when he reached Menardville.

2

Sixty-year-old George Angleton was the owner of the Rocking A, a five-section ranch in eastern Menard County. He had started the ranch a few years earlier when he inherited the land, along with eighty head of longhorns, from his father-in-law. Though small, by Texas standards, the ranch was situated in prime cattle country. Perennial grasses were abundant, with plenty of shade and a water supply that included the San Saba River. Indeed, everything a longhorn needed in order to thrive was usually right under its nose.

Though otherwise in seemingly good health, Angleton sometimes suffered from a back ailment that hindered his actions considerably and on more than one occasion had confined him to bed. He never knew what originally brought on the condition, or why he could sometimes go for months without suffering. At times, he could stack hay with the best of them. Then sometimes all he could do was sit on the porch and watch, for working or riding a horse was out of the question.

He knew little about the cattle business when he inherited the ranch, for he had been a carpenter. He hired two men almost as old as he was to manage the cattle, then proceeded to put his own vocation to good use. Within the first year, he built a two-story house, a large barn, two corrals and, though small, the most elegant bunkhouse in the county.

Angleton and his wife, Bama, had raised three daughters. All had married and left Texas at the first opportunity. The youngest had left for Louisiana the same year her parents moved to the ranch. Bama Angleton had been overjoyed with the move, for she was a lifelong student of nature. The new way of life also meant that her husband would sleep in his own bed at night, instead of sometimes being off working on a building project a hundred miles from home.

She wasted no time putting in a large garden, and filled enough jars during the summer to make sure that everyone on the premises had green vegetables throughout the winter. Five years younger than her husband, the small, gray-haired lady was full of life, and loved by all who knew her.

The Rocking A cattle had been allowed to reproduce unmolested for more than four years now, and the herd was not so small these days. In fact, Angleton had contributed five hundred head to a community trail drive to Kansas the year before. John Calloway, a drover from San Antonio who was reputed to be among the best, had bossed the drive.

Calloway had delivered two thousand head of longhorns to a buyer in Dodge City, and was paid for the herd in cash. He paid off each of his trail hands in the same fashion. Then, being a serious man, and somewhat religious, he found himself a room at a boardinghouse, declining all invitations to join in the partying and hell-raising that had come to be expected of cowboys whose pockets jingled with newly acquired coin.

Next morning at sunup, accompanied by Bill Fisher and Joe Plenty, Calloway headed for Texas. Once there, he would deliver the money to the three men who owned the herd, each

rancher's percentage of the poke being dictated by the number
of cattle he had contributed to make up the drive.

John Calloway never reached Texas. The second day out,
he and his two companions made camp at a small stream two
hours before sunset. They had scarcely brought their coffee to
a boil when five men rode into their camp. None of the
campers was alarmed, however, for the riders were all well
known to them: the very same men who had helped deliver the
herd to Dodge City.

It was over in less than a minute. The riders dismounted;
then, at some kind of prearranged signal, every man drew his
gun and started shooting. Each of the campers was shot more
than once, for the idea, of course, was to leave no witnesses.
A few minutes later, after taking the money for the herd and
robbing the pockets of the drovers, the renegades remounted
and left the area.

All of these details were known because, although he had
been shot four times and left for dead, and later lost both an
arm and a leg to a surgeon's saw, Joe Plenty had survived.
More dead than alive, he had been found by some trail hands
two days after the carnage occurred. With the cook playing
the role of nursemaid, Plenty was hauled back to Dodge City
in the chuck wagon and turned over to a young doctor.

Minus the limbs that had been shattered by gunfire, Plenty
was quickly on the mend. He was back in Austin three months
later, telling the story to all who would listen, including a few
seemingly disinterested lawmen.

Camp Houston listened to the story attentively and ab-
sorbed every detail, for John Calloway had been a personal
friend. Houston also had a soft spot in his heart for George
Angleton. Holding down the job of ranch foreman, Camp
had once lived on the Rocking A, and had come to love
George and Bama Angleton like family.

He had visited the couple two weeks earlier, and stayed on
the ranch for three days. That was when he informed them
that he had waited as long as he intended to for action by

U.S. marshals, that he himself was about to take up the trail of the men who had slaughtered and robbed the trail hands.

Angleton sat staring between his knees for a while, then nodded. "I guess you'll be needing some traveling money, then."

"No, no," Camp said quickly. "At least, not yet." He was on his feet now, looking toward the corral. He shook the skinny, gray-haired man's rough hand, then hugged the lady of the house.

"You need something, Camp, you just holler," Bama said, squeezing his arm as tightly as she could. "We've got a little money. We can help."

Ten minutes later, the Angletons stood on the porch waving as Houston rode down the hill. He stood in his stirrups with his hat in his hand for a moment, then he was out of sight.

He was in Austin four days later, where he spent several hours talking with Joe Plenty. The gaunt, hollow-eyed skeleton of a man presented a pitiful picture. His voice was clear and easily understood, however, and he seemed to be in complete control of his mind. He described the incident thoroughly, and supplied the name and description of every man involved.

"I was looking right at Walt Turner," Plenty said with a growl, his hatred for the man obvious. "Looking right at the sonofabitch when he started pumping lead into us. Then all of them were shooting; must have fired at least twenty rounds. We didn't have no chance to fight back, 'cause they caught us off guard. We didn't have no reason to expect trouble from them. Hell, we knew every one of them; been working with them for months. Looked to me like Walt Turner was the head honcho. At least he was the first one to draw a gun. His first shot hit me in the chest. Went clear through me without hitting any vital organs, is what the doc said. Otherwise, I guess I wouldn't be here, huh?"

"Guess not," Houston agreed.

When Camp asked if there was something that he could do to make life a little more enjoyable for the man, Plenty shook his head. "Don't need anything," he said. "Mama keeps me fed good, and I quit smoking cigarettes on the very first day that I didn't have two hands to roll one."

When he left Austin, Camp not only had the names and descriptions of all five of the killers, he had some information that might prove to be much more valuable: somewhere in San Antonio, where the trail drive had originated, there was a picture.

"Bill Fisher was the one who found the photographer," Plenty had said. "Hired him to take a picture of the whole crew. Bill wanted it to put in a scrapbook. We all got together and posed for it, looking silly with our guns out and all. Even Mr. Calloway was there, but he didn't take his gun out, like the rest of us. The photographer told Bill he could pick up the picture at the end of the week, but Bill said he wasn't going to be there, that he'd come by for it after the drive was over. Of course, Bill never made it back."

"Do you think the photographer would still have the picture?" Camp asked, getting to his feet.

"Don't see why not," Plenty answered. "I can't think of anybody else that would buy it, and besides, I think fellows like him keep copies of all their work."

"Do you remember exactly where his business is located in San Antonio?"

Plenty shook his head. "Never did know. He came to the livery stable to take the picture, wanted the stable and the corral to be showing in the background. Don't reckon I ever heard his name called, so I wouldn't know it either."

Camp stood thinking for a while. "Several livery stables in San Antonio," he said finally. "Do you remember which one it was?"

"Sure don't, 'cause I don't know the town. Never been there but that one time. I do know that the stable's on the west side, though. We stayed at a little hotel close by, and rode out of town early next morning."

Now, in the town of Menardville, Camp sat at a table for a long time after finishing his meal. Drinking one cup of coffee after another, he was busy reliving the events of the past two weeks and making plans for the immediate future. His decision to get on the trail of the killers and stay there till he had located every last man was final: cut and dried.

Sid Blankenship, the local liveryman, after hearing of Camp's decision to take up the hunt, had offered the loan of a packhorse and anything else that was needed. Today, Houston would inform Blankenship that he was accepting the offer, after which he would take a room at the Menardville Hotel. Then, after resting himself and his roan for two days, he would head southeast. If the picture of the trail hands was in San Antonio, he intended to find it.

3

Two days later, astride the big roan and leading a ten-year-old black gelding, Houston rode out of Menardville. The pack animal carried everything Camp would need for the trail, including two small sacks of grain for the horses and a one-man sleeping tent that he would probably never use. Today he was headed for San Antonio, which was, unless a man pushed his animals, a four-day ride. Being a man who seldom rode his horse more than thirty miles in one day, Houston would be taking his time. There was no hurry; the killers would keep.

He crossed the San Saba at a rocky ford where the water was less than a foot deep. Then, heading the roan in a southeasterly direction, he spent the day riding steadily, never once pushing the animal past a walking gait.

An hour before sunset, and a few miles after crossing the Mason County line, he halted at the Llano River. He stripped the saddle from the roan, and the pack from the black, then watered and picketed both animals. Neither would receive a portion of grain tonight, for green grass was plentiful. The grain would be saved for hard times, when no grass of any kind was available.

He found deadwood easily enough, and soon had a fire going. He moved out from under the big oak tree, and pitched his bedroll where there was nothing but clear sky overhead. He had long ago learned about camping under trees. Birds roosted in trees and shit all over everything underneath.

When his coffeepot came to a boil, he removed it from the fire and placed his skillet on the bed of gray coals. He dropped several slices of German sausage into it, then added two biscuits. As the bread and meat slowly heated, he sat peeling two of the hard-boiled eggs he had bought from the hotel cook. He was soon enjoying a good meal, after which he extinguished the fire and crawled into his bedroll. He lay there in the darkness for a long time, thinking.

He had not the slightest intention of giving up the hunt until he had found all five of the killers. Nor did he intend to bring the law into the picture. The law had already had more than enough time to make some headway. Even now they were claiming a jurisdiction problem, saying they had been unable to establish whether the crime had been committed in Kansas or in Indian Territory. "The lawmen are lying through their teeth," Joe Plenty had said. "I told every damn one of them exactly where it took place. Told them every creek, bush and rock in the vicinity. They know damn well it happened in Kansas. They just don't give a shit. You can just forget the U.S. marshals and the Kansas lawmen, too. Ain't none of them gonna do a damn thing. Just plain scared, is what they are."

Though Camp agreed with Joe Plenty to a certain extent, he also knew that the description did not fit all lawmen. He personally knew one sheriff who was not afraid of the devil himself. The man hounded criminals day and night, and had more than a few times laid his life on the line against the rowdy element.

Camp believed that it was men such as that particular

sheriff, whose jurisdiction was limited to one county, who should be U.S. marshals, with unlimited jurisdiction. Appointments to those positions were usually political, however, and rarely based on merit.

Though he had no desire to be a lawman, and had declined several opportunities to wear a badge in the past, Camp would be on the trail of the killers just as soon as he could find a starting place, and follow it to the last man. Nor would he turn any of them over to the law. Awaiting them all was the same fate that had befallen the unsuspecting trail hands in a Kansas gully.

Three days later, Houston rode into San Antonio from the west. He stopped at the first livery stable he came to and questioned the owner, who introduced himself as Ralph Hicks. Camp had not expected it to be so easy. "Yeah," Hicks said, getting to his feet and nodding several times. "I remember 'em takin' that picture. Must've been somewhere around June of last year, 'cause I remember it was hotter'n hell."

Camp seated himself in the chair he was offered, then continued. "The reason I'm asking questions, Mr. Hicks, is that I'm looking for the man who took that picture. I was hoping you could help me."

Hicks was a beefy, red-faced man, who appeared to be about fifty years old. He wiped sweat from his brow with his sleeve, then spat a mouthful of tobacco juice through the open doorway. "Could be," he said, wiping his mouth on the same sleeve. "His name is O'Malley or O'Bannon or sump'm like that. Hell, he wouldn't let me forget him. He was down here earlier this year tryin' to get me to pay for that picture. I told him I didn't order no damn picture, that he'd hafta take the matter up with the trail hands." He dropped his eyes to the floor and began to speak more softly. "I hear that some of them didn't make it back from the drive."

"You heard right, Mr. Hicks." Camp told the liveryman the whole story.

"You don't mean to tell me!" Hicks said, his voice now reverberating around the small office. "You're tellin' me that the same men who helped Calloway take the herd to the rails were the ones who killed and robbed him on the way back?"

"Exactly."

"Well, I'll be damned! Hell, I knew one of 'em, old Red Bentley, from down around Corpus Christi. Sure wouldna never thought he'd be in on sump'm like that, though."

"Neither did the trail hands," Camp said, shaking his head. He paused for a few moments, then continued. "A man named Joe Plenty was the only survivor, and I've had a long talk with him. He named Red Bentley as one of the men who did the shooting. I have the name and description of every man involved, Mr. Hicks, but I'd sure like to get my hands on that picture."

"You aim to go huntin' 'em up?"

Houston nodded.

"Well, I see that little fellow who took the picture around town pretty often." The liveryman walked to the front of the building, and Camp followed. Hicks pointed north. "He operates out of a little hole in the wall beside Berry's Restaurant, three blocks from here."

Camp nodded. "I appreciate the information, sir." He walked to the hitching rail and untied his horses, then led them forward, handing the reins to Hicks. "I'll be leaving them with you for a while, if you don't mind."

"Mind?" the hostler asked, smiling. "It's the way I make my living, young fellow." He led the animals down the wide hall toward the stables.

Houston began to walk north at a fast clip, his saddlebags across his shoulder. He found the "hole in the wall" easily enough, and quickly decided that the liveryman had aptly described the photographer's headquarters. The building was about ten feet wide, and probably no more than twice as deep. A weathered sign over the front door read simply, PHOTOGRAPHY, then went on to inform one and all that Abner Overton was the proprietor.

A bell attached to the top of the door announced Camp's arrival when he stepped inside. Then, climbing over or around one obstacle after another, a small man made his way to the front of the cluttered building. He stepped behind the counter. "Hello," he said in a high-pitched voice. "My name is Ab Overton. May I help you?"

"I hope so," Camp said, introducing himself and offering a handshake. Overton grasped the hand and pumped it a few times as Houston continued to talk. "I'm here to talk about a job you did nearly a year ago. Do you remember taking a picture of some trail hands down at Ralph Hicks's livery stable?"

"Of course, I remember it. I never took but one picture down there. A man named Bill Fisher talked me into doing it, but he didn't tell me till later that he wasn't going to be around to pay for it. Finally told me that he was going on a trail drive, that he'd pick it up when he got back. Well, I'm still waiting."

"Do you still have the picture?"

"Of course. I never discard my work. I tried to sell it to the newspapers back when they were all printing stories about the trail drives, but none of the editors was interested." He paused for a moment, then asked, "Just what is your interest in the picture, Mr. Houston?"

"John Calloway was the trail boss, and he was my friend. He's dead now, and I'd like to have a picture of him. Bill Fisher won't ever be coming back to pay you anyway, for he's dead, too. They died together, killed and robbed by outlaws."

In an honest show of emotion, all color drained from the little man's face, and he looked as if he might cry. "Oh, my Lord," he said, his voice sounding almost feminine. "Couldn't the outlaws have robbed them without killing them?"

Houston shook his head emphatically. "No. Not men like John Calloway."

Overton said nothing else, just went about the room looking on shelves and pulling out drawers. After several minutes, he laid the picture on the counter.

Camp spotted John Calloway immediately, and the man

beside him bore a striking resemblance to what was left of Joe Plenty. The picture was of very good quality, and Houston stared at it for a long time. Every feature was so clear that it seemed as if his old friend should be able to speak.

"I'll say one thing for you," Camp said, reaching into his pocket. "You certainly know how to take a picture." He had his purse in his hand now. "I'll be happy to pay whatever you think it's worth."

Overton dropped his eyes to the counter. "Don't know," he said slowly. "Don't guess I ought to charge anything, since the trail hands had such bad luck. Seems sort of like taking money from the dead."

Houston spoke quickly: "Those men being dead has nothing to do with the fact that you should be paid for your work, Mr. Overton. Besides, it's my money you'll be taking; I'm alive."

The little man smiled. "Guess you've got something there," he said. "I believe I told Mr. Fisher that it would cost a dollar. Does that sound reasonable?"

"Absolutely." Camp laid the money on the counter, then turned to leave. "It was nice meeting you," he said, "and I'm sure glad you hung on to this picture." He shoved it into his saddlebag, then added, "If I ever need your services in the future, I know where to find you." Then he was out on the street.

A few minutes later, he rented a second-story hotel room one block west of the livery stable. He paid for the room, then, without climbing the stairs, walked back to the street. It was almost suppertime, and he was very hungry. He chose a small restaurant two doors west of the hotel.

A tall, gray-haired man stood behind the counter. He greeted Camp with a toothy smile, and told him to choose any table he wanted. Houston was soon sitting near the back wall, close to the kitchen. Once seated, he became even hungrier, for the establishment was very clean, and he could smell the strong aroma of something baking.

A young waitress, who was obviously of Mexican descent, was soon at his table. "Thank you for coming to the Beacon, sir," she said in perfect English. "May I bring you something to eat?"

"I'll have one of your best beefsteaks," he said, "and everything that goes along with it. And I'd like some of whatever that is I smell baking."

She chuckled softly, and continued to offer a beautiful smile that seemed genuine. "It's fresh bread, sir, and I think you're just in time." She tucked the bill of fare under her arm, then headed for the kitchen.

Half an hour later, he was enjoying a meal he would not soon forget: steak, potatoes, greens, beans, and a large slab of peach pie. The buttered, freshly baked bread was hot and delicious, and if he had ever drunk a better-tasting cup of coffee, he could not remember where or when. He took more time than usual with his meal, and sipped more coffee afterward. Then, leaving a dime on the table to show that he appreciated good service, he paid for his food and left the building.

He bought a newspaper on the street, then walked to the livery stable. He informed Ralph Hicks that he had been successful in his meeting with the photographer, and thanked the hostler again for his information. Then he retrieved a change of clothing from his pack, along with his razor and his shaving mug. A few minutes later, he was back at the hotel.

Once in his room, he tested the mattress immediately. The bed was soft, yet firm. Like everything else in the room, it was clean, and it had two feather pillows. There was a medium-sized table against the wall, on which rested a large pitcher of water. A washbasin was also there, along with soap and a washcloth.

There was a foot-square mirror on the wall behind the table. It had obviously been placed there by a woman, or at least a short man, because Camp had to stoop until his body was in an uncomfortable position in order to see his image. He smiled, then took off his shirt. He placed both pillows in a

chair, then pulled it up to the table and took a seat. Now he
was looking into the mirror dead center.

He shaved his face and washed his body as best he could,
then sat down on the bed and began to study the picture. The
trail hands had posed around a few bales of hay, with the corral and several horses in the background. John Calloway sat
on one of the bales, a serious expression on his face. Behind
and on either side of him stood the remaining trail hands. All
wore silly grins, and each man had a gun in his hand.

Camp had written Joe Plenty's descriptions of the men in
a small notebook. Now, holding the photograph in one hand
and the notebook in the other, he had no problem putting a
name on every man pictured. He sat for a long time, commit-
ting each man's face and description to memory. Finally, he
slipped the picture back into his saddlebag, convinced that he
would recognize any of the men on sight:

Walt Turner, who was thought by Joe Plenty to be the
leader of the pack, was about thirty years old. A six-footer
who weighed about one-ninety, he had coal-black hair and
dark eyes. He had near-perfect teeth, and smiled often. Plenty
believed that Turner came from Fort Worth, for during their
months on the trail together, the man had mentioned that particular town more than any other when talking about bygone
days.

Red Bentley was considerably smaller. He stood no more
than five-seven, and weighed about one-forty. As his nickname implied, his hair was fiery red, and his face was covered
with freckles. He openly boasted about rustling cattle in the
past, and always carried a roll of money. Plenty had once
heard one of the other hands use the nickname "Lightning"
when referring to Bentley. Did the man's use of that particular word mean that Bentley was exceptionally fast with a six-
gun? Plenty believed that it did. So did Camp Houston, and he
had made a mental note of it.

Bill Wiggins had originally come from Brackettville, and
very often said as much: "I'm Bill Wiggins, from down Brack-

ettville way," he would inform any man whom he was meeting for the first time. Tall, skinny and bowlegged, Wiggins wore sideburns that reached below his ears and blond, stringy hair that he allowed to grow to his shoulders. Though Plenty said that the man was in his late twenties, he knew little else about him. Wiggins was the quiet type, he said, and appeared to spend much of his time daydreaming.

Sam Lott was a twenty-one-year-old braggart from Waco. Plenty said that Calloway had finally begun to put Lott on early guard duty every night because the serious-minded trail boss had grown tired of listening to the young man's high-pitched voice. If allowed to remain in camp after supper, Lott thought nothing of keeping the other men awake with his boasting.

He was quick to say that he himself might very well be the fastest gun alive, that he had never seen a man who could match his draw. A six-footer who weighed about one-sixty, Lott was a blue-eyed blond. He seldom if ever shaved his face, for his beard amounted to little more than a sparse crop of white fuzz. The young outlaw would surely die with a gun in his hand, Joe Plenty had said, for he was anything but smart.

Among the five outlaws, both Camp Houston and Joe Plenty thought Jack Little was the poorest excuse for a human being. The man had been on three trail drives with John Calloway. He had always received top dollar for his work and, on occasion, what some of the hands thought was preferential treatment.

"You oughta seen the sonofabitch buddying up and trying to kiss Mr. Calloway's ass," Plenty had said. "Always pretending to be his friend. They usually ate their meals together, and slept side by side under the chuck wagon at night. I know for a fact that they once shared the same room in Dodge City. I tell you, it gripes my ass just to think about it. We all trusted that sonofabitch, then here he comes pumping lead into us. I saw it with my own eyes, just before I passed out."

Jack Little was a twenty-five-year-old native of Corsicana.

He was obviously a good cowhand, for John Calloway, a man widely known for his keen knowledge of the cattle business, had hired him on at least three occasions.

At six foot three and two hundred twenty pounds, Little was by far the largest of the five. He had brown hair and gray eyes, with the right eye having a permanent squint. Though slightly stoop-shouldered, he was nevertheless a very strong man, and known to be handy with his fists. Plenty did not know how good a gun hand Little was, but said that he always carried a Peacemaker in a low-hanging, cutaway holster.

Camp slipped the notebook into his saddlebag beside the picture, then dozed off. He slept for more than three hours, and awakened to a dark room. He was on his feet quickly, and touched a burning match to the wick of the coal-oil lamp.

He dressed in clean clothing and buckled on his gun belt, then headed for the stairway. Moments later, he was out on the street.

He was hungry again. As much as he had enjoyed his meal earlier in the afternoon, one glance at the Beacon told him that the restaurant was closed. Camp smiled, and nodded. The owner was probably smart, he was thinking: the man obviously stayed open throughout the daylight hours, fed all the people who were serious about eating a quiet meal, then closed early enough to avoid all the nighttime drinkers and hell-raisers.

He walked past the Beacon, and continued west. A few doors down, and on the same side of the street, he came to a large, well-lighted building. The signs over the door and on the windows gave no hint as to the name of the establishment, but stated that food, drink and the game of billiards could be found inside. Camp counted a total of nine saddled horses at the two hitching rails.

He stepped inside and stood against the wall for a few moments, looking over the layout. A three-sided bar stood in the middle of the room. The kitchen and eating area were on the west side, with the billiard tables on the opposite. The poker tables were all located along the rear wall, past what appeared to be a small, hardwood dance floor. At the moment, no cardplayers were present.

Nor was there any action at the billiard tables. From where Camp was standing he had a good view of everything in the building and, try as he might, he could not see half enough men to ride off all of those horses out front. There were only three men sitting at the bar. Camp walked forward and spoke to the fat bartender. "Kitchen still open?"

The man nodded and finished off his drink, then wiped his mouth and pointed. "Just knock on the wall over there, then have a seat. She'll be with you pretty quick."

Camp did as he had been told, and a middle-aged woman was at his table immediately. "I was jist about ta call it a day," she said tiredly. "Shore hope ya want sump'm simple."

"How simple?" Camp inquired.

"Well, sump'm it don't take all night ta fix." She pulled a strand of gray hair out of her eyes and tucked it behind her ear, then continued. "Tell ya what I could do. I could warm ya up some stew purty quick, 'cause I've prob'ly still got some red coals in th' fahrbox." When Camp was slow to speak, the lady continued. "I made it outta fresh beef, an' it was mighty good at dinner." She looked Houston in the eye for a moment, then added, "Ya git a good-sized bowl fer a dime, fifteen cents if ya want biscuits an' coffee."

Camp nodded, then offered a big smile. "Sounds like just what I need," he said. "Bring me the whole works."

As he sat enjoying his meal, it soon became obvious that the men who owned those horses outside were definitely in the vicinity. Camp watched as a man came through the back door and spoke to one of the men sitting at the bar. Then the drinker gave up his stool to the newcomer, and himself walked through the back door. Camp sat smiling as he realized that he might well be dining in the biggest whorehouse in Texas.

After he had eaten and paid for his meal, Houston walked to the bar and ordered whiskey. Never once making eye contact, the bartender poured the drink. "Dime," he said, holding out his hand. Camp ignored the hand, and laid the money on the bar. The man scooped up the coin, then turned his back and walked away.

When Camp turned his head toward the far end of the bar, he could see that the drinkers were staring at him. When he returned their inquisitive looks with a steely stare of his own, all three men quickly averted their eyes. A moment later, Houston upended his drink and set the empty glass on the bar. Then, without a word, he walked through the front door and headed for his hotel room. He wanted to get an early start next morning, but first he must decide where he was going.

Long after he had blown out the lamp, he lay on his bed, thinking. He finally decided that, since it was closer to his present whereabouts than any of the other towns he would eventually have to visit, he would begin his search in Brackettville. Plenty had said that Bill Wiggins seemed proud, maybe even boastful, of the fact that he had been born and raised there.

Camp knew that most wandering men occasionally return to the place of their beginnings, however short the visit might be. He was hoping the pattern might hold true in the case of Wiggins. Plenty had said that the man was a daydreamer. Had one of his dreams been to come back to Brackettville with a pokeful of money? Was he at this very moment living in a fancy home while passing himself off as a successful investor?

After thinking for a while longer, Camp discarded the latter possibility. Though one share of the proceeds from the robbery might well be enough to build a fancy home, it was hardly the kind of money necessary to secure an impressive position on the social ladder of even a small town.

Nope, the take had simply not been big enough for five men to live the good life forever. John Calloway had been carrying thirty-five thousand dollars, which, split evenly, would have put only seven thousand dollars into the pockets of each of the robbers.

Camp Houston doubted, however, that there had been an even split. Outlaws were usually not very bright, and any man in the bunch who was actually capable of putting together a workable scheme could easily convince the others that he should be the leader of the pack, and that his extraordinary brilliance entitled him to a lion's share of the booty. A lopsided split usually followed all robberies that were committed by more than one man, with Boss Thief often claiming as much as half the take.

As did Joe Plenty, Houston believed that Walt Turner had bossed the robbery in Kansas, and probably kept the larger portion of the money for himself. If that was the case, and if Turner's underlings had been living high on the hog for the past year, they should all be running short of money just about now. Especially since they had received less than an equal share.

Lying on his bed in the dark, Houston nodded at his thoughts. One thing he knew for sure was that when a man's funds began to run low, he changed his habits. He ate, drank and slept in places that he might have shunned when his bankroll was adequate. Camp believed that a man who was down and out could be much harder to find than one whose poke was full.

A man who was well-off got noticed, for he usually dressed well, ate in expensive restaurants and stayed at the better hotels, places whose business it was to know who their customers were. A man whose poke was empty, however, would likely drop his bedroll behind any old bush, and avoid crowds altogether. Then when he did come to town, which he would eventually have to do if he hoped to better his circumstances, he would inevitably head for the seamy side, where seedy characters mostly looked at each other through unseeing eyes. There he could move about freely, and often be remembered by nobody.

Nodding again, Camp pulled a blanket over himself and turned on his left side, his normal go-to-sleep position. In the morning, he would get on Bill Wiggins's trail, and he would assume that the man was broke, or nearly so. He fluffed up his pillow, then closed his eyes. He was asleep quickly.

It was past ten o'clock when he rode out of San Antonio next morning. He was getting a late start because he had waited for some of the stores to open. He had first retrieved his animals from the livery stable, then ridden to the Shebang. There he bought two half-gallon glass jars, complete with lids and sealing rubbers. He also bought a smoked ham and a bag of crackers.

Then he rode to the establishment in which he had eaten supper the night before. He ignored the fat bartender as he walked past the bar. When he knocked on the kitchen wall, the lady opened the door quickly. She looked him up and down, then smiled. "Lord, whatcha gonna do with them?" she asked, her eyes taking in the jars he held in his hands.

"I was hoping you would put something to eat in 'em," he said, his smile as big as her own. "Do you have enough leftover stew and beans to fill 'em?"

She chuckled softly, and reached for the jars. "Guess by gosh I do. Been wonderin' what th' heck I wuz gonna do with it all." She turned toward the kitchen, then spoke over her shoulder: "I'll put th' lids an' rubbers on th' jars, then brang 'em out here fer you ta seal. I ain't near strong enough in my hands to do it, nowadays."

Ten minutes later, she brought the jars to his table. One was almost full of beef stew, and the other was filled with warmed-over red beans. Camp gave each of the lids a hard twist. The jars were now sealed, and would not leak.

He ordered a ham-and-egg breakfast, then asked the lady to bake him an extra pan of biscuits and put them in a bag. "I'll be on the trail for a while," he said, "and I like my biscuits."

She nodded. "Won't take long. Th' oven's already hot."

Half an hour later, he was headed west at a fast trot. The roan could hold this pace all day long, and Sid Blankenship had said that the same was true for the packhorse. Camp expected to be halfway across Medina County by nightfall.

He reached Hondo Creek an hour before sunset. *Hondo* was a Spanish word meaning "deep," and the creek had been aptly named. He quickly decided to camp on the east bank, for he could see no place where fording was possible. He would seek out shallow water in the morning, for he had no intention of swimming the animals across and wetting everything they carried.

He dropped his pack and his saddle beside a willow, then watered and picketed the horses. Grass was at least adequate along the creek, so he would save the grain for another day.

He raked a pile of leaves and twigs together, then broke up a dead limb across his knee. He needed only a small fire for boiling his coffee and heating his stew; then he would rake several handfuls of dirt over the coals.

After a pleasing supper of hot stew and biscuits, he put out the fire and crawled into his bedroll. He lay staring at the stars for a long time, thinking about the ranch he intended to build on Calf Creek, a few miles north of the Mason County line. He had bought three sections of land there four years earlier, and if all went well, he would make the last payment to John Butterworth next January.

Once he had a clear deed, he would build a home and some outbuildings, then stretch his credit to stock the property with cattle. He would start with longhorns because they were cheap, but he fully intended to buy some Hereford bulls at the first opportunity. He would allow the bulls to run free with the cows, and keep none of the half-breed male offspring. After a few years, the longhorn strain would be gone, and he would have a herd of Herefords.

The ecology of the Calf Creek property was ideal for the raising of livestock. The vegetation consisted of open grasslands and oak savannahs. Woodlands occurred along the water courses, and shrubs were restricted to very shallow soils and steep slopes. The property also had a history of its own:

On November 21, 1831, James Bowie, Rezin P. Bowie, David Buchanan, Cephas D. Hamm, Matthew Doyle, Jesse Wallace, Thomas McCaslin, Robert Armstrong, James Coryell and two servants, Charles and Gonzales, fought a twenty-four-hour battle with more than a hundred fifty Caddo and Lipan Indians.

Though the Bowie party suffered no casualties, they killed eighty warriors before the Indians withdrew. James Bowie, who would later die at the Alamo, erected a marker of sorts, proclaiming Calf Creek the location of the battle.

Camp would build his home very near the conjunction of McCulloch, Menard, and Mason Counties, where Calf Creek emptied into the San Saba River. Moving about in the area should be a little safer now that the shooting had ceased in what had come to be known as the "Mason County War." Newspaper writers had very quickly begun to use the term "Hoo Doo War" when writing about the deadly hostilities.

During and for several years after the Reconstruction period, lawlessness in general, and cattle rustling in particular, were prevalent along the entire Texas frontier. State lawmen were of little help, for being a very corrupt organization, they themselves were part of the problem. The problem reached major proportions in Mason County in 1875.

Rustling had been going on for years when the newly elected sheriff, John Clark, intercepted a large herd of cattle being driven to Llano. When ownership of the cattle could not be determined, Clark arrested nine men and took them to the Mason County jail. All were soon out on bail provided by local citizens.

The men were ordered to remain in the town of Mason until their hearing took place. When Sheriff Clark learned that they were not in town, as their bonds stipulated, he rearrested the five men that he could find, and placed them in jail.

Several nights later, a group of unknown men held the sheriff, deputy sheriff, and a Texas Ranger named Dan Roberts at bay while making off with all five of the prisoners. Three of the alleged rustlers were killed, one was brought back to the jail, and the fifth was never heard from again.

During the next few months, several arrests were made on charges of cattle rustling, and a group of unknown assailants killed one man even while he was in the custody of a deputy sheriff.

Men from other counties soon became involved in the fighting, and during the summer of 1875 the killings increased dramatically. First, a rancher was shot from ambush. Then a deputy sheriff was killed, followed closely by two men from out of the county. Another stockman and a gambler were killed soon after.

The newly reorganized Texas Rangers, under the leadership of Major John B. Jones, were ordered to send a force to Mason County. A small contingent, which included Major Jones, arrived at the Hedwig's Hill community, in the southern part of the county, during the afternoon of September 28, 1875.

Then, hearing rumors of trouble in the Loyal Valley community, Jones turned south and headed there, instead of continuing on to Mason, as had been the original plan. Next morning, a county official was shot and killed from ambush while walking down the street in Mason.

The male population of the county was by now split into three groups. One group remained neutral and tried to keep the peace, while the other two fought at every opportunity. The line between the two feuding groups had never become clear. Nor had the reason for all the bloodshed.

Supposedly, Sheriff Clark was the leader of one of the factions, but the leader of the other was never identified. Many names appeared, but nothing was ever proved.

Sheriff Clark and nine of his "faction" were charged with minor offenses stemming from the initial arrest. All but Clark were found innocent in October, 1876. The sheriff posted bail, and was never heard from again.

The following winter, a stockman was killed at his home in Llano County. Then, in what was hopefully the last act of the Hoo Doo War, the Mason County Courthouse was torched on January 21, 1877. It was believed by all and stated by many that the building had been burned to destroy all evidence that was to be used against those involved.

Most of the county's residents believed that by now, the leaders of both factions either were dead or had left the area. At any rate, the killing stopped just as suddenly as it had begun. And though many names were mentioned, no charges were ever filed concerning the courthouse fire.

Camp Houston had not fired a shot during the Mason County War, for he had spent the entire period working as foreman of John Butterworth's Lazy B Ranch, in Mills County. He had nevertheless been acquainted with some of the men who had died in the senseless feud, and believed that he knew who had killed them. Even so, his lips were sealed, for it had long been his policy to stay clear of other men's squabbles.

The night air finally turned cool, and after turning over in his bed for the tenth time, Camp dozed off and slept like a log.

He awoke with the sun shining in his eyes next morning, and lay still for a few minutes trying to remember how long it had been since he had slept so soundly. He had not even gotten up during the night to relieve himself, as was usually the case. He smiled, and reached for his boots.

He was soon on his feet gathering dead grass to start his morning fire. Both of his horses began to whinny when they saw him moving about. The breakfast of oats they were hinting at would not be forthcoming this morning, for they had grazed most of the night. Good grass would become more difficult to find as he moved farther west, however; then the animals would have to be grained at least once a day.

When his coffeepot came to a boil, he pulled it off the fire. With his folding knife, he cut several slices of the smoked ham into his frying pan, added some of the biscuits, then placed the pan on the hot coals. He poured himself a steaming cup of coffee and added a spoonful of sugar. A few minutes later, he was enjoying a tasty breakfast.

An hour later, he was riding north along the creek, looking for a place that was shallow enough to ford. After traveling for half a mile, he gave up and reversed his direction. A mile to the south he found a natural ford with a rocky bottom, where the water ran less than two feet deep. His animals took to the water eagerly, and he stopped midstream and allowed them to drink their fill.

He crossed the Sabinal River shortly after noon, and arrived at the Frio an hour before sunset. Flowing directly out of the mountains and through Frio Canyon, the Frio River was cold and clear, and usually ran shallow enough to be forded at almost any location.

Hondo Creek last night had been the exception, for it had long been Houston's policy to cross a stream before bedding down. A hard rain anywhere upstream could drastically change the character of a creek or river within a matter of hours, making it difficult or impossible to cross for several days. He watered his horses, then waded them to the far side. He would make camp on the west bank.

He had eaten a supper of beans and biscuits and was sipping a cup of coffee when a covered wagon drawn by two horses crossed the river and stopped a few yards from his camp. A couple who appeared to be in their thirties sat on the seat, and Camp could see at least two youngsters poking their heads around the canvas. He waved at the newcomers, and his greeting was returned.

He dashed his coffee grounds over his shoulder, then walked to the wagon. "Deadwood's mighty scarce in this area," he said, speaking to both the man and his wife. "My fire's still burning, and you're welcome to use it. I'll move my gear a little farther down the river."

"Well, now," the man said, stepping down and offering a handshake, "I'd say 'at's mighty white uv ya. Been wonderin' how'n th' heck I wuz gonna git Maggie a fahr started, now here ya come offerin' us yore'n. Yessir, 'at's white uv ya . . . mighty white."

Camp grasped the man's hand. "My name's Camp Houston," he said, "and I'm just passing through. I've already eaten my supper, and like I said, you folks are welcome to my campfire."

"My name's Ed Crane," the man said, pumping Camp's hand. He pointed to the wagon. "Th' lady on th' seat there's my wife Maggie, and them two young uns ya see peepin' aroun' th' canvas is our ten-year-old twins, Mark an' Sarah."

Camp waved to the woman and the kids, then turned to walk away.

"Ya don't hafta move none o' yer stuff," Crane called to him. "We c'n use 'at fahr with ya settin' right whur ya been settin'."

Houston turned halfway around. "No, Mr. Crane. You folks just take over my campsite and get yourselves a good night's sleep. I'll be moving." Within a matter of minutes, he had moved his belongings fifty yards downriver. Half an hour later, he was sound asleep.

He rode west at sunup, after washing a breakfast of cold ham and biscuits down with water from his canteen. Though he usually began his day by drinking at least two cups of steaming coffee, this morning would be the exception, for there had been no wood available for a fire. Maybe later in the day he would come across some fuel; then he would dig out the coffeepot.

He supposed that the Crane family would also have to eat a cold breakfast, for they had no wood in the wagon, and the area around the campsite had been picked clean. It would probably be some time yet before the Cranes concerned themselves with that problem, however, for although Houston had made no particular effort to prepare for his departure quietly, no member of the family had stirred.

The two humps beneath the wagon probably represented father and son, Camp was thinking, with mother and daughter sleeping in the wagon. Just before riding out of sight, he took one last look. The humps were deathly still. He smiled, and nodded. The folks had obviously been tuckered out completely, and would sleep until the heat of the day awakened them.

He held his animals to a fast walk. He expected to ford the Nueces River by noon, then camp on the west bank of the West Nueces before nightfall. He would wake up in Kinney County in the morning, and should be in Brackettville by midday.

Several times during the morning he dismounted to pick up deadwood, adding it to the packhorse's burden. When he reached the west bank of the Nueces, he first fed each of the horses a hefty portion of oats. Then he finally had his morning coffee and a hot meal as well. He ate the last of his beef stew, then, after washing out the empty jar with sand and water from the river, returned it to his pack. He had every intention of acquiring a refill in the very near future. If not another jar of beef stew, he'd find something else that he liked.

5

It was an hour past noon when Houston arrived in Brackettville next day. The weather was hot and dry, and little clouds of dust sprang from the hooves of his animals as they walked down the wide street. He was headed for the livery stable, which he could already see three blocks ahead. The few men he passed paid him no mind. Most were soldiers, no doubt stationed at nearby Fort Clark.

Fort Clark was the sole reason for Brackettville's being, for the settlement had originally been established in 1852 as nothing more than a supply village for the cavalry units stationed there. And though the town had by now become a trade center for surrounding ranches and irrigated farms, the prosperity of many local merchants was still largely dependent upon the military, especially the men who owned the hotels, restaurants and saloons.

Most civilians slept and ate their meals at home, and a respectable number of men did their drinking there. Consequently, there was a never-ending campaign among the town's watering holes to separate the soldiers from their pay, and a few of the saloons even allowed those in good standing to drink on credit.

Over the years, the drinking establishments had several times been placed off limits to all military personnel, usually to punish the soldiers for one infraction or another, but a few times to teach Brackettville's businessmen a lesson. The lesson was learned quickly, and each occasion sent the saloon owners to Fort Clark, begging the camp commander to lift the restrictions. Then, when the commander complied and the soldiers were once again in town with their money, they were welcomed enthusiastically, and could get away with anything short of murder in almost any saloon in town.

Camp continued down the street till he reached the livery stable. The stable and corral stood at the end of the street, with ample room for two-way traffic on either side. There was an open-air blacksmith shop beneath the wooden awning, and two wagons and a buggy bearing FOR SALE signs were parked nearby. Houston dismounted and led his horses to the watering trough.

A tall, hatless man with gray hair stood in the wide doorway. "Saw you coming more than a mile away," he said, beginning to walk toward the trough. "Seems to me that it's just too damn hot for traveling." He nodded in the direction of the horses. "You gonna leave them for a while?"

Camp nodded, and handed over the reins. "They're probably at least as tired as I am," he said, "and you're right about the weather being hot." He unsheathed his rifle, then extracted his razor and a change of clean clothing from his pack. "Don't know how long I'll be in town," he said, "but I'll trust you to take care of my animals till I need them."

"I'll treat them like they were my own," the man said. He offered a handshake, adding, "My name's Rufus Bunt."

Houston accepted the hand. "I'm Camp Houston," he said.

Camp felt Bunt's firm grip turn to mush, and the man extracted his hand quickly. "I . . . I guess I don't have to tell you this," he said softly, "but that name is well known around this town—around this whole area, for that matter."

Camp nodded curtly, then changed the subject. "Any particular hotel in town that you'd recommend?"

"Don't guess so," the hostler said. He pointed up the street. "Three hotels in town, and you just rode past all of them. I'd say they're all about the same, but the Frey has the most business. That's where most of the soldiers and the cowboys hang out. The hotel bar downstairs is crowded every night of the week. Plenty of gambling and easy women, if a man's hunting that sort of thing."

Camp smiled faintly. "I'll be at the Frey," he said. He patted the roan on the rump, then walked down the street.

A middle-aged man wearing a straw hat sat behind the counter at the hotel, and offered Camp his choice of an upstairs room or one on the first floor. "I'd rather sleep upstairs," Houston said, signing his name to the register.

The clerk stared at the signature much longer than was necessary, and Camp knew that once again his name had been recognized. He had considered using a name other than his own for his manhunt, but had decided against it. Now he was not so sure that had been wise. Maybe he should reconsider picking a name out of the air for hotel registers.

"Thank you for choosing the Frey, Mr. Houston," the clerk said. He dropped the key to room number twenty in Camp's hand, adding, "I certainly hope you have a nice stay, and if there is anything I can do to make it more enjoyable, just let me know."

Houston dropped the key into his vest pocket. "I'm sure everything will be all right," he said. "I don't know how long I'll be in town, but I'll settle with you before I leave."

"Yes," the clerk said nervously. He nodded several times. "Yes, of course. There was never any doubt in my mind."

Camp picked up his gear and headed up the stairway, then

paused momentarily to look over his shoulder. The clerk had already stepped away from the counter, no doubt eager to head for the barroom with the news that Camp Houston was in town. Camp shook his head, and continued up the stairway.

He unlocked the door to number twenty, then stepped inside. He stood still for a few moments, pleased with what he saw. Though the Frey Hotel was hardly impressive from the outside, the room he had rented was exceptionally nice, and much larger than he had expected.

The window had curtains, and there was a colorful spread on the bed. There was a chest of drawers in one corner, and a large table in another. A smaller table with two chairs was closer to the center of the room, and held a coal-oil lamp and a pitcher of water. A pan of water, a bar of soap, a washcloth and two towels rested on the corner table, and a medium-sized mirror hung on the wall. There was even a small recess in the wall that could have been called a closet, with an overhead rod for hanging clothing.

Camp laid his gear on the corner table, then sat down on the bed. The mattress was springy, yet firm. He fluffed up one of the pillows, and smiled. The hotel clerk had given him a quality room all right, well worth the dollar-twenty-a-night price tag.

He stripped and washed himself, then lathered and shaved his face. He pushed his rifle as far under the bed as he could reach, then dressed in clean clothing. A few minutes later, he walked down the stairway and into the restaurant. He took a seat at a table on the far side of the building, with his back against the wall.

The restaurant and the barroom were separated by nothing more than a thin wall, with batwing doors that even a short man could see over. And as he took his seat, Camp could see the heads of several men peering over the doors, no doubt wanting to see if Camp Houston was as big as his reputation. When Camp smiled and waved to them, every head disappeared quickly.

Houston ordered a plate of chicken and dumplings from the Mexican waiter, then sat sipping coffee as he waited for his meal. He cast his eyes toward the barroom occasionally, but saw no one else peering over the doors. He had already decided that, as soon as he finished off his meal, he would belly up to the bar and give them all a good look. He blew air into his cup, then took another sip.

Half an hour later, he pushed his way through the batwing doors and moved quickly to one side, waiting for his eyes to adjust to the dimmer lighting. Standing just inside the doorway, he was the center of attention. None of the men wanted to be singled out, however, and all found something else to look at each time Camp attempted to make direct eye contact. The room was eerily quiet.

Houston himself broke the spell. "Howdy!" he said loudly, his deep bass voice bouncing off the back wall. A few men mumbled a soft greeting, then quietly resumed their previous conversations. There was an empty stool at the corner of the bar, against the wall, and Camp walked there now. He leaned across the bar on his elbows, then spoke to the young bartender. "Have you got any Bourbon County whiskey?"

The bartender, who appeared to be still in his teens, laughed bravely. "Not so you could tell it," he said. "Ain't never been no Kentucky whiskey in this place that I know of." He laughed again. "Only thing I can offer you is some stuff that was cooked up in San Antonio about three months ago. Can't guarantee it to be good, but I can sure guarantee it to make you drunk."

Houston chuckled softly, then nodded. "Give me a bottle and a glass."

The young man complied, then held out his hand. "Sixty-five cents," he said. Once he had been paid, he skedaddled to the other end of the bar.

Camp poured whiskey in his glass, then offered a drink to the man on the next stool. "Don't mind if I do," the man said, reaching for the bottle. He poured his glass full, drank half of it, then filled it again. Then the pitifully thin man, who appeared to be at least sixty years old, looked at Houston through bloodshot eyes. "That bartender knows what he's talking about," he said. "This stuff'll turn your head around." He gulped another mouthful.

"I can certainly believe that," Camp said, retrieving his bottle and placing it near his left elbow, well out of the old man's reach.

The old-timer sipped at his drink noisily, then began to speak again. "Ain't never set next to nobody like you before," he said. "Ain't never even talked to nobody famous."

Houston wet his lips with whiskey, and said nothing.

"No, sir," the old man continued, "it ain't every day that a man like Camp Houston shows up around here. It's my guess that you're hunting somebody, otherwise you wouldn't be caught dead in a godforsaken place like Brackettville."

Looking over his shoulder, Camp spotted an empty table behind him. He spoke to the old man: "Why don't we move to that corner table, old-timer? If this bottle runs out, we'll get a new one."

The old man led the way, surprising Houston with his steadiness. They seated themselves, and Camp poured whiskey in both glasses. "Looks like you already know my name," he said, "but I don't recall hearing yours."

"The name's Jack Fondon," the old man said. He licked his lips and took another drink.

Camp scratched at the label on the whiskey bottle with a thumbnail. "You say you think I came to town hunting somebody," he said. "What if I did?"

"Hell, I don't know," Fondon answered. "I was just thinking, kinda wondering who it might be. Reckon I know about everybody who lives here, and a whole lot of people who don't."

Houston got to the point. "Do you know a man named Bill Wiggins?"

"Used to," Fondon said, a smile playing around the corners of his mouth. "Don't no more."

"What does that mean?"

"It means that he ain't around no more; been dead since last winter. A man from Waco gunned him down right out there at the hotel's hitching rail, two days before Christmas. Wiggins took two shots in the gut and one in the mouth, and died without ever speaking."

Camp sat thinking for quite some time, continuing to scratch at the label. "The man who shot Wiggins," he said finally, "was his name Sam Lott?"

"Sure was," Fondon said quickly. "How'd you guess?"

"It wasn't entirely a guess."

The old-timer poured more whiskey in his glass. "Lott claimed Wiggins drew on him," he continued, "but I never believed it. Wiggins wasn't no fast gun, and he knew that better'n anybody else. He never would have tried to pull on no damn gunslinger. Of course, his gun was lying there in the dirt, but I damn sure don't believe he was the one dropped it. The town marshal said it appeared to him like nothing more than a shootout between two enemies, and since there weren't no witnesses to the actual shooting, he had no choice but to take Lott's word for what happened. He ordered Lott to get his ass out of town and stay out. The county buried Wiggins next morning, 'cause his wife said she sure didn't have no money.

"Now, Lott claimed that Wiggins had been in debt to him for a long time, and when he came to town to collect, Wiggins went for his gun. Now, he might have owed Lott money, maybe a bunch of money, but he damn sure didn't go for no gun." The old man helped himself to another drink of Camp's whiskey, adding, "I'd bet a hundred million dollars on that."

Camp pushed back his chair and got to his feet. "Where's the marshal's office? What's his name?"

"His office is one block east, on the opposite side of the

street, and his name is Seth Ringling. He's one of the nicest young fellows you'll ever meet, but he don't put up with no shit out of nobody. He's damn sure man enough to back up whatever he says, too."

Camp pushed the bottle across the table. "Here," he said. "Drink up and enjoy yourself." A few seconds later, he stepped out on the street and headed east.

After introducing himself he was soon shaking hands with Marshal Seth Ringling, a very muscular man who appeared to be in his late twenties. The lawman offered a firm grip, speaking as he pumped his visitor's hand. "Camp Houston, huh?" he asked, then pointed to a chair.

Camp nodded, and seated himself.

"No use in me pretending that I haven't heard your name before," the marshal said. "In fact, I doubt that a week ever goes by when I don't hear it." He took a seat behind his desk. "Is there something I can do for you?"

"I don't really know. I came to town looking for Bill Wiggins, but I hear a man from Waco already found him."

Ringling nodded. "A fellow named Sam Lott shot him dead in front of the Frey Hotel last Christmas. Claimed Wiggins drew on him."

"Did you believe Lott's story?"

The marshal shuffled some papers around, then sat thinking for a while. "What I believe or don't believe is not worth a hill of beans," he said finally. "What I can prove is the only thing that counts, and in this case, I can't prove anything. What I found when I arrived on the scene was the same thing I've seen at every other shootout I've ever investigated: a dead man with a cold Peacemaker lying at his feet, and a live man holding another Peacemaker with a hot barrel and three spent shells."

Ringling got to his feet and began to pace about the room. "Hell, no, I didn't believe Sam Lott's story, but my hands were tied. He claimed he shot Wiggins in self-defense, and no jury in Texas would have convicted him. I believed then and now that he was guilty of murder, but there were no witnesses, and his word was law." He walked to the opposite side of the room, then returned, stopping in front of Houston. "You say you came to town looking for Wiggins. Was he a friend of yours?"

"Not by any stretch of the imagination," Camp said, getting to his feet. He told the marshal about John Calloway's trail drive, and the cold-blooded murder of the drovers in a Kansas gully. "I was looking for Bill Wiggins because I intended to kill the sonofabitch."

Ringling shook his head very slowly. "Since Sam Lott and Wiggins were both in on the robbery, maybe the gunplay here in town really was over money," he said.

Camp stood quietly for a while. "That's altogether possible," he said finally, "but it's my guess that Wiggins was killed because the others were afraid he might decide to do some talking. They probably gave Sam Lott the job because he had the fastest gun and the weakest mind. A fellow who knows him very well told me that Lott barely has sense enough to come in out of the rain."

"I talked with him a few minutes the day of the shooting," Ringling said. "He seemed to me like a backwoods kid that just never did quite grow up." The lawman stood in the doorway looking down the street for a moment, then spoke over his shoulder: "I suppose you'll be calling on Mr. Sam Lott before long, huh?"

"Guess I'll take a trip to Corpus Christi first," Camp said, moving closer to the door. "Fact is, I intend to get a good night's sleep and head out in the morning." He stepped out on the small porch. "Good-bye, Marshal. I'm glad to have met you."

"Same here," Ringling said. "Damn shame I can't go with you."

Houston spent the next hour sitting on a barstool in a rundown saloon two doors east of the marshal's office. When Camp ordered a beer, the bartender served, collected, then moved away, obviously evading any questions Houston might want to ask.

Two beers later, Camp suddenly decided that he had drunk enough for one day. Besides, he was tired of trying to understand the muted conversation around him. The room had grown strangely quiet when he entered; then the incessant mumbling had begun. That he himself was the topic, he had no doubt. He slid off his stool and nodded to the bartender, then headed for the front door.

He ate a light supper in the hotel restaurant, then climbed the stairway to his room. He undressed, put his Peacemaker under the extra pillow, then stretched out. The wide, comfortable bed put him to sleep in short order.

6

Camp was at the livery stable shortly after daybreak. The hostler was already up, standing in the doorway sipping from a steaming coffee cup. "Good morning," Houston said, pointing toward the corral. "I've come for my horses."

"Figured as much," Bunt said. He took a coil of rope from a wooden peg, then headed down the hall. "Pot of hot coffee on the stove there in the office," he said loudly just before he disappeared around the corner. "Drink all you want."

"No, thanks," Camp said to himself, for the liveryman was already out of sight. Unlike most western men, Houston liked a little sugar in his coffee, and it never failed to interfere with his appetite if he loaded up early in the morning. He would have breakfast at the hotel restaurant a few minutes from now, and he would drink his coffee then. He pulled up a nail keg, then sat down to await the delivery of his horses.

When the hostler returned, he was leading both animals.

"Fed 'em more'n an hour ago," he said. "They ought to both be raring to go."

"Just like me," Camp said. He saddled the roan and shoved his rifle into the boot. Then the liveryman helped him balance and fasten his packs to the black's packsaddle. He rolled up the soiled clothing he had taken off yesterday, and placed it in one of the packs. Mother Nature would take care of his laundry while he slept tonight.

Camp had used to hunt up a washerwoman every time he accumulated a sack of dirty clothing. He still did that occasionally, but not when he was traveling. He had hit upon a way of washing his own clothing several years earlier, and nowadays he used it with regularity when he was on the trail, especially in hot weather.

He almost always camped beside a stream with a strong current, and it was a simple matter to stake his clothing out in swift, shallow water before going to bed. In the morning, all he had to do was wring the water out of the garments and hang them on his packhorse. The sun would dry them quickly after he began his day's traveling, then he would roll them up and place them in his pack. They were always clean, and smelled good.

Houston said good-bye to the liveryman, then mounted the roan and yanked on the black's lead rope. A few minutes later, he tied both animals to the hotel's hitching rail. The restaurant had its own separate entrance, and Camp pushed the door open and stepped inside. He had no problem getting the cook's attention, for there were only three customers in the restaurant at this early hour.

The middle-aged cook smiled and nodded when Camp handed him the jars and requested that they be filled with something edible. "Got half a pot o' chili and a couple pounds o' roast beef that I'm dyin' to get rid of," he said, chuckling. "How does that sound to you?"

"It sounds just right," Camp said. "I'll have a platter of flapjacks and eggs for my breakfast. Then if you'll bake a pan of biscuits and bag them for traveling, you'll be making me happy all around."

The cook chuckled again. "Your breakfast'll be ready in a jiffy," he said. "The rest of your order'll take a little longer." He headed for the kitchen.

Less than an hour later, Camp was riding east on the same road that had brought him to Brackettville, with his horses no doubt stepping in their own tracks occasionally. His hat was pulled low over his eyes, for the rising sun he was facing seemed both hotter and brighter than usual, and appeared to be exactly at ground level.

He held his animals to a fast walk hour after hour, expecting to make the West Nueces River by midafternoon. Once there, he would lie down under a willow and spend the remainder of the day enjoying the cool breezes that blew across the water. He also knew that his horses would appreciate the location, for there was green grass in abundance.

All morning long he kept an eye out for anything that would burn, for he knew that a search for fuel anywhere near the river would be fruitless. Not only had all of the deadwood been used, but low-hanging limbs from many of the trees had also been burned. And just as if there would be no tomorrow, campers had even chopped off as many of the living trees' roots as they could find running along on top of the ground. Most of the trees had survived, but some had not.

By the time Houston reached the West Nueces, he had as much bark, dry grass and deadwood on the packhorse as he was likely to need, since a small blaze would be sufficient to reheat his precooked food and boil his coffee.

He watered his animals, then forded the shallow river, selecting the same campsite that he had used on his way to Brackettville. He rubbed his horses with handfuls of grass till their backs were dry, then released them on long picket ropes. He would move the animals to new grass about sunset, for they would eat everything they could reach by then.

He built his fire underneath the willow, then dug his coffeepot and an iron skillet out of his pack. He was very hungry, and had been thinking about food for the past two hours. He filled the coffeepot with water from the river, then dumped in a handful of grounds. Then he twisted the lid off one of the jars and poured the skillet half full. A short time later, he seated himself on his bedroll and began to wolf down the hotel cook's chili right from the skillet.

He had eaten only a few bites when he suddenly stopped chewing and set the skillet down. He spat the contents of his mouth into a bush, and very quickly made a beeline for his canteen. He drank several swallows, then sat for a long time sloshing water around in his mouth.

He remembered hearing the cook say he was "dyin' to get rid of the chili." Small wonder. Camp had always liked food with a peppery taste, but the concoction he had tried to eat just now was nothing short of ridiculous. Nor did he believe that any other man really preferred his food fiery enough to peel the inside of his mouth.

Though Camp had once seen a man eat a large pod of red chili without the benefit of additional food or water, Houston knew that the man was weak in the head, and trying to impress a group of other men. Camp considered the act silly, and had no doubt that it might be harmful to the man's health.

He was still staring into the skillet when he heard a splashing sound. He raised his eyes to see a rider fording the river from the west. Camp was on his feet quickly, for both man and animal looked familiar. The rider halted his horse in midstream, pointing and laughing. "Tell me that my eyes don't deceive me," he shouted loudly. "Tell me that I'm looking at a fellow named Camp Houston."

Camp complied. "All right," he said. "You're looking at a fellow named Camp Houston." He doffed his hat, and motioned the rider into camp. "Come on over, Runt. The coffee's still hot."

The two men were soon shaking hands and patting each other's back. Camp took the extra cup from his pack and filled it with coffee. "Drink this," he said. "It won't cool you off, but it might taste good."

As the man accepted the coffee and began to sip, Houston continued to talk. "Damn, Runt," he said, shaking his head. "I wouldn't have thought of you for the world. How long has it been since I've seen you? Three years? Four?"

"Be five years this coming winter. Don't reckon I've seen you since you went to work for George Angleton, on the Rocking A." He refilled his cup, then placed the coffeepot back on the dying campfire.

The man had been christened Hiram Fowler shortly after birth, but few men knew him by that name. He had stood six foot six and weighed two hundred fifty pounds on his eighteenth birthday, and had acquired the nickname "Runt" along about that time. He had grown no taller since his late teens, but was probably twenty or thirty pounds heavier nowadays.

And although Fowler possessed all of the necessary capabilities, a brawler he was not. He was simply an oversized, good-natured man who was liked by all who knew him, and though it was obvious that he held a physical advantage over most people, and could quite easily kill a man with his bare hands, he had never been known to lift a finger in anger.

Though he could not move about as quickly as the skinny fellows, especially in hot weather, Fowler was a dependable cowhand, and always knew what needed doing without being told. He had no ambition whatsoever, always content as long as he had enough to eat and a roof over his head. Exactly the type of man most ranch owners liked to have around.

Houston and Fowler had been friends for many years. They had made cattle drives up both the Chisholm and the Western Trails together, and walked the streets of Abilene and Dodge City side by side.

Fowler had thick, brown hair that looked as if it belonged on a brush, and he kept it cut short year-round. His eyes were also brown most of the time. At other times they took on a metallic hue, more like copper. Despite having two rows of perfect teeth, his face was nevertheless homely, with a potato nose and large ears that stood out from his head. The young women he loved to look at always avoided him, and the only way he could get any attention from them was to pay for it.

Other than a younger brother, who had left for California several years before, Fowler had no family. He had never known for sure who his father was. His mother had been a saloon whore who dropped out of sight more than twenty years earlier, and it was doubtful that she herself knew who had fathered her sons. Newt Fowler, a man who claimed to be their uncle, had raised the boys on his ranch near Laredo.

The boys had asked few questions about their parents as they were growing up, for Uncle Newt was always quick to tell them to get their minds on whatever jobs they had been assigned. Consequently, Runt had been almost grown when one of his relatives told him that Uncle Newt was not his uncle at all, that the man was most likely his father.

By that time each of the brothers weighed more than two hundred pounds, and were no longer afraid of Newt Fowler. When they cornered him about the extent of their blood relationship, the man insisted that he was their mother's brother, then refused to discuss the matter further. Neither of the young men believed what he was being told, and both left home shortly thereafter.

Both Runt and his brother Milton were good ranch hands, and quickly found jobs on separate neighboring ranches. They kept in close contact for a year or so; then Milt came by with the news that he was headed for California. Twelve years had passed since then, and Runt had heard nothing from his brother.

Houston nodded toward the grassy slope. "Stake your horse out there with mine, Runt. You're not going anywhere else today."

"Nope. Not after running into you, I ain't." He dropped his saddle and bedroll beside the willow, then led his horse away.

Camp laid on another stick of wood and blew on the coals till he had a flame, then headed for the river to get water for a fresh pot of coffee. When he returned, Fowler was busy spreading his bedroll a few feet from the willow. "Never did like to sleep right under a tree," the big man said. "You never know what the hell you'll have on you when you wake up."

Houston nodded, and put the coffeepot on the fire. Then he seated himself and motioned toward the skillet. "Plenty of chili there," he said, a mischievous smile playing around the corners of his mouth. "I've already eaten all I wanted."

Without a word, Fowler set the container on the fire and began to stir the chili with the spoon. A few moments later, he crumbled two biscuits into the skillet and devoured its entire contents before coming up for air.

Camp had watched closely. The laugh he had expected to get at Runt's expense would seem out of place now, for the man was still holding on to the skillet and licking his lips. Houston shook his head and reached for the jar, which was still more than half full. "More chili in here," he said, handing it over. "Eat it all, if you can, so I can wash out the jar."

Fowler emptied the jar into the skillet, heated the chili, and ate it all. Then he walked to the river, where, using one handful of sand after another, he scrubbed both jar and frying pan until there was no trace of grease in either.

Camp sat quietly rethinking his opinion about men and pepper. Maybe some men really did like the taste of red chilies. After all, he had just watched Runt eat almost half a gallon of fire, and the man had never even stopped licking his lips. Camp shook his head again, and forced himself to think about something else.

"Where have you been, Camp?" Fowler asked when he returned to the fire. "And where are you going?"

"I'm looking for some men, Runt." Camp related the story of the murdered drovers, and Fowler listened attentively.

"Hell, I knew Bill Wiggins," he said, "knew him for at least ten years. I heard about him getting killed in a gunfight, but nobody seemed to know what brought on the shooting. Guess you'll be going after that fellow in Waco now, huh?"

"I'll get around to him. At the moment, I'm headed for Corpus Christi." Camp filled both cups with coffee, then continued. "I'll ask you the same question, Runt. Where have you been, and where are you going?"

"Been down in Maverick County to get some money that was owed me. Guess I'll go on up to Mason or Menard County and see what I can find. I hear all the shooting's stopped around Mason, that the so-called Mason County War's over."

"I believe so, Runt, at least for now."

Fowler smoothed out his bedroll, then stretched out. "You still got that land on Calf Creek, Camp? Did you ever do anything with it?"

"Yes and no."

"Yes, you've still got it, and no, you haven't done anything with it?"

"Right."

Fowler raised himself up on an elbow. "A hell of a lot of good it's doing you just lying there. I know that Calf Creek area like the back of my hand, Camp, and it's some of the best ranching property in Texas. You need to build something on it."

"I know, Runt, but every time I get ready to start on it, something else always comes up. I'll eventually get around to it. I intend to build a log house right there on the hill where I showed you, and leave those two big oaks standing in the front yard."

"I remember exactly where it is," Fowler said, sitting upright now. "One of the prettiest places I ever saw."

Darkness had settled in now, and both men were quiet for a long time. Finally, Houston's eyelids grew heavy. He was just dozing off when Fowler's deep voice startled him. "Want me to build that house for you, Camp?"

Houston did not answer right away, for he was busy thinking. He had no doubt that Fowler could handle the job. He remembered a log barn that Runt had built for John Butterworth several years earlier. The barn was not only a solid building, it looked better than the house Butterworth lived in. "Did I hear you right, Runt?" Camp asked finally.

"Sure. I can build the house while you're running around the country. It'll give me somewhere to be, and something to do."

"I'll give it some thought, Runt. One thing I have to figure out is how much I can pay you."

"That ain't no problem," Fowler said quickly. "You don't have to pay me anything till I finish the job, then just pay me whatever you can. I ain't gonna hurt none. I've got enough money to tide me over till next spring. The first thing I'll do is build myself a small shelter close to the homesite, something tight enough to winter in. Then I won't have to be in any hurry on the house, just take my time and do it right. I'll build a barn and some corrals, too."

"Let me think myself to sleep on it, Runt," Camp said after a time. "You'd sure be needing a lot of things that cost money."

"Yeah? Like what?"

"Like a team and a wagon," Camp began. "Like tools, chains, lumber to seal the inside and build the floors, and either tin or shingles to build a damn roof. Not to mention several kegs of nails and a stove to cook your grub on."

"Well, yeah," Fowler mumbled. "Stuff like that, sure."

Once again Camp told his friend that he would think on the idea, that they would discuss it further in the morning. Houston was still thinking on it when he went to sleep two hours later, but he had reached a decision: he would soon be the proud owner of a fine homestead on Calf Creek, and Runt Fowler would be his builder.

They ate a breakfast of smoked ham and biscuits next morning. Then Camp spent the next half hour drawing pictures and directions in the sand with a stick. Fowler studied the drawings intently, nodding all the while. "I know exactly what you want, Camp. You told me the day you showed me the property."

"Sorry, Runt." He slapped Fowler on the back and threw away the stick. "I didn't mean to keep harping on it. I just wanted to be sure you understand the layout I want. If you build something in the wrong place, you're stuck with it."

Camp dug around in his pack for a while, spent a few moments writing, then handed Fowler a bank draft for two hundred dollars. "Take this by the bank in Mason," he said, "and Roy Holder'll give you the cash. Then go on to Menardville and talk to Sid Blankenship, at the livery stable. Tell him I said to let you have a good team and wagon, that I'll settle with him when I see him. Do as much of your trading right there in Menardville as you can, 'cause the community needs the money. Any merchant in town'll bend over backward to help you, and there's not a shyster in the bunch. I suppose about all the teenage boys around there are out of work. Hire one of them when you need some help."

Fowler looked at the draft, nodded and put it in his vest pocket. "Guess by God it's time I was heading for Calf Creek, huh?" He dashed his coffee grounds into the bushes, and headed for his big piebald.

A short time later, the men shook hands and Fowler rode north. Houston stood watching till Runt disappeared from sight, then stepped up into his own saddle and turned the roan's head southeast.

7

The town of Corpus Christi was situated on the Gulf of Mexico, and Camp expected the ride to take at least a week. He allowed the roan to choose its own pace. He crossed the Nueces River at noon, halting only long enough to eat some ham and biscuits and feed his animals. Then he continued in a southeasterly direction. He skirted the town of Uvalde just before sunset, and made camp on the west bank of the Frio.

He found good grass for his horses easily enough, and although there was plenty of deadwood lying around, he built no fire. He washed the cold beef and biscuits down with water from his canteen, then spread his bedroll. By the time full darkness came on he had surrendered to his drowsiness and the blood-sucking mosquitoes that would feed on him all night.

He continued to spend most of every day in the saddle, and almost always held his animals to a walking gait. This was certainly not the time of year to be in a hurry, for the weather was very hot, and horses had been known to fall dead from heat stroke with no warning.

He arrived in Corpus Christi at four o'clock in the afternoon, eight days after leaving Brackettville. He had been enjoying the cool breeze from the gulf for the past several miles, and it had dried not only the shirt he wore, but the backs of his horses as well.

As he rode down the street toward the livery stable, he was quickly reminded that he was in a tourist town, for few of the men he encountered were dressed in western garb. Instead, they wore every color of shirt that could be imagined, and some even wore light-colored hats that appeared to be made from leaves. Camp smiled, and rode on.

At the livery, he draped his saddlebags across his shoulder and dismounted. He unsheathed his rifle, then handed the reins to a middle-aged man. He did not introduce himself, nor did he ask the hostler's name. "Need to rest my horses for a couple days," he said. "Traveling in this heat's taking its toll on 'em."

"Yep," the liveryman said, flashing a standard commercial smile. "It's showing on 'em, all right." He handed the roan's reins to a teenaged boy, saying, "You heard the man, Trent. Put 'em in them two new stalls and rub 'em down. Then grain 'em good and give 'em two blocks of hay apiece. Leave the doors open, now, so they can get fresh water out there in the corral."

Knowing that every word spoken by the hostler had been designed not to instruct the kid but to impress the customer, Camp stifled a chuckle. The youngster appeared to be at least sixteen years old, and had no doubt grown up around the stable; hardly the type who would have to be told how to take care of a horse. Nevertheless, the hostler was not quite done yet. He offered Camp the same toothy smile, then shouted down the hall toward the stables. "Rub them horses till they're good and dry, now, Trent!"

Then the liveryman spoke to Camp again: "He'll leave your packsaddle back yonder, but he'll bring all your packs up here." He pointed over his shoulder to a windowless room at the front of the building. "I keep all that kind of stuff in the office, under lock and key."

Houston nodded. "That's nice to know," he said. "I need to get my razor and some clean clothing out of one of those packs, anyway."

A few minutes later, Camp walked up the street toward the nearest hotel, his saddlebags across his shoulder, his rifle and clothing in his hands. The hostler had asked him to pay in advance for the lodging of his horses. The exorbitant fee only served to once again remind him that he was in a tourist town: back in Menard County, the same money he had just paid for a two-night stay would have bought enough oats to feed his horses for a month.

He walked west till he reached the corner of the next block, then stopped at the Lighthouse Hotel. The desk clerk greeted him with the same commercial smile as the hostler, and charged him two prices for the key to an upstairs room. Houston climbed the stairway, found his room and turned the key in the lock.

Standing just inside the doorway, he began to feel a little better about the price he had paid, for the room was spacious and very well appointed, almost elegant. A chest of drawers, two chairs, a large table, and even the bedstead appeared to be made of mahogany, and a full-length mirror was attached to the closet door.

The usual coal-oil lamp and a pitcher of water rested on the table, along with a washcloth, soap and towel. Closer to the closet, and about a foot from the wall, was an oversized washtub that was half full of water.

A sign on the wall informed Houston that, should he so desire, hot bathwater could be had. All he had to do was make that desire known to the management and pay a "small" fee.

Camp smiled, and dunked his hand in the tub, deciding that splashing around in the cool water for a few minutes was exactly what he needed.

An hour later, he stepped out on the street. He had shaved, bathed and changed into clean clothing, and most of the weariness had left his body. He walked about the town for a while, occasionally being jostled by someone attempting to hurry along the crowded street.

He was paying close attention to the number of horses hitched in front of the various buildings. He was searching for a crowded saloon, for according to Joe Plenty, Red Bentley spent a large portion of his time in such places. Besides, Camp was not quite ready for supper. He would have a much stronger appetite after having a drink or two.

He finally chose a place called Mookie's, which sported a sign boasting that drinking, gambling and dancing took place inside. The two hitching rails held as many horses as they could accommodate, as did two rails across the street where businesses had closed for the day.

He pushed his way through the large building's batwing doors, then stepped aside quickly, leaning against the wall. Once his eyes had adjusted to the dim lighting, he immediately recognized the bartender as Casey Holbrook, a man he had known for many years.

Holbrook was a jack-of-all-trades, and every time Camp had ever seen him, the man had been working at a different type of job. A dark-haired six-footer, in his early thirties, Holbrook knew how to do any number of things, and do them well. He had shifted from one profession to another all of his adult life, and moved from place to place anytime he felt the urge, usually with the changing of the seasons.

He had even worked on the Lazy B for a while, where Houston had been his foreman. And although he had been a good cowhand, he had a strong aversion to sixteen-hour days in the saddle, and had quit just before the fall roundup began.

After a while, the bartender's face broke into a broad

smile, and he motioned Houston over. Knowing that he had also been recognized, Camp stepped forward and pushed his right hand across the bar. "Good to see you, Casey," he said, pumping the man's hand. "Whoever said it was a small world sure knew what the hell he was talking about."

Holbrook released the hand, then grabbed Houston's shoulder, giving it a little shake. "I don't think I've ever been so surprised to see a man, Camp." All the while, he had been reaching under the counter with his left hand. "I keep the good stuff under here," he said, chuckling. "Have a seat."

Houston seated himself, and Casey poured him a stiff drink, refusing payment. "Didn't think I'd ever see you again, Camp," he said. "Not unless I went back up around Butterworth's place, and I ain't likely to do that."

Houston sampled the whiskey, then wiped his lips with the heel of his hand. "Well, I don't know, Casey," he said. "Sometimes I think a man's likely to end up most anywhere in the world except where he thought he'd be."

"You just said a mouthful, Camp." Holbrook stood thoughtful for a while, as if trying to make a difficult decision. Finally, he poured a glass half full of whiskey, clinked it against the one held by Houston and proposed a toast: "To old times."

"To old times," Camp repeated, and touched his glass to his lips.

Neither man spoke for a while. When Holbrook finished his drink, he set the glass down noisily. "Excuse me for a minute," he said. He untied his apron and rolled it up, then moved away. He unlatched a small gate at the end of the bar, then headed for a separate room that was probably the office.

Camp sat at the bar alone for what seemed like a long time. He had finished his drink and was thinking about finding another saloon when Holbrook appeared beside him. "I took the rest of the night off," he said. "Let's go somewhere else."

Houston was off the barstool quickly. "Lead the way," he

said. "Are they gonna have something to eat where we're going?"

Holbrook stood quietly for a few seconds, then smiled. "Hadn't thought about you being hungry," he said. "How about the Fisherman's Wharf? They've got the best seafood of any restaurant in Corpus."

Camp pointed toward the front door. "Lead the way," he repeated.

They walked north till they reached the blue waters of the gulf, then turned east. After passing boathouses, bait houses and a few small dwellings, Holbrook pointed out the Fisherman's Wharf, located in a small cove. Most of the building hung out over the water, supported by pilings of heavy timber, and as the name implied, a wharf made of thick planks led to its front door.

They stepped onto the wharf and headed for the restaurant. The sound of their bootheels striking the hardwood boards brought a smile to Camp's face. He began to make a conscious effort to walk more quietly, but was unsuccessful.

A beautiful, dark-haired hostess, who was obviously of Mexican descent, greeted them at the door. A blond-haired waiter, who appeared to be still in his teens, escorted them to a table, then headed elsewhere. Still another waiter, a gray-haired man who was probably past fifty, brought a pitcher of coffee. He filled two cups with the steaming liquid, left each man a copy of the bill of fare, and then he too disappeared.

When yet another waiter appeared, pad and pencil in hand, Houston waved him away. He spoke to Holbrook softly: "I'm not used to this much attention, Casey. I don't need all this shit."

Holbrook laughed aloud. "It's designed to make a man think he's somebody special," he said, "so he won't hit the ceiling when he sees the bill. I don't ever worry about the bills, 'cause I don't have to pay 'em. I treat people here several times a month, and just charge it to the saloon." He patted Camp's hand and laughed again, adding, "So, my good man, just make your wishes known. Even though Mookie Mitchell don't know you, your supper's on him tonight."

Holbrook crooked his finger at the waiter, then spoke to Camp again. "Order anything you want," he said, "but the seafood platter's the best thing in the house: shrimp, clams, flounder, stuffed crab and a big bowl of oyster gumbo on the side."

Houston nodded. "I'll take your word for it," he said. "Order for both of us."

The meal was just as good as Holbrook had promised, and they sat at the table long after the food disappeared. Even as they ate, they had discussed Houston's mission. "Red Bentley ain't a hard man to find," Holbrook said. "You can usually hear him bragging long before you see him. He hangs out in Rockport, about twenty miles up the coast. He bought Kate King out about a year ago, so he's got his own saloon now. He probably stays pretty close to home nowadays. You see, Rockport's a small town, and Bentley likes being a big duck in a little puddle.

"I guess the story is as old as time, and you've certainly known men like Bentley before. The sonofabitch is pissed off at the rest of the world because he himself is such a damn runt. I've heard some pretty knowledgeable men say that he's fast with a six-gun, though, so I guess he is. He killed a man named Dave Hunter last winter, but one man who saw it said that Hunter was so drunk he couldn't find his ass with both hands. I believe every word of that, Camp, because I know Red Bentley."

Holbrook had just snuffed out a cigarette, and was busy rolling another. "By the way," he added, as he licked the paper and gave it a final twist, "Bentley's given name is Calvin, and that's what he likes to be called. I've heard it said that he once threatened to shoot somebody for calling him Red."

Camp leaned closer, for the restaurant was noisy. "Did you say Calvin?"

"Yep. And he gets madder'n hell if anybody mentions his red head."

Houston nodded. He would remember the things he was hearing. "What's the name of Bentley's saloon?" he asked.

"Used to be called Kate King's Korner, and the place is so well known that I can't imagine Bentley changing the name. You can't miss it if you go looking. When you ride into town from the west you'll be on First Street, and the saloon's right there on the left-hand corner."

Camp sat for a while digesting the information, then spoke softly: "Who's the town marshal in Rockport?"

"I don't believe they have one right now. Whittaker resigned several months ago, and I don't think anybody else has shown any interest. The marshaling job don't pay enough for an honest man to live on, and it's dangerous as hell besides.

"Clyde Cash is sheriff of Aransas County, but he don't give a shit what goes on in Rockport, even though it's the county seat. They say that he's afraid of his shadow, and even more afraid of Red Bentley." He held up the empty coffeepot for a few moments to get the waiter's attention, then continued talking. "Clyde Cash ain't gonna give you any shit, no matter what you do to Bentley. And Bentley ain't gonna be a problem for you either. Hell, he's never been up against anybody with know-how. He's made his whole reputation shooting drunks and inexperienced men who scarcely knew one end of a six-shooter from the other. He runs off at the mouth constantly, and I've heard it with my own two ears. He brags about how good he is to anybody who'll listen, and I think that he really believes it. Overconfidence is a dangerous thing, Camp, and if the truth was known, it's probably what gets most of the animals in the woods killed.

"I'd even bet that a rabbit gets a little braver every time he gets away from a small dog. And after he does that a few times, the next thing he'll do is sit around in the tall weeds somewhere and convince himself that he can outrun a damn hound. Then it ain't very long till he don't have any problems of any kind."

Houston chuckled. "You sure have a way of putting things, Casey, but I doubt that anybody's ever gonna mistake your meaning."

"I hope not," Holbrook said, getting to his feet.

At the door, both men flirted with the hostess, then stepped outside. Although the night was as black as pitch, several lighted lanterns hung from posts along the wharf, lighting it all the way to the street. They returned to the saloon by the same route they had come. They continued to talk as they walked, sometimes having to raise their voices in order to be heard above the din of barking dogs.

When they reached Mookie's Saloon, Camp stopped at the front door. "I guess I'll get on back to the hotel, Casey. I don't want to drink any more, and I need a good night's sleep. I'll be heading for Rockport in the morning."

"You gonna come back to Corpus when you get done up there?"

Camp nodded. "Yep, I'll have to. I'm gonna leave my packhorse here at the livery stable, so I'll have one less thing to worry about. I don't expect to be gone long."

Holbrook put a hand on Houston's shoulder and squeezed. "You take care, old buddy, and be sure you don't let that bastard get the drop on you." He stepped inside the saloon, continuing to speak over the top of the batwing doors. "I hope you'll let me know something as soon as you get back."

"Count on it," Camp said, then disappeared down the shadowy street.

The sun was straight overhead when Houston rode into Rockport next day. He saw very quickly that Bentley's ego had overruled his business sense, for he had indeed changed the name of the saloon. According to the sign out front, Kate King's Korner was no more, and the place was now Cal Bentley's Saloon and Recreation Hall.

Camp tied the roan at a hitching rail across the street, then seated himself on a sidewalk bench in front of a hardware store. He leaned his shoulders against the wall and relaxed, for he was in no hurry. He was in town on business, and it would be handled in a businesslike manner.

From where he sat he could see up and down both sides of the street, and had a good view of Bentley's saloon. He had spoken to no one, nor did he intend to until it became necessary. He planned to sit tight for a while, hoping that he might spot his quarry going in or coming out of the saloon.

An hour later, however, he changed his mind, for he was very uncomfortable. The noonday sun shone directly on the bench, and his shirt was already wet with sweat when he got to his feet. He led the roan across the street and tied it at the saloon's hitching rail, then stepped up onto the plank sidewalk.

He leaned against the saloon for a while, trying to decide on some way to flush Bentley out. He had about decided to take the bull by the horns and go in after the man when he heard a clattering sound behind him. He turned to see a middle-aged man who was obviously headed for the saloon, his peg leg striking the planks noisily as he hurried along.

As the man drew abreast, Camp spoke to him softly: "I was wondering if you'd do me a favor, mister. I—"

"Whatcha want done?" the man interrupted.

Camp withdrew a dollar from his pocket. "Well, I need you to carry a message to Calvin Bentley, and I'm willing to pay for it."

The man accepted the money and shoved it into his vest pocket, then raised his eyebrows questioningly, waiting for further instructions.

"Just tell him that I want to see him out here at the hitching rail," Camp said.

The man nodded, and walked through the swinging doors.

He was back in less than two minutes, shaking his head nervously. "He says to tell you that if you want to see him you'll have to come to his office, like everybody else does."

Houston stood quietly for a few moments, thinking. He believed that if he challenged Bentley publicly, the man would come through the front door immediately. And he believed that Bentley would come alone, for his ego would forbid his asking for help, thereby admitting that he was afraid to face another gunman.

Houston moved away from the building, readjusted his gun belt, and spoke to the man again: "Make sure all of Bentley's friends hear you when you give him the second part of the message: Tell him that I stayed out here because I don't want to make a mess in there. Tell him that I'm here to kill him."

The man nodded, and disappeared inside the building.

Camp pushed his hat to the back of his head and stood waiting, his body bent slightly forward and his feet spread apart. When the noise inside the saloon ceased abruptly, he knew that the message had been delivered.

A few moments later, the batwing doors flew open and Bentley, red-faced and thoroughly antagonized, was suddenly on the sidewalk. He looked Houston in the eye, and spoke loudly: "You the one out here shootin' his mouth off? Who in th' hell—"

"The name is Camp Houston," Camp interrupted.

All color suddenly drained from Bentley's face. He had heard the name many times, and was well aware of the reputation associated with it. "Camp . . . Hou—" Just as if he had come down with lockjaw, he stopped talking for a moment. Then he held his left hand out, palm forward, and began to stammer again: "Now, they ain't no use'n . . . ain't no use'n me an' you—"

Houston cut him off again: "I'm here about John Calloway, Bentley. He was a good man, and he was my friend."

"I . . . uh . . . I didn't—"

"You shot him down like a rabid dog, you sonofabitch." Camp shifted his feet again, and pointed to the Colt hanging low on Bentley's hip. "Make your play, fellow! It's the only chance you've got!"

Bentley hesitated for only a moment, then made his play. And even as he took a shot in the mouth he got off one of his own, with the slug knocking splinters off a board between Camp's feet. The man had been fast, all right, quite possibly the fastest gun Camp had ever faced.

Two men stepped to the sidewalk to inspect the body, and several more stood just inside the saloon, staring over the batwing doors.

Houston still held his Colt in his right hand. He untied his horse with his left, and stepped into the saddle. Then he spoke loudly, almost shouting. "Listen up, men, and listen good!" When he had the attention of all, he related the story of the hapless drovers. When they heard that there was a survivor who pointed the finger directly at Red Bentley, and even called him by name, the men began to nod back and forth, talking excitedly among themselves.

Camp turned his horse's head, and continued to speak: "If it turns out that the U.S. marshal wants to pursue this matter, he can find me if he comes looking. My name is Camp Houston." Then, still clutching his Peacemaker, he kicked the roan to a canter. He did not reholster the weapon until he was out of sight.

8

Houston was back in Corpus Christi an hour before sunset. He dismounted at the livery stable, and handed the lathered roan's reins to the hostler. "Take good care of him. He's had a hard day."

"Always do," the man said, taking the reins. "By the way," he added, loosening the saddle girth, "my name's Hullet." When Houston said nothing, the liveryman continued, "I don't reckon I heard your name."

"The name's Camp Houston."

"Oh," Hullet said. He turned to lead the big horse away, adding, "I was wrong about not hearing it. I've been hearing it for years."

Houston entered Mookie's Saloon a few minutes later, and Holbrook was on duty. He sat on a stool behind the bar doing absolutely nothing, for this was the slack period of the day. Only three drinkers were in the building, all of them seated at the far end of the bar.

Casey was on his feet quickly, reaching for a bottle. Houston took a seat on a barstool, and Holbrook poured a glass half full of whiskey. "You already been to Rockport and back?" he asked.

Camp nodded, and wet his lips with whiskey.

Holbrook smiled, and lowered his voice. "Did you take care of that piece of business?"

Camp nodded again, and took a big swallow from his glass. The whiskey went down easily, for it was a premium brand. Casey had poured the drink from the special bottle, which he had quickly returned to its hiding place under the counter.

"Did that piece of business put up a fight?"

Camp nodded again.

Holbrook leaned forward, both elbows resting on the bar. "By God, you're a talkative cuss tonight, Camp. Don't know when I've had anybody feed me so much information."

Houston chuckled, and took another drink. "There ain't really a whole lot to say, Casey. I called the man, and he accepted the challenge. That's about all there was to it."

Holbrook laughed loudly, but continued to talk softly. "All there was to it? Humph. Must have been a little more than that to it, 'cause here you sit drinking the best whiskey in town. I'd bet a damn dollar that he ain't up there in Rockport doing the same thing."

Camp looked Holbrook in the eye for a moment, then shook his head slowly. "No, Casey. He won't be needing a drink tonight."

They were quiet for a while as Camp finished off his drink. He set the empty glass on the bar noiselessly, then slid off the barstool. "I'm gonna eat supper and call it a night early, Casey," he said, pushing his right hand across the bar for a parting handshake. "It's been a pleasure running into you again, and I appreciate the hospitality. Guess my place on Calf Creek'll be up and running by this time next year. If you're ever out that way, stop by and stay as long as you like."

Holbrook squeezed the hand, pumping it a few times. "I know the place," he said. "I don't expect to be out there, 'cause life's treating me pretty good here on the coast. Of course, like you said last night, a man never knows which road he might be taking in the future. I'll remember the invitation."

Next morning at nine o'clock, Houston rode out of town. And although his destination was otherwise, he would first have to ride west for several miles. Then, as soon as he had left the big water behind, he would turn the roan's head due north. The trip ahead would be a long one, for he had decided to pay a visit to Jack Little, in Corsicana. He expected to be in the saddle for twelve or fourteen days, for the distance was more than four hundred miles.

Houston had eaten breakfast in the hotel restaurant. Then the cook, after having filled Camp's jars with precooked beans, wrapped up a dozen biscuits and a cake of leftover corn bread. As Camp began his journey, everything he was likely to need was on the packsaddle, including two fifty-pound sacks of grain for the horses.

He traveled steadily all day, and, an hour before sunset, forded Medio Creek. He halted on the north bank, and, after feeding each of his animals a portion of oats, picketed them on long ropes. Finding deadwood was no problem, and he soon had a fire going. Half an hour later, he was eating warmed-over beans and corn bread, washing it down with sugared coffee.

Darkness did not actually come this night, for when the sun disappeared over the western horizon, it was replaced by a full moon. Lying on his bedroll, Camp could even see his horses grazing in the small meadow more than fifty yards away.

He had not even unrolled a blanket, for it was simply too hot for covering. He had taken off his boots, but did not undress, for his clothing offered a certain amount of protection against the mosquitoes. As he lay slapping at his neck, he decided that he would make camp a hundred yards from water tomorrow night, hoping that fewer of the pests would find him.

Sleep was slow to come, for Camp had many things on his mind: Runt Fowler should be settled in on Calf Creek by now, he was thinking. The man had had enough time to build livable quarters for himself, and would probably be starting on Houston's log house anytime now.

That the house would be something he could be proud of, Camp had no doubt, for Runt Fowler was not to be taken lightly. He was not only an honest man but a master builder, and would never take on a project unless he was confident of the outcome. Houston smiled at his thoughts. He was thinking that he might have the pleasure of selecting furnishings for his new home by Christmastime.

And once he had his own home and a herd established on Calf Creek, he would travel to Little Rock to visit his father. And this time, Camp really meant to do it. He had thought about making the trip many times in the past, but always decided that he would do it next year. Next year had always turned into next year, however, and now more than ten years had passed.

Camp would have been hard pressed to explain why he had written only two letters to John Houston, and both of those during the first year after leaving home. It had certainly not been due to ill feelings, or that Camp did not love and respect his father. The elder Houston had always treated his son well, and the two had parted on good terms.

John Houston had even given his son a thousand dollars on the day of his departure, no doubt suspecting that the young man might have difficulty making it on his own.

Camp had indeed made it on his own, however, and even after ten years, the thousand-dollar stake was lying in the bank in Mason gathering interest. Of course, he would soon be using both the interest and the principal to furnish his home and stock his ranch. Then he would travel to Little

Rock. Maybe his father would even return with him to Texas, and spend some time on Calf Creek.

He was still tossing and turning an hour later, his mind now on the business at hand. He knew that Waco was closer to his present position than was Corsicana, but he had a burning desire to face Jack Little as soon as possible. Though all of the killers were equally guilty, Little's betrayal of John Calloway rankled Camp more than the actions of all the others combined.

The others had been hired simply because they happened to be available when Calloway needed men. Little, however, had probably been hired because he was a friend, with the fact that he was a good cowhand being secondary. At any rate, he had been the first man hired. According to Joe Plenty, John Calloway had hunted the man up with a job offer several weeks before the drive began.

Camp had to grit his teeth each time he thought about Jack Little. Calloway had given the man work on three separate occasions, and had obviously paid him well. They had worked, eaten and slept together for months on end, and even shared a hotel room in Dodge City.

The very thought that Little had turned traitor and pumped lead into his longtime friend for no reason other than money stuck in Camp's craw like glue. He spat toward the bushes, as if ridding his mouth of a bad taste, then turned over again. A few minutes later, he finally went to sleep.

He reached the town of Giddings five days later, and put his animals up at the livery stable. Then he rented a hotel room, for he intended to rest himself and his horses for a while. For three days now Camp had been traveling only in the early morning and late afternoon, but the hot weather had nevertheless taken its toll on both man and animals.

"No use in the world in a man having to travel in this kind of heat," the hostler had said, when Camp turned over his horses. "Friend of mine dropped dead from a heat stroke a year ago this month, just fell out of his saddle right out there in the middle of the street. After I saw I couldn't do him no good, I caught up his horse, but two hours later, the horse was dead, too."

Camp nodded, and said nothing. With his saddlebags over his shoulder and his Henry cradled in the crook of his arm, he soon stood in the lobby of the town's only hotel, located half a block from the livery stable. A bald-headed man with a white goatee sat behind the counter. "If ya want a room, ya better git it now," he said, pointing up the stairway with his thumb. "Ain't got but one left. Th' price is a dollar a night."

"I'll take it," Camp said. He produced the money as the clerk handed him a key. Houston reached for the hotel register and signed "*W.C. Fanning*," a surname that he had recently read on the label of a pickle jar.

Inside the room, he pushed his rifle under the bed, then washed his face and hands. He had deliberately left his razor and his clean clothing in his pack at the livery stable. He did not intend to shave his face in the near future, and changing clothing in this kind of weather was unlikely to make a man smell better for more than a few minutes. Even as he splashed water on his face, Camp could feel beads of sweat rolling down his back.

He raised both of the windows and tied back the curtains, hoping to create a crosscurrent of air that would eventually cool the room. Then he locked the door and headed for the stairway. He knew that he was unlikely to find a place that was cool enough to be comfortable, but believed that a cold beer would make the heat seem more bearable. A moment later, he stepped out onto the street.

Now Camp sat in a small saloon, three doors down from the hotel. The table he had chosen was at the front of the building, near a double window, and he had a good view of the sidewalk, the street beyond and the passersby who used both. He was in the act of pouring his third glass of beer from the pitcher he had bought when the skinny bartender, who had no other customers at the moment, approached his table. "Would your name happen to be Camp Houston?" he asked, his green eyes darting around the room nervously.

Houston shook his head. "The name is W.C. Fanning," he said. "Been traveling north for about a week now, but I decided to stop in your town and try to cool off some. I was concerned that the heat might kill my horses, and it certainly wasn't getting any easier on me."

The bartender continued to stand beside the table, absentmindedly twisting the corner of his apron. "They're saying this heat wave is gonna be over by the end of the week," he said, making no attempt to explain exactly who "they" were. He pulled out a chair and took a seat at a nearby table. "Have you ever seen Camp Houston?" he asked.

Camp did not offer a direct answer to the question. He took the last sip of beer from his glass, then wiped the foam from his lips with the heel of his hand. "I've been told before that I look like Camp Houston," he said, pouring more beer from the pitcher.

The bartender began to drum his fingers on the table. "Whoever told you that was sure telling the truth, 'cause it's a fact." He leaned forward, appearing to study Camp's face more closely. "I saw Camp Houston up in Waco a few years back," he continued, "just a few minutes after he shot Dick Manville. Now, I didn't see him up real close, mind you, 'cause the sheriff and several other men were standing around talking to him. Houston did look my way a few times, though, and judging from what I saw that day, I'd call you a dead ringer."

Camp sipped at his beer again. "A dead ringer, huh?"

"You sure look more like him than anybody I've ever seen. Truth of the matter is, there ain't many folks around who are as big as Camp Houston—just a few men like you, and maybe Jack Little."

Jack Little! The name hit Houston like a sledge. His hand

froze in midair for a moment, then set the glass on the table noiselessly. "Who's Jack Little?" he asked, in the most nonchalant tone he could muster.

The answer came quickly: "Little owns that feed store at the edge of town. Not only that, but it's my understanding that he's doing a land-office business with his freight wagons. He's got several of 'em, and most of the time they're on the road day and night. Reckon he must have some kind of franchise deal with the H&TC Railroad, 'cause his wagons are the only ones allowed to pick up freight at the depot. I mean, just about every train that comes through here drops off something on that platform. Then about once a week they sidetrack a boxcar. Jack Little's wagons haul the freight on to wherever it's supposed to end up.

"Little moved to Giddings sometime last fall. Don't think he ever told anybody where he came from, but he must have brought some money with him, 'cause he went into business right away. He's done right well, too. He's got a lot of people working for him, but he don't seem to be afraid of getting his own hands dirty. Even now, he usually drives one of the wagons himself; makes more money that way, I guess."

"I guess," Camp repeated. He asked no more questions concerning Jack Little, for he had learned as much as he needed to know.

Nevertheless, the bartender continued to talk. "They say that the best way in the world for a man to get his ass whipped is to go sassing Jack Little. I don't know all that for sure, now, but I've certainly seen the scars on his knuckles. I've also been told that Little is the main reason every gunslinger in Texas gives this town a wide berth. He's mighty fast, according to all the talk going around."

Camp continued to sit quietly, and placed his hands in his lap so that the scars on his own knuckles could not be seen. A short while later, the bartender, no doubt tired of talking to an unresponsive listener, got to his feet and returned to his stool behind the bar.

Houston was on his feet quickly, headed for the front door. "Gonna hunt up something to eat," he said to the bartender. "The beer made me hungry."

Established on the H&TC Railroad when track was laid from Brenham to Austin in 1871, the town of Giddings was chiefly settled by Wendish immigrants who moved to the railroad from the original community, six miles to the south. Because of its proximity to the railroad, and the fact that it was surrounded by prime farming and ranching country, the small town prospered right from the start, and was soon named the seat of Lee County.

Now, after walking up one side of the street and down the other, Camp stood leaning against a building, admiring the scenery. Evidence that the town had been put together by master German builders, who were obsessed with practicality, could be seen in any direction: a six-horse team and wagon could be turned around in the middle of the street, and every building in town looked as if it belonged exactly where it had been erected, and nowhere else.

Even from where he stood, Camp could see Jack Little's feed store, but he would go no closer. Neither would he approach the railroad depot, which was also within eyeshot. Since the bartender had said that Little often drove one of his freight wagons himself, Houston would bide his time. He felt that if he did not rush things, he would eventually be able to face his man in open country, well away from the town limits of Giddings.

Camp was even hungrier now that he had walked around for a while. He chose a small place that he had walked past earlier, which had painted-over windows and signs advertising hot food. Standing in front of the restaurant, he took a last look up and down both sides of the street, then entered.

He selected a table at the rear of the building, where he could sit with his back to the wall. He had no idea how successful he had been in his effort to convince the bartender that his name was W.C. Fanning, but he was taking no chances.

The skinny man had talked as if he were at least an admirer of Jack Little, and getting word to him that there was a man in town who bore a strong resemblance to Camp Houston would be a simple matter.

He sat for a while reading the bill of fare, then laid it down and got to his feet. At that very moment, a dark-haired waitress arrived at his table. She smiled, and spoke softly: "I'm sorry to have kept you waiting, sir. May I bring you something to eat?"

He nodded. "Bring me some German sausage and sauerkraut to this table," he said. "I've got a short errand to run, but I'll be back by the time you are."

He walked through the front door and headed down the street with long, quick strides. When he reached the saloon, he pushed his way through the doors and stepped inside. The drinkers who had been present earlier were gone now, and the bartender was alone in the building.

Houston leaned over the bar and spoke to the skinny man: "Do I still look like Camp Houston to you?"

"Well, now," the bartender began nervously, "you sorta . . . you kinda—"

"You were right the first time," Camp interrupted, "but so far, you and I are the only two people in this town who know it. I'm asking you to keep this information under your hat."

"Oh, you can count on me doing that," the man said, his lower lip quivering slightly. "You can sure count on me."

Camp nodded, turned to leave, then stopped in his tracks. Deciding that he had not been firm enough with the man, he returned to the bar. "Look," he began. "Lots of people have promised me things in the past that didn't necessarily turn out that way. I'm gonna take your word that you'll keep quiet about this, but if you don't, I think you should know that I'll be back. If you tell one single person that I'm in this town, you're gonna answer to me." He stared into the man's eyes for a while, then added, "And it won't be pleasant."

"No, sir, Mr. Houston," the barkeep said shakily. "Not a word to anybody."

Camp was soon back in the restaurant, arriving at his table just as his food was being served. He smiled at the waitress and pulled out a chair, his eyes sizing up the platter of steaming food. "Looks good," he said.

"Bread pudding with raisins for dessert," she said gushingly. "I believe the cook's taking it out of the oven just about now." Before he could speak again, she was gone to the kitchen. She returned with his pudding a few minutes later, and Camp never saw her again.

The sun was disappearing in the west when he left the restaurant. He stood on the corner for a few moments, looking up the street to the depot. No boxcar stood on the sidetrack, nor was there any freight on the platform. According to the bartender, that situation might very well change with the arrival of the next train, however. If the picture did change, Camp would certainly know about it, for he almost had a bird's-eye view of both the sidetrack and the platform from the window of his hotel room.

He bought a newspaper at the drugstore, then decided to get off the street, for he wanted to be seen by as few people as possible. He headed for his hotel room and the coal-oil lamp, for darkness was coming on fast. Tonight would not be the first time he had used the *Fort Worth Democrat* to read himself to sleep.

He was soon lying on his bed enjoying the cool of the evening. The windows he had opened earlier in the day had created a draft, and the temperature in the room was now pleasant enough. So pleasant, in fact, that he went to sleep with the lamp burning. He was still reading the front page when his eyes closed and the newspaper fell to the floor.

A loud, clanging noise woke him, and he immediately recognized the sound. He shielded his eyes from the lamplight with one hand, and reached for his pants with the other. He looked at his watch, and was not surprised to learn that it was three o'clock in the morning. He had slept for more than seven hours.

He sat on his bed for a few moments listening to the sound that had awakened him: a train was at the depot, pulling forward, then backing up, jerking and clanging the boxcars against each other. Knowing that a freight car was being uncoupled on the sidetrack, Camp slipped on his pants, then blew out the lamp.

As the clanging noise continued, he walked to the window and stood looking toward the depot. By the light of the flickering lanterns they carried, he could make out the forms of several men walking up and down the track. Through the open window he could very clearly hear them shouting back and forth, and even understood some of their words.

Feeling his way around the dark room till he found a chair, he pulled it over to the window and sat watching. He knew that he would be able to see better in just a short while, for daylight came early in the summertime. A number of the townspeople had already touched fire to the wicks of their lamps, for now Camp could see lighted windows where darkened buildings had stood only moments before. He had obviously not been the only one awakened by the train.

He was still sitting by the window when the black of night turned to gray, and he began to make out a certain amount of movement on the street. He saw no mounted men, however, just a few people moving hurriedly from one building to another. Then, as dawn chased away the last remnants of darkness, he pulled the flimsy curtain between himself and the window and continued his vigil.

Just as the first rays of sunshine hit the street, Camp heard the sound he had been waiting for. Even as he sat listening, two wagons rolled into view from the east. The heavy freighters, with their oversized wheels, were coupled together and pulled by six large mules. The vehicles rolled right under

Camp's window, and he could easily see the double-barreled shotgun behind the seat of the lead wagon.

He also got a look at the driver. Though the hat pulled low over his eyes hid much of his face, the man was the right size, with the same stooped shoulders that Camp had been told about. And though a teamster wearing a sidearm was a rarity, the man driving the mules under the window wore a Peacemaker on his right hip.

Camp had seen enough, and had no doubt that the man on the wagon was his quarry. He seated himself on the bed and slipped on his boots, for he had been sitting at the window barefoot. Then he gathered up his things and was out of the room quickly. A few minutes later, he was at the livery stable.

"I need to use the roan for a while," he said to the hostler. "I'll just leave the packhorse here for the time being."

The liveryman nodded, took a coiled rope from a peg on the wall and headed toward the corral. When he returned a few minutes later, he was leading the roan. He handed the reins to Houston. "Want me to saddle him for you?"

"No," Camp said. He saddled the animal, shoved his Henry in the boot, then mounted. With his saddlebags still lying across his shoulder, he rode through the doorway and up the wide street. There was a small restaurant on the corner, just before the street reached the railroad. He tied the roan at the hitching rail, then stepped inside.

Seating himself at a table by the window, where he could easily see the freight car on the sidetrack, he ordered breakfast from a middle-aged woman. While he was waiting for his order, he took the picture of the drovers from his saddlebag and slipped it into the pocket of his vest. Then he sat sipping the coffee the lady had brought, his eyes on the action at the depot.

The sliding doors on each side of the boxcar were open now, and several men were moving about. And though it appeared that at least one of the freighters was on each side of the car, the dual hookup that had passed under Camp's window was on the near side. After being driven as close as was practical to the boxcar, the sideboards on one side of each wagon had been removed, and the grunting men were now busy sliding heavy crates down a wooden ramp and onto the lead wagon. The mules would no doubt be driven a few steps forward when it was loaded, then the process would be repeated with the second vehicle.

Camp had finished eating his steak and eggs and was drinking his third cup of coffee when he saw the workers put the sideboards back on the wagons. Then the big man climbed to the seat and turned the mules around, heading them right back through town. Houston held his seat as the wagons passed. This time his view was much better, and there was no doubt about it: the man on the driver's seat was none other than Jack Little.

Camp left the restaurant and stood beside the hitching rail for a while, then mounted and headed east, riding down the street very slowly. He halted at the edge of town and sat watching, waiting to see which way the wagons headed. At the fork in the road, two hundred yards east of town, Little took a left-hand turn in the direction of Caldwell, in Burleson County. Camp waited till the wagons had disappeared around the bend, then he guided his horse onto the dusty road.

Though he did not intend to let Jack Little reach the town of Caldwell, Camp would have been more than happy to hold off on a showdown till after the man crossed the county line. The Burleson County sheriff, a man named Henry Pugh, had been a friend of Camp's for many years. In fact, on Houston's very first cattle drive, when he had helped push two thousand steers up the Chisholm Trail to Abilene, Pugh had been the trail boss. The two men had gotten along very well, and though they seldom saw each other nowadays, the friendship was still intact.

Although he had no way of knowing if Henry Pugh had personally known John Calloway, Camp thought it was highly possible, since both men had for many years been in the same line of work. However, even if Pugh had not known Calloway, Houston believed that the sheriff would empathize with the pitiful plight of a fellow drover. Camp shook his head. No, sir, he was not the least bit concerned about leaving Jack Little's remains in Sheriff Henry Pugh's county.

Camp continued his pursuit from a distance of several hundred yards, always making sure that he could not be seen. Then, after he had followed the wagon across Yegua Creek and moved into Burleson County, he turned off the road and kicked the roan to a canter.

He made a wide half circle to the southeast, then north. When he returned to the Caldwell road, he was a few minutes ahead of the wagon. Afraid that his horse might whinny and give away his presence, he dismounted and tied the animal a hundred yards from the road. Then, remembering that Little had been sitting on the left end of the wagon seat, Camp crossed to the north side of the road.

He took up a position at the base of a small hill, behind a clump of tall bushes. His wait was not a long one. No more than ten minutes passed before he began to hear the rattling of chains and the sound of the oversized wheels crushing the dry, hard earth. Then the mules were upon him, trotting down the hill to stay ahead of the wagons that literally pushed them along, in spite of the fact that Little was busy yanking on the brake.

Then, just as the animals leaned into the harness to begin the hard pull up the incline, Houston stepped into the road. He raised his left hand high into the air, signaling the driver to stop. His right hand held a Colt .45 that was pointed at the man's head. The mules halted in their tracks. "Tie up the reins and get down, Little!" Camp said loudly, motioning with his gun barrel to emphasize his words. "You've got some business with me!"

Little sat with his mouth half open as his face literally changed colors. Even his right eye—the one with the permanent squint—was wide open now. "I . . . I think I know who you are," he said through quivering lips, "and I sure ain't got no squabble with you."

"Get down!" Houston ordered, even louder now.

Little complied. He wrapped the reins around the brake, then jumped to the ground, facing his antagonist.

Camp did not keep him waiting. "John Calloway was a friend of mine, Little. I suppose that should tell you why I'm here." He stood quietly for a few moments, then added, "I'd also like to have a talk with your old buddies Walt Turner and Sam Lott. Now, where would I be likely to find them?"

As Camp had expected, the man did not answer the question. Little continued to fidget nervously, then began to stammer, "Well, I don't guess I . . . what I mean is . . . I've got money now. Why, I can give you—"

"I'm sure that you do have money now," Camp interrupted, "but I wouldn't be interested." He slowly holstered his Peacemaker, spread his legs apart and leaned his body slightly forward. "I'm here to collect more than money, fellow. Go for your gun, you no-good bastard!"

Little shook his head. "I . . . I know exactly who you are now," he said. "You're Camp Houston, that's who you are, and I ain't about to draw against you." Then, as if to make sure there was no misunderstanding, he clasped his hands together behind his back.

Houston continued to stare into Little's eyes, surprised at the man's actions. "You pretended to be John Calloway's friend for years," he said, "then by God you shot him in the back for nothing more than the money he was carrying. I'm giving you the chance that you never gave him, Little: I'm gonna count to three, then I'm gonna start shooting."

Little continued to stand with his hands behind his back even as the count began. True to his word, when Camp reached the count of three, he drew his Colt and put two slugs in Little's chest. Only then did the man unclasp his hands. He grunted loudly, then fell on his face at the side of the road.

When Houston was convinced that Jack Little had taken his last breath, he moved the wagons off the road, then unhitched and unharnessed the mules and turned them loose. Then he walked to his saddler, mounted, and took a shortcut to the Giddings livery stable to pick up his packhorse.

9

Five days later, Camp crossed the Brazos River on the long, swinging bridge that separated Waco east from west. He knew the town well, for his very first job after coming to Texas had been on the Flying W, a nearby ranch owned by a man named Albert Wells.

He turned south after crossing the bridge. Riding down the street toward the livery stable, he scanned along the sidewalk for a familiar face, but saw none. He even had to look around him occasionally to pinpoint his exact location, for though all of the prominent landmarks remained the same, Waco had changed much in recent years.

The fact that the Chisholm Trail ran right through town had brought prosperity to most of Waco's merchants. Many had put new faces on their establishments, while others had erected new buildings altogether. The majority of the merchants who had rebuilt had relocated, giving the street an entirely different look from the one Camp remembered.

The Bryan Hotel still looked the same, however, as did the Texas Saloon. He rode past both buildings on his way to the livery stable, which was located at the end of the street. At the stable, a teenaged boy relieved him of his horses, promising to treat them as if they were his own.

After renting a room at the hotel, Houston walked to the adjacent barbershop, where he bought a shave and a bath. Then, after changing into clean clothing, he was on his way to the Texas Saloon, for he remembered that the establishment used to serve what was widely referred to as the best Mexican food in Texas.

In bygone years the Texas had employed Mexican cooks in its kitchen, and their south-of-the-border concoctions had been one of the saloon's main drawing cards. Knowing that good businessmen were reluctant to change a winning combination, in this case good food, good whiskey and pretty women, Camp thought it highly unlikely that owner Al Foster had allowed the quality of the food to deteriorate.

A few minutes later, he pushed through the saloon's batwing doors and headed for the dining room, which was nothing more than a roped-off area adjoining the kitchen on one side and the dance floor on the other. A smiling, flirting, dark-haired waitress was there quickly. She first served him a cup of steaming coffee, then took his order for an enchilada dinner.

"Your food will be at least half an hour in coming, sir," she said, moving his silverware around while deliberately leaning across the table to offer him a good look at her ample bosom. "If you need more coffee in the meantime, just lift your empty cup and wave it around a little." She laughed, then was gone to the kitchen.

He sat looking around the large room while waiting for his food. There had been few changes over the years, and Camp well remembered his visits to the saloon when he was a young greenhorn. It was on one of those visits that he had experienced his first intimate contact with a woman, with the encounter taking place in a fifty-cent bedroom at the top of yonder stairway.

He had spent many a Saturday night dancing on that hardwood floor, and had probably eaten off the same table at which he was now sitting. And there was the same fifty-foot bar, with stations for three bartenders. On weekends there was a man at each of the stations, for the Texas was by far the busiest saloon in McLennan County.

An hour later, after having enjoyed his dinner, Camp walked to the bar and seated himself on a stool. "I'll have whiskey and water," he said to the tall, skinny bartender, who appeared to be in an unsound state of health. His complexion was a sickly-looking sallow and the skin on his face hung loosely, suggesting that he had once been a much heavier man. His short, coal-black hair grew almost down to his eyebrows, not unlike some of the animals Houston had once seen in a zoo.

Limping noticeably as he moved about, the man set two glasses on the bar, one of them half full of water. Then he reached into a cabinet under the counter for a bottle of whiskey, setting it on the bar noisily. "I usually let a man pour his own, if he ain't too drunk," he said. "That way, nobody ever accuses me of slighting 'em."

Camp nodded, and poured himself a drink of what, according to the label, was an acceptable brand of whiskey. He smiled at the thought, however, for he knew that labels meant very little in most saloons: a saloon owner or a bartender could simply take a bottle bearing a respectable label and fill it with rotgut. Then it would take its place on the shelf beside the good stuff, and any man ordering a drink from that particular bottle would be charged a premium price.

Bartenders seldom poured from such bottles if a man was ordering his first drink of the day. Once he had consumed several drinks, however, the man who could tell the difference between rotgut and premium whiskey was rare. And even if a bartender did get a complaint, he could always shrug, turn his palms upward and play dumb. The trick was to pour the fraudulent bottles a little less than full, so the customer would expect the seal to be broken.

Camp took a sip from his glass, and quickly decided that the whiskey was genuine. He had expected no less, for even though Al Foster was a high-stakes gambler, he had the reputation of being a square shooter. And during all of the years he had known the man, Houston had never heard anybody say otherwise.

The bartender stood quietly for a few moments, then poured himself a drink. He inhaled the whiskey in one quick gulp, then dropped the empty glass into a pan of water. He continued to eye Houston for a while, then spoke: "Didn't you used to work out at the Flying W?"

Camp nodded. "Worked out there for several months in '68," he said. "Been living farther west since then."

"Well, I thought I'd seen you before. Then I remembered that you used to come into my place with the Flying W hands. You probably don't recognize me, but I owned the Longhorn Saloon back then. A man cut a tree down on my right leg three years ago, and I lost the business while I was laid up. Lost everything I owned, in fact."

"I'm sorry to hear that," Camp said. He continued to look the bartender over, glancing elsewhere occasionally to keep from staring. Then the man's identity hit him, and he spoke quickly: "Are you Flint Hastings?"

The man wiped at a wet spot on the bar and began to nod, smiling broadly. "One and the same, my boy. I didn't expect you to know me; hell, I've lost a hundred pounds since you saw me. I stayed in bed for nearly a year. Then when I did get up I wasn't worth a damn. No, sir, you ain't the only one that don't recognize me nowadays. I can't even recognize myself. My poor little wife's been having to shave my face every morning for the past two years. I quit using mirrors a long time ago. Got tired of looking at a damn corpse."

Not wishing to dwell on the bartender's health problems,

Camp poured himself another drink, then changed the subject. "How's Albert Wells doing these days, Flint?"

Hastings chuckled softly. "Albert Wells is doing the same thing he's always done, getting richer by the day." He poured himself another drink, then continued, "I know I don't have to tell you what a good layout that ranch is. Wells bought several sections that bordered him on the west, and the Flying W reaches all the way to the Bosque River now. He's got thousands of longhorns, perennial grasses, and he'll never have to worry about water again. I know for a fact that he's sent three herds north to the rails this year, and I hear that the Kansas buyers paid his asking price for all of 'em. I'm talking about the first two herds, of course, 'cause the third one ain't got there yet. It just left here ten days ago."

Houston sipped at his drink. "I sure don't envy those drovers," he said. "This is the hottest time of the year, and half of the grass is already dead. I wonder why Albert waited so late to send up this last herd."

"I don't think he planned it that way. From what I hear, Wells wasn't gonna send this bunch up till next spring, but one of the buyers got real anxious, wanted two thousand head of longhorns right now. Fellow told me that the buyer offered Wells a bonus big enough to cover the entire expense of getting the herd up there, including the salaries of the drovers. Now, you and I both know that Albert Wells ain't gonna pass up a deal like that."

Camp shook his head. "Can't think of anybody who would." He emptied his glass, then refilled it. "Don't guess there's a soul left out at the Flying W that I'd know," he said. "After all, it's been ten years since I was there."

"Not much chance," Hastings said. "It's a whole new bunch out there now, all of 'em what you and I would call youngsters. Even the foreman's a loudmouthed, blond-haired kid with a squeaky voice. Ain't got a bit of hair on his face, and he sounds like he might not have none on his balls."

Camp was suddenly very interested. "What's the foreman's name?" he asked.

"You wouldn't know him. Kid named Sam Lott. Grew up right here in Waco."

Houston sat quietly for a while. He sipped at his drink nonchalantly, showing no sign that he had heard the young foreman's name before. "Like I was saying," he began, raising his voice for emphasis, "I sure don't envy those drovers. During these first few weeks it's gonna be the hottest drive any of 'em ever made, then they'll probably freeze their asses off coming home. I've been on those Kansas plains in the fall of the year, and that wind can make a man wish he'd never seen a damn longhorn. It's liable to blow hard and cold for weeks, twenty-four hours a day, then dump a foot or two of snow on you before you can find a hole to crawl into."

"Know what you mean," Hastings said. "I've done some traveling myself, and I've certainly felt that November wind whipping across the wide-open plains. The drovers are gonna feel it too, 'cause there ain't no way in hell that they can get back here before Thanksgiving Day."

Camp nodded, and finished off his drink. "Thanksgiving Day sounds about right to me," he said. Houston had heard enough. He had no business in this town at the present, and knew that he would be heading for Calf Creek at sunup. Then, come the last week of November, he would be visiting Waco again. He slid off the stool, paid for his drinks and waved good-bye to the bartender.

As Camp reached the front door, Hastings called after him: "You never did say what your name was!"

"The name is Bo Granger," Houston said over his shoulder. He stepped onto the sidewalk and headed for his hotel room. He would get a good night's sleep, then head for Menardville.

10

★

The ride to Calf Creek took six days, and Camp arrived at midafternoon. He topped the hill above his homesite and sat his saddle for several minutes. He could hear the sound of hammers, but saw no workmen. Nevertheless, he was pleasantly amazed at the scene below: the outer walls of his home, built of foot-thick logs, appeared to have been completed.

Sporting a shiny tin roof, the building had been placed exactly where Camp suggested, with the two large oaks in the front yard, and the spring only a few steps from the back door. A pole corral with a shed and tack room at one end had been constructed farther down the hill. And even from where he was sitting, Camp could see that a ditch had been dug to reroute the spring's runoff through the corral, so the horses could water themselves.

A rock chimney had been built on the north side of the house, and a joint of stovepipe that was no doubt connected to the kitchen stove protruded from the roof closer to the middle of the building. A stack of what appeared to be planed lumber had been placed on the south side, and even as Camp watched, a man he had never seen before approached the stack and sighted down the edge of a board to determine its quality. He repeated the process with several of the boards, then, apparently satisfied that they were straight enough, put them all on his shoulder and disappeared around the corner of the house.

Camp knew that he was listening to the sound of more than one hammer, and that the action was taking place on the opposite side of the house. He guided the roan down the hill and stopped in the front yard. Runt Fowler and two young men were in the process of flooring a porch that ran the length of the building. Since Camp had approached from the south, and all three of the workers were on their knees facing north, none of them saw him ride into the yard. Nor did they hear him, for they were making too much noise with their hammers. He sat watching for a while, more than a little pleased with what he was seeing.

When Fowler finally turned around to get another handful of nails, he spotted Houston. "Well, I'll be damned!" he said loudly, getting to his feet. "I've been thinking about you just about all day, Camp. I sure didn't expect you back this soon, though."

"Neither did I," Camp said, dismounting. He tied the roan to a post. "I ran into a little problem, and thought I might as well do my waiting at home. I'll be going out again in the fall." He walked backward for several yards to get a better look at the place, then smiled and shook his head as he returned to the doorsteps. "It looks mighty good, Runt, but I sure didn't expect you to be this far along with it."

Fowler smiled broadly. "I've had a lot more help than what you see," he said. He pointed to his helpers, who appeared to be in their late teens. "These are the Wooten brothers, Willie and Randy, and they've been with me right from the start. I guess you know Cornell Wooten, don't you?"

"Sure do. Good man."

Fowler pointed to the boys again. "Well, these two are Cornell's sons. Cornell himself helped us for the first three weeks, him and his oldest son, too. They both had to leave on account of an earlier commitment, but they damn sure knew what they were doing." He made a sweep with his arm to indicate the entire layout. "It don't take five good men forever to get something done."

"I believe you, Runt." Camp stepped onto the finished portion of the porch, and shook hands with each of the young men.

"I've sure heard a lot about you, Mr. Houston," the boy named Randy said. "Been hearing about you since I was little."

Camp gave the youngster a serious look. "You probably shouldn't believe everything you hear," he said.

"Most times I don't," the boy said. "But it ain't all just something I heard. I read a whole lot of it in the newspaper."

Camp bit his lip. "Well, they don't always get their stories straight either," he said. He placed his hand on the boy's shoulder and looked him squarely in the eye. "No matter what you hear or what you read, Randy, don't try to be like me." He stepped off the porch and untied his horses, then led them to the corral.

He unburdened the animals and loosed them into the corral, then stowed his saddle, the packsaddle and the grain bag in the tack room. He spent a few minutes in the shed inspecting the oversized wagon, which appeared to be almost new, then walked to the corral to look over the draft horses, for which he no doubt owed Sid Blankenship a bundle. Solid blacks with blaze faces, the two animals stood in the opposite corner of the corral, as if separating themselves from the saddle horses by choice. After seeing that Camp did not have a rope in his hand, they moved in his direction and stood staring.

Camp stood at the gate for several minutes, taking in the size of the horses. Runt had certainly chosen a team that was big enough to get the job done. Any job. Their feet were as large as dishpans, and Camp decided that each of the animals would weigh at least fourteen hundred pounds. And they would, of course, eat accordingly, he was thinking as he headed for the house.

"We started spreading our bedrolls in the house last week," Fowler said as Camp took a seat on the edge of the porch. "Soon as we got the roof on, we moved in."

Houston nodded. "Like I said before, Runt, I'm surprised and pleased. I'll be spreading my own bedroll inside the house about sundown." He sat looking down the hill for a few moments, then continued, "I like this homesite even better now that I see something on it. You did everything just the way I envisioned it, Runt, and I won't be forgetting it."

Fowler chuckled softly. "I hope not," he said. "Hell, I expect you to be a rich man one of these days."

Camp changed the subject. "I noticed the stovepipe, so I guess you've already got a cookstove in the house."

Fowler nodded. "Sure do. Got it from old lady Sommerville up in Brady." He smiled broadly. "She sold it to me too cheap, but she set her own price and I sure as hell wasn't gonna argue with her. She said she'd let me have it for two dollars 'cause it used to be a bunkhouse stove, and it was real old. Hell, Camp, an old stove is just as good as a new one, if it ain't got no cracks in it. I looked it over, then me and Randy put 'er in the wagon right quick. It had been in the barn for a long time and had a little rust on it, but I got that off real easy. It even has a hot water tank, and the oven works perfect. I baked corn bread in it just last night."

Camp smiled. "Maybe I should let you do all of my shopping, Runt." He got to his feet and stepped inside the building. Fowler walked beside him, talking all the while. "That's three bedrooms back there," he said, pointing to the east side of the house. "We ain't floored 'em yet, 'cause we didn't think there was any hurry. We'll do that tomorrow, 'cause I expect you'll be wanting to put a bed in at least one of 'em."

Camp nodded, and continued to inspect the building.

Planed, tongue-and-groove lumber had been used to floor the living room, and the boards fitted together so tightly that the floor appeared to have been made from a single piece of wood. And the story was the same in the kitchen. Back in the living room, Houston ran his hands over both the inside and the outside of the fireplace. He took a long look up the chimney, then spoke: "You've done a good job on everything, Runt. Have you checked this chimney to make sure it'll draw?"

Fowler shook his head. "I haven't built a fire in it, but it'll draw all right. Hell, I built it just like I built a dozen others, so it can't do anything but draw."

Camp smiled. "I'm inclined to take your word for it, Runt." They returned to the front of the house and took a seat on the doorstep. "I guess you wrote down how much money I owe," Camp said, "and who I owe it to."

"I didn't write anything down," Fowler said, "didn't have anything to write. I only did business with two men, and both of them said they'd settle with you later. I bought the team and wagon from Blankenship, and all of the tools and building material from Spike Nettleton's hardware store. He said he'd give you a discount on everything, but even at that, I'll bet the price of that damn tin is gonna be outta sight."

"I expected no less," Camp said. "But it won't leak, and it'll last a mighty long time. A whole bunch of men who ought to know what they're talking about have told me that a tin roof is the best way to go nowadays."

"I would agree with that," Fowler said. He fished around in his pocket for a moment, then offered Camp a small roll of bills. "Since you're home now, I guess you ought to be keeping track of your own money. Roy Holder cashed the check you gave me, and I spent a little of it for food. Most of what I spent, though, went for wages. Cornell and his boys didn't charge me but a dollar a day apiece, so I've still got nearly a hundred dollars here."

Camp shook his head. "Keep the money, Runt," he said. "You've still got a lot of building to do, and you need those boys to help you. Besides, I'm gonna be mighty busy for the next few weeks, and I won't be spending much time around here. I will take the wagon to town with me tomorrow, though. I'll be bringing back a load of stuff for the house, so make a list of the things you need." He got to his feet and stepped into the yard, adding, "Just go ahead and put a floor and a ceiling in that southeast bedroom. I'll probably be gone for several days, but I'll have a bed with me when I get back."

As the workmen resumed their hammering, Camp walked past the corral and down the hill to the east bank of Calf Creek. He stopped at a fallen log and sat thinking, his chin in his hands and his elbows on his knees. He remembered that he had been sitting on this same log with a fishing pole in his hand the day he decided to discuss buying the property with John Butterworth.

The rancher had not only been willing to sell, but had even seemed eager, and made Camp an offer that he could not resist. Camp would pay the final seventy-five-dollar payment within the next week or two, then he would own the three-square-mile area free and clear. The property was all located in McCulloch County, but bordered both Mason and Menard Counties on the south.

Butterworth also owned three sections of land directly across the county line, and had offered to sell it to Camp on the same easy-payment plan. Now, Camp smiled and nodded at the thought, for within the past few minutes, he had decided to take the rancher up on his offer. Then he would own six square miles in three counties, all of it prime grazing land.

The sun was dropping over the western horizon when Houston left the creek. He walked up the hill slowly, stopping at the tack room to get his bedroll. When he reached the house, all three of the workmen were sitting on the porch eating from clay bowls. "Some pretty good soup in there,

Camp," Fowler said. "I just put a little of everything I had in the pot, then baked some corn bread to go with it."

Camp nodded, and headed for the kitchen. Moments later, he rejoined the men on the porch, a bowl of soup in one hand and a steaming cup of coffee in the other. He took a seat on the top doorstep. "I'll try to find a decent buy on a table and some chairs while I'm in town," he said to no one in particular.

"You can buy some chairs if you want to," Fowler said around a mouthful of food, "but I don't think you oughta rush into buying a table. The way I've got it figured, we're gonna have enough of that tongue-and-groove lumber left over to build one. A damn sight better table than you could buy, too."

Camp chuckled, and mimicked a British accent: "Very well, sir, I shall heed your words." He got to his feet and dashed his coffee grounds into the yard. "I'm still gonna look around some while I'm in Menardville. Even if the wagon's loaded, I can tie a few chairs on it somewhere." He walked across the porch and paused at the door. "I don't know about you fellows, but this day's over for me. I'm gonna spread my bedroll in there by the fireplace." Five minutes later, he was sleeping soundly.

At sunup, he ate a breakfast of smoked ham, flapjacks and maple syrup, then headed for the corral. He harnessed and hitched up the team, then took the wagon road to Mason, a journey that would take most of the day. As he drove around the bend, he could hear that the hammering had already started again. The sound was like music to his ears.

Less than an hour of daylight remained when he arrived in Mason. He parked the wagon outside the livery stable and turned the team over to the hostler, a man named Hamm Harrison. Although probably past sixty years of age, Harrison was apparently in good health, and had been the town's liveryman for many years. He was well known and respected throughout the county.

"Ain't seen you in a coon's age, Camp," he said, accepting

the team's reins. "I think I remember hearing somebody say you went hunting. Any luck?"

"Not much," Houston said, with a tone of finality meant to discourage further questions. He held the hostler in high regard, but the old man was a talker, and Camp did not intend to furnish him with the details of his manhunt. He pointed to the corral, and changed the subject. "Didn't I just see Will McDavid's chestnut out there?" he asked.

"Yep. Will wants me to try to sell the animal for him. From the way he talked, I'd say he needs the money pretty bad."

Camp headed for the corral and stood leaning on the top pole. Tossing its head about friskily, the chestnut walked directly toward Houston till it was halfway across the corral. Then, just as if making its own attempt to attract a prospective buyer, the beautiful animal stopped in its tracks and made a quarter turn, offering a broadside picture. Houston spoke to the hostler, who had followed him to the corral: "Best-looking quarter horse I've seen in a long time," he said.

Harrison nodded. "About as good as they get, I reckon. I doubt that Will really wants to get shed of the horse, but like I said, I believe he needs the money."

Camp, who was something close to an expert on horse-flesh, crawled between the poles and walked into the corral for a closer look. The animal stood its ground and made no attempt to evade Houston's probing hands as he began his head-to-hoof inspection.

As a man who had grown up around fine horses, Camp had long been aware of the peculiarities possessed by outstanding quarter horses: the head is neat, but distinctly shorter than that of the Thoroughbred, and the muzzle is small. The knees must be big, broad and flat. Like the other joints, they should be hard, with no sign of puffiness. The belly is longer than the back, and should contribute to the chunky impression and the compact symmetry of the outline.

The cannons are short. The hocks are set low to the

ground and have a high degree of flexion. The horses normally stand sixty to sixty-three inches in height, and their heavy, muscular quarters, which give them a chunky appearance overall, are characteristic of the breed.

After running his hands over the gentle animal and inspecting every single detail, Camp decided that he might very well be looking at the best of the best. Indeed, the chestnut seemed to have it all. Camp Houston not only knew how an outstanding quarter horse should look, but knew the history of the breed.

He knew that the quarter horse was the oldest all-American breed. First bred in Virginia in the seventeenth century, they were used for many purposes, including work on the farm, rounding up cattle, hauling goods and lumber, drawing carriages and riding. They were also frugal horses, demanding less food than most breeds. Versatile though they were, the most prized characteristic of these early horses was their ability to sprint over short distances from an explosive standing start.

The sports-loving English settlers raced their horses over quarter-mile stretches laid out most anywhere they had room, usually within easy walking distance of towns or villages. For this reason the new breed became know as the "quarter horse" or "quarter-miler."

The power and muscular conformation of the quarter horse were ideally suited to this type of racing. By the year 1656, quarter horse racing was well established in Virginia, and the breed was widely recognized as the supreme short-distance racer.

Later, when the Thoroughbred was introduced to the United States, oval tracks were constructed and the sport of long-distance racing began to thrive. As a result, the popularity of the quarter-mile sprints quickly declined, and within a short time these races were abandoned altogether in the eastern states.

The quarter horse then shifted to the West, where it quickly adapted to the job of herding cattle. It moved at such high speed that it was said to be able to "turn on a dime from an all-out gallop, and toss you back nine cents change." Indeed, the breed early on exhibited a high degree of "cow sense," and within a few years every rancher in the West was firmly convinced that its speed, balance and agility, as well as an uncanny instinct for the job, made the quarter horse the best cow pony in the world.

Houston took one last look at the chestnut's teeth, and decided that the animal was six years old. He spoke to the hostler again: "Did Will put a price on this horse, Hamm?"

"Yep. Said he wants a hundred and forty dollars. I told him I didn't believe he was gonna get that much."

"Neither do I," Camp said. He gave the horse a pat on the rump, then walked to to the wagon and retrieved his rifle. "I'll be staying in town overnight, Hamm. Got some business to take care of in the morning."

"Well, I'll be around here all day tomorrow, so you can get your team anytime you take a notion." He turned to lead the team down the hallway, then stopped. "I couldn't help but notice how close you looked that quarter horse over," he said, smiling broadly. "You want to make an offer on him, just in case Will decides to take a little less than he's asking?"

Camp stood thinking for a while. "I'd pay ninety dollars for the horse real quick," he said finally. "Might pay a hundred after I rode him." He turned to leave, continuing to speak over his shoulder: "Just tell Will that I don't mean to insult him, but if he wants to let the animal go for a hundred dollars, I'll be at my place on Calf Creek."

"I'll tell him," Harrison said, chuckling loudly at something that Houston did not understand. "Probably be several days before I see him, though."

Camp nodded, then headed up the street, his rifle cradled in the crook of his left arm. He ate a supper of stuffed pork chops at a small restaurant, then rented a room at the town's only hotel. A few minutes later, he locked the door, blew out the lamp and crawled into bed. He was asleep quickly.

He was back on the street at sunup, and walked to the edge of town, where he had breakfast at Ma Franklin's boardinghouse. He had eaten in the establishment many times before, and knew that the food was some of the best the area had to offer. The lady had a vested interest and did her own cooking; therefore, the food was consistently of the highest quality. Although well past the age of sixty, she was spry and apparently in good health, and ran the business year-round with the help of only one hired hand, a middle-aged Mexican woman.

One of the few three-story buildings in the area, the house had been built in the late 1840s by James and Edward Franklin as a place to raise their families. And though they collectively produced five children, both men had died at a relatively young age. Edward had been killed by Indians, and James had been kicked in the head by a mule.

The Franklin brothers' offspring, all of them boys, had now scattered to the four winds, leaving Edith, widow of James, sole owner of the property. Now referred to as "Ma" by everyone in the community, the lady had several years earlier turned the huge residence into a boardinghouse, and business had been good right from the start.

As Houston walked down the hall and into the dining room, he could see that the lady was already busy clearing dishes from the long table. "Am I too late for breakfast?" he asked.

"Nope." She smiled, and pointed to a chair at the end of the table. "Good to see you, Camp. Take a seat right there."

"I could have been here a long time ago," he said, "but I had no idea that you served breakfast so early."

"I have to feed my boarders at daybreak," she said. She placed a steaming cup of coffee before him, jokingly adding, "Some men have to work for a living, you know."

He faked a dejected look. "I suppose that means you think I don't work, huh?"

She did not answer the question. "I've got ham and sausage cooked already," she said, beginning to walk toward the kitchen. "I can fry eggs and heat up some biscuits pretty quick."

He continued to sip at the coffee while he waited. A look at his watch told him that it was a quarter past seven, and he decided that he was right on time. As soon as he ate breakfast, he would head for the livery stable and hitch up his team. By then it would be close to half past eight, at which time the bank would open.

An hour later, he tied the team at the bank's hitching rail. Being a few minutes early, he stepped onto the sidewalk and took a seat on the narrow wooden bench that the bank provided for its customers. He was still sitting there when Roy Holder, the bank's vice president, walked down the street and put a key in the lock. "Good morning, Mr. Houston," he said as he pushed the front door inward. "Been waiting long?"

"Just a few minutes," Camp said, getting to his feet. "I need to withdraw some money, then I've got some more business I'd like to talk over with you."

The frail, middle-aged man's smile seemed almost as wide as his shoulders. "Well, you've certainly come to the right place," he said, "and I'll help you any way I can. Please step inside."

Later in the morning, Houston drove the team west toward Menardville, knowing that it would be well past dark when he arrived there. He had had a long talk with Roy Holder, and the banker had readily agreed to advance him the money to stock his property with longhorns. "I wouldn't feel very comfortable financing more than two hundred fifty head, however," Holder had stated plainly. "Not if you only have three sections of land."

Houston had expected to hear those very words. "I understand," he said. "But I expect to own six sections by this time next week."

"Very well," Holder said quickly. "In that case, I see no reason not to go with five hundred head."

Camp was on his feet now, offering a parting handshake. "I guess that about covers it, then. I'll get back with you after I make a deal with John Butterworth." A few minutes later, he drove the team out of town. He traveled continuously till midafternoon, with the wagon jostling over the rough road so badly that it eventually gave him a slight backache. When he halted for an hour at Big Rock Spring, it was more to rest his back than to let his animals blow.

He sat on a rock beside the spring, thinking of the well-stocked ranch that he would soon own. In fact, he had thought of little else throughout the day. He had little doubt that he could deal with Butterworth, for at one time the man had even tried to talk him into taking the three sections off his hands.

All of which was easily understandable, for Butterworth's Lazy B Ranch was in Mills County, with all of San Saba County and more than half of McCulloch County separating it from the three sections in question. Indeed, the rancher had never intended to actually use the property. He had simply taken advantage of a bargain, and bought the land as an investment.

Camp's ranch would be mortgaged to the hilt, of course, as would every cow that fed on its perennial grasses. And even though he intended to make the last payment on his original three sections within the next few days, the deal could still fall through unless he could convince John Butterworth to hand over a clear deed to the additional property, with nothing more than Camp's promise to pay for it. And a clear deed was a must, for expecting Holder's bank to stock the six sections without holding a first mortgage on every head of cattle and every acre of land was out of the question.

An hour later, Camp climbed back to the wagon seat and returned to the rough, rocky road. He had business to attend to in Menardville, part of which was paying Sid Blankenship for the team and wagon. He whipped the horses to a fast trot, hoping to arrive there before the liveryman's bedtime.

II

Ten days later, Houston was at the Lazy B Ranch, in Mills County. It was midafternoon when he rode the roan through the gate, past the big red barn that Runt Fowler had built, and into the ranch house yard. He sat his saddle quietly for a while, looking toward the bunkhouse. When he detected no sign of life there, he rode to the porch and helloed the house.

Seconds later, Nellie Butterworth opened the door and stepped onto the porch. Though past the age of sixty, she was nevertheless a striking woman. Standing almost six feet tall, she was probably just as slender now as she had been when she married John Butterworth, forty-two years ago. With copper-colored eyes that sometimes appeared to be too big for her face, she had been a brunette in her youth. Now, only a trace of that color could be seen atop her milky-white head.

She stood just outside the front door for a few moments, shading her eyes from the sun with her hand. She smiled, then hurried down the steps and into the yard. "Campbell Houston!" she said excitedly. "Of all the people I didn't expect to see today, I guess you'd be at the top of the list. What in the world brings you to Mills County?"

He threw his right leg over the horse's neck and slid to the ground, taking the lady's small hands in his own. "You mean to tell me that you don't know?" he asked, releasing her hands. Not waiting for an answer, he led the roan to the hitching rail just outside the yard, then climbed the steps to the porch, accepting the cane-bottom, ladder-back chair the lady offered. "I still owe you and your old man some money," he said, seating himself. "Remember?"

She smiled again and shook her head. "I can honestly say that I didn't, Camp. Not till you mentioned it. I don't concern myself with things like that anymore, and I don't believe John spends much time thinking about money. Not the way he used to, back when he had to keep track of every penny."

Camp nodded. "I'm truly glad that John doesn't have to worry nowadays," he said, "and this place couldn't have happened to a better man. I've ridden over every mile of it, and I know that it's one of the finest ranches in the state. I also know that he started it with nothing but a keen mind and a lot of determination. I think he told me himself that he was broke when he first came to Texas."

"Well, not exactly broke," she said, laughing aloud. "We had forty-two dollars. Forty-two dollars, two skinny horses and a wagon, a turning plow and a fifteen-year-old milch cow. But just as soon as John saw this place, he said to dig in, and that's what we both did: dug in." She folded her hands in her lap and sat quietly for a while, then added, "Life has been mighty good to us, and I can't think of another thing that we need. We've raised two fine daughters who both married well, and I reckon the good Lord must have taken a liking to my dear husband right from the start. John didn't have the slightest idea what he was doing when he first started out, no more'n I did, but he's made more right decisions over the past forty years than any man on Earth is entitled to. Every move he's made has turned out well, and he gives thanks to the Almighty every day. You see, John knows just as well as I do that he didn't make all those good decisions alone."

Camp sat quietly for a while, digesting her words of wisdom. He held both the lady and her husband in high regard, and knew that John Butterworth possessed the same degree of humility as did his wife. "You're a smart woman, Nellie," he said finally, "and you married a very smart man. When I get my own place up and running, I'd be happy to accept any advice I can get from either of you."

"Oh, I'm sure John'll help you any way he can," she said, getting to her feet. "He decided several years ago that he liked you, and he talks about you often. He liked it when you were his foreman, and he hated it when you quit. I've heard him say so plenty of times." She stood in the doorway for a moment, then added, "He left for San Saba early this morning to take care of some business and pick up a few things for the cook. He took the buggy and a fast-stepping mare, so he should be back anytime now." She pointed toward the corral. "You just take care of your horse, then come on back. I've got some cool cider in the cellar."

He nodded, and stepped into the yard. At the barn, he unsaddled the roan and led him down the hallway. Camp shook his head and smiled as the big animal jerked on the reins and headed straight for the last stable on the right, the same one that had been home to him during the time his master had been employed at the Lazy B. No doubt about it, the horse knew exactly where he was. He began to neigh immediately, and did not stop till Camp poured a bucketful of oats in the trough.

A short while later, Houston stood leaning against a corral post, reminiscing and looking things over. Other than the fact that a new corral had been built and the bunkhouse painted, the place looked the same as when it had been home to him. He had spent some happy times on these premises, and no man had ever treated him better than had John Butterworth. Camp had been paid well, and his only reason for leaving was that he intended to start a ranch of his own somewhere. When he explained that to Butterworth, the man was eager to help, and offered him a once-in-a-lifetime deal on the property in McCulloch County.

Camp was still standing at the corral when he saw Butterworth's buggy come around the bend. After passing under the Lazy B's welcome sign, the rancher stopped the buggy and jumped to the ground, swinging the gate open wide. Then, of her own accord, the mare pulled the vehicle through the opening and forward just far enough to allow the gate to be closed. Then she halted again, and waited patiently till her master had reclaimed his seat.

Always quick to appreciate a good horse, Camp smiled as he watched. The mare had probably done the same thing a hundred times before, he was thinking. She had been trained to do exactly what she did, and she would never forget.

As the buggy closed the distance, Houston headed for the cookshack, for he expected that to be the rancher's first stop.

Butterworth began to talk before the vehicle even came to a halt. "Think of the devil, and there he is!" he said loudly. He dropped to the ground, beaming. "I've been thinking about you off and on for most of the day, Camp. Don't ask me why, 'cause I don't know." He pumped Houston's arm and patted his shoulder. "Things been going all right?"

"At least as well as I could expect." Camp tied the mare's reins to the hitching rail. "I can tell at a glance that you're doing all right, John. I believe you look healthier right now than you did the first time I ever saw you. Have you got some kind of secret that I ought to know?"

"Nope, don't reckon there's any secret to it. What I do, anybody can do. You see, I always take some time out to talk to the Lord, and it sure ain't time lost. Now, I don't take up His time asking Him for a whole lot of stuff for myself. He already knows what I need and don't need. I don't recall ever asking Him for anything more than good health for Nellie and me, but He sure must've heard my prayers, 'cause neither of us has ever been sick with anything worse than a bad cold."

Though John Butterworth stood less than six feet tall, he was nevertheless a large man, with long arms, thick chest and broad shoulders. Today he had his shirtsleeves rolled up against the hot weather, and even though he was well into his sixties, his bulging biceps and muscular forearms were conspicuously noticeable.

Looking at the rancher nowadays it was easy to see how he had attracted such a beautiful woman as Nellie when he was younger, for even now, he was a handsome man. He had dark, intelligent eyes, and his complexion was the color of well-tanned leather. And though its color had turned to salt and pepper, he still possessed most of his hair. He had a disarming smile, which he used now. "If you'll help me unload this buggy, we'll put up this mare and go to the house. I've got something good to drink in the cellar."

Camp nodded, and picked up a fifty-pound can of lard. "Nellie already offered me some cider."

"Humph!" the rancher said, hefting a bushel bag of dried beans to his shoulder. "I had something a little different in mind."

When they had transferred the supplies from the buggy to the cookshack, the rancher made the introductions between Camp and the cook, a man named Hubie Biddle. When Biddle appeared to be bored by the entire proceedings, mumbling and staring over Houston's shoulder while offering a limp handshake, Camp's reaction was quick. "Pardon me all to hell, fellow!" he said loudly. He jerked his hand away. "I just decided that I'm about as interested in this damned meeting as you seem to be." He headed for the yard, and did not look back.

Butterworth was there immediately. "I hope you won't feel too hard at Hubie, Camp. That's just his way."

"Well, I don't care much for his way."

The rancher laughed. "I can see that," he said, "and I'd even make a bet that Hubie knows it now. Let's stable this mare, then go get us a bottle of wine."

Nellie met them at the porch, carrying a tray containing a pile of cookies and two glasses of cider. "These cookies'll hold the two of you over till supper," she said, "and the cider ought to cool you off some."

The rancher winked at Camp, and accepted the tray. He patted his wife's hand. "Why, thank you, my dear," he said softly. "This is mighty thoughtful of you, and I'm sure the cider is just what we need."

No sooner had Nellie returned to her household duties than Butterworth slid off the corner of the porch and headed for the cellar, a deep excavation beneath the house that could be entered from the outside as well as the inside of the living quarters. Houston heard the rusty hinges squeak each time the rancher opened and closed the cellar door.

A few moments later, Butterworth rounded the corner and handed him a gallon jug. "I believe this is a little older than that cider," he said. He wrapped his hands around the corner post and pulled himself to the porch. Smiling from ear to ear, he dashed the cider into the yard and reclaimed his seat. Then he removed the cork from the jug and poured both glasses full of dark red wine, handing the first one to Houston. "I think you're gonna like this a little better," he said.

As both men sat sipping, Butterworth proceeded to extol the so-called benefits of wine consumption. "Drinking wine is probably one of the healthiest things a fellow can do," he began. "I even heard a doctor say one time that a man would live a lot longer if he drank some good wine every day." He held his glass up in front of his eyes, squinting at its contents. "And this is good wine, Camp, about as good as wine ever gets." He closed one eye and peered into the glass again. "At least it ought to be—it's been down there in the cellar for about two years, maybe three."

Camp tilted his glass again, then wiped his mouth with the

heel of his hand. "I don't know that I've ever tasted better, John. Did you make it yourself?"

"No, no. A Bohemian family up in the northern part of the county makes it. I just did a little trading with them; wound up with twenty gallons."

Camp nodded, then chuckled. "Well, I suppose that ought to be enough wine to keep you healthy for a long time," he said.

They spent the remainder of the afternoon on the porch, sipping and talking. When the ranch hands rode in and paraded to the bunkhouse, Camp saw no one that he knew, and with his introduction to Hubie Biddle still fresh in his mind, he made no effort to meet any of them.

He spent an enjoyable night with the Butterworths, and when he left the Lazy B Ranch next morning, he was a happy man. After eating a supper fit for royalty, he had paid the rancher the final installment on the three sections of land north of the county line, and expressed his desire to own the three additional sections to the south. His only problem, he told Butterworth, who was listening attentively, was that he needed a clear deed to all six sections, so he could mortgage the property to the bank. Otherwise, obtaining financing for the five hundred head of breeding stock that he had in mind was out of the question.

Butterworth slid his chair away from the table noisily. "Roy Holder?" he asked loudly. "That sorry sonofabitch?" He turned to Nellie and begged her forgiveness for using such language, then continued, "I know that no-good bastard well, Camp. So does every other man in this country who's been around for a while, and we all know him for the horse's ass that he is. The sonofabitch'll cheat you out of your underwear even while you're looking at him." He walked to the washstand and drank water from a gourd dipper. "The next time you see Roy Holder," he continued, "you tell him to kiss your ass." He dropped the dipper back into the bucket and returned to the table. "You just go on to bed and get yourself a good night's sleep while I think on it. I'm sure I can figure you out a better deal than you're ever gonna get from Roy Holder."

Butterworth had announced his decision at the breakfast table this morning, offering Camp another once-in-a-lifetime deal: "I'm gonna give you a clear deed to the whole six sections, Camp, but I can't bring myself to stand by and watch you mortgage it all to Holder's bank. I've figured out a way to stock the place that I think will be beneficial to you and me both. You see, I've got more breeders than I actually need. In fact, my north range is in danger of becoming overstocked unless I get some of that old stuff off of it within the next few months."

He dumped several spoonfuls of jelly onto his plate, then sat thoughtfully while he buttered himself a biscuit. "What we'll do is drive five hundred head of my older cows down to your place. Then at roundup time, you can touch every third calf with my iron, and put your own brand on the rest. Won't be too long till you have a herd of young stuff of your own, and you'll be indebted to no man. As for the property in Mason and Menard Counties, just pay for it any way you can, at the same price you paid before." He took a sip of his coffee, then laughed. "I guess the best part of the deal, as far as you're concerned, is this: if I happen to die before you get the money to pay me, you won't have to pay anybody, 'cause you'll already have a clear deed." He smiled, and patted his wife's arm. "Of course, you could give the money to Nellie here, and I'm sure she wouldn't go putting a time limit on you."

The lady shook her head, and said nothing.

Camp had been staring into his plate. He pushed his chair away from the table and got to his feet. "I don't think I know the right words to tell you how much I appreciate this, John," he said, attempting to swallow the lump that had suddenly appeared in his throat. "But I will tell you that I'll hold up my end of the bargain, and you can rest assured that I'll pay Nellie for the land in case you're not around."

Continuing to stand beside the table, he thanked the lady for her hospitality, then shook the rancher's hand. "I'll be getting on back to Calf Creek now," he said. "I've got a lot of things that need doing before we move the cows down there."

As Camp saddled the roan at the corral, Butterworth stood by talking. "You don't have to break your back getting that place ready, Camp; you've got plenty of time. We'll wait till after the first of the year to move the cows, maybe late March or early April. The next time I'm in San Saba I'll have my lawyer spell out our arrangement on paper. I'll get your copy down to you before long."

Camp tightened the cinch another notch, then climbed into the saddle. "Like I said before, John, I appreciate what you're doing, and I won't be forgetting it."

Butterworth shook his head. "Don't give it another thought," he said, waving his hand back and forth as if to dismiss Camp's words of gratitude. "You just go on and take care of yourself." He took a few steps toward the house, then stopped and turned halfway around, adding, "Don't go hiring up no bunch of men to make the drive, now. When the time comes, my riders will deliver five hundred cows to you. Five hundred cows and twenty bulls." Then he headed for the house, and never looked back.

Heading the roan in a southwesterly direction, Houston kicked the animal to a canter, a gait that he would hold for most of the day. He would travel steadily till he reached his new home, for he was completely unprepared for a night on the trail.

12

It was close to midnight when he rode into his own yard. He helloed the house loudly, and Fowler answered quickly. "Just wanted you to know that it was me moving around out here," Camp said. "Go back to sleep." He rode to the shed and sat his saddle for a few moments, staring into the corral. Though the moon was only in its first quarter, and provided no more than a faint glow of light, it was enough for Camp to recognize the chestnut quarter horse that he had seen in the corral at Hamm Harrison's livery stable.

Once he had unsaddled and fed the roan, he spoke to the chestnut. The horse answered with a soft nicker, then walked to the middle of the corral and snorted loudly. Standing just outside the enclosure, Houston leaned against a fence post.

Pleased with what he was seeing, he came to a quick conclusion: Harrison had no doubt passed Camp's bid of a hundred dollars on to Will McDavid, who had accepted the offer and delivered the horse himself. Camp knew of no other explanation for the animal being in his corral. McDavid would hardly be making a social call, for he and Houston had never been more than casual acquaintances. Camp smiled, and headed for the house. He would put the chestnut under a saddle in the morning and find out if he had gotten his money's worth—if the animal was actually worth the one hundred dollars that he now owed to Will McDavid.

At the house, he moved around in the dark quietly till he found his bed, then stretched out. Although he was very tired, sleep did not come right away. He lay for a long time thinking about the deal he had made for the cattle, and how his former employer had bent over backward to help him establish a herd of his own.

And it should take no more than two years for him to get that herd. Some of Butterworth's cows would no doubt already have calves following them when they arrived next spring, and most of the others would be pregnant, for they all ran with the bulls year-round. Two calf crops was all Camp would need to stock his place, then he would return the old cows to Butterworth. The rancher could either make room for them on the Lazy B or send them to the rails in Kansas.

Then Houston's thoughts returned to his newly acquired quarter horse. Tomorrow he would put the animal through its paces. He had no doubt that the chestnut would be fast, maybe even faster than a Thoroughbred, for the first few hundred yards. Of course, a quarter horse could not be expected to stay with a Thoroughbred over a great distance. The swift sprinters were bred for short races, while the Thoroughbreds were both bred and trained for the long haul.

Quarter horses were even excluded from the Kentucky Derby, a Thoroughbred race that had been organized in Louisville in 1875. The race had been run on the first Saturday in May for the past four years, and Camp had read somewhere that this year's winner was a horse named Day Star. In fact, he had read several pieces of published literature concerning the Derby. Most stated that the decision to make the race exclusive to Thoroughbreds had been reached early on. No other breed could be expected to hold up under such a hard run, for the fathers of the Derby had set the distance of the race at one and one-half miles.*

Camp fluffed up his pillow and turned over in bed. He was thinking of the Kentucky Derby and what a grueling test of endurance the race must be. He doubted that he himself had ever owned a horse that could run all-out for a mile and a half. Nor would he ever attempt to push an animal that far at top speed. Not unless it was a matter of life and death.

He tossed and turned for a while longer, then managed to clear his mind. When he finally dozed off, he slept soundly.

The sun was two hours high when he rolled out of bed next morning. Sensing that he was alone in the house, he headed for the kitchen, where he filled a tin cup from a coffeepot that had been pushed to the back of the stove. When he stepped out on the porch, he could see Fowler moving around down at the shed. Camp took a seat on the doorstep and began to sip his coffee.

Fowler spotted Houston quickly enough, and came lumbering up the slope. "I thought about checking to see if you were still alive," he said, "but then I decided that you probably rode all the way from the Lazy B without any rest."

"You decided right," Camp said, taking a sip from his cup, then dashing the remaining coffee grounds into the yard.

Fowler took a seat on the doorstep beside Camp, then pointed down the hill. "I've been up since daybreak," he said. "Took that horse for a three-mile run right after sunup." He nodded toward the corral. "Guess you saw my new horse last night, huh?"

Camp sat thinking for a moment, and did not answer the question.

*Distance changed to a mile and a quarter in 1896.

"Quarter horse," Runt continued, "and he can take you for the ride of your life. Yessir, fellow gets on him, he damn sure better hang on to his hat."

Houston nodded, and continued to listen.

"I bought the horse from Will McDavid yesterday morning," Runt was saying. "Will actually came up here looking for you, but of course you weren't home. Then when I noticed that quarter horse he was leading, I made up my mind right away that I was gonna have that animal, and damn the price. Will just started hemming and hawing around when I first let him know that I was interested, but I wound up getting the horse anyway." Then Fowler filled Camp in on the story:

He had been stacking firewood on the corner of the porch and just happened to be looking down the hill when he noticed a large black dog trotting around the bend. The animal was soon followed by a man riding a tall, gray Appaloosa and leading a muscular chestnut whose weight Runt guessed to be somewhere around a thousand pounds.

As man and animals continued up the hill, Fowler eventually recognized the rider as Will McDavid, and walked into the yard to meet him. "Get down and rest yourself, Will," he said, taking hold of the Appaloosa's bridle. "I can stir up the fire and put on the coffeepot in short order."

McDavid shook his head. "I don't have time," he said, and did not dismount. "I just rode up to see Camp. Is he around?"

"Nope. He's up at the Lazy B Ranch, in Mills County."

McDavid nodded. "I know where it is. John Butterworth's been a friend of mine for years." He drew in and exhaled a deep breath, then turned the Appaloosa's head in the direction from whence he had come. "No telling when he'll be back, so I guess I'll be getting on home. I just rode up 'cause Hamm Harrison said that Camp told him—"

"How come you're leading such a good-looking quarter horse around?" Runt interrupted. "You want to sell him?"

"Well, that's what—"

"How much you want for him?" Fowler interrupted again.

"Well, I was asking a hundred forty dollars, but—"

"Hundred forty?" Runt asked loudly. "Hundred forty dollars? You've got it, mister. Just turn him into the corral down there, then write me a bill of sale. I've got the money on me." McDavid did as he had been told, and rode off the hill a few minutes later with Fowler's money in his pocket.

Houston continued to sit on the doorstep. "Did Will ever say why he wanted to see me?"

"Nope. I asked him if he wanted to leave a message for you, and he said no, said it wasn't necessary."

Camp nodded, and headed for the kitchen to refill his cup. He smiled as he poured the coffee, and made himself a promise that he would never reveal the whole story behind Fowler's quarter horse deal. Runt would never know that Will McDavid had actually ridden to Calf Creek to deliver the animal to Camp for a hundred dollars.

Fowler was obviously pleased with his purchase, and Camp could certainly find no fault with McDavid for accepting more money than he had expected to get. Houston shrugged, and shoveled a spoonful of sugar into his coffee. Things usually happened for the best, he was thinking. He didn't really need another horse anyway, for his current saddler was still relatively young. And though not a good cow pony, the roan was an exceptional animal for traveling, always eager to hit the road.

And the packhorse that Sid Blankenship had lent him was still in the corral. Camp had mentioned it the day he paid the liveryman for the team and wagon, and offered to return the animal immediately. Blankenship had said that was completely unnecessary, and suggested that Houston keep the horse at his own place until he was sure that he would not need it again. Moreover, when he learned that Camp would be going hunting again in a few weeks, the liveryman offered him money to help with his traveling expenses. Houston declined.

Camp took a sip of his coffee to test its sweetness, then returned to the porch. "I saw that quarter horse down at Hamm Harrison's stable a while back," he said to Fowler, who was still seated on the doorstep, "and I looked him over good. I'd say you're gonna be plenty satisfied."

The big man's homely face brightened, and he smiled broadly. "I already am satisfied," he said. "Smoothest horse I've ever been on. He don't even bounce you around when he's trotting. Want me to saddle him up so you can see what I'm talking about?"

Camp shook his head. "Maybe some other time." He finished his coffee and set the cup aside, then changed the subject. "I guess you'll be busy enough right here for the rest of the year, Runt. What do you intend to be doing next spring?"

Fowler peeled a splinter off the wooden handrail, using it to pick his teeth. "Hell, I don't know," he said. "I never plan that far ahead. Why do you ask?"

Camp sat staring down the hillside. "Because yesterday I made a deal for five hundred head of cows and twenty bulls. They'll be delivered to me right here in March or April."

"Five hundred head?" Fowler was on his feet now, shaking his head. "Seems to me like that's driving it up mighty tight, Camp. I mean, three sections is enough land that a man can shit anywhere he wants to, but it ain't all that much when you start talking about running five hundred head of cattle. On top of that, every damn one of the cows is gonna have a calf following her around before long. You'll either have to sell your calves or get rid of your breeders after the first year, 'cause you'll be outta room."

Camp chuckled. "I'll get rid of the breeders, Runt, but I won't have to do it the first year. While I was dealing yesterday, I acquired three more sections south of the county line." He explained the details of the arrangement he had made with John Butterworth.

Fowler guffawed, then began to speak slowly, still chuckling intermittently. "Now, let me be sure I understand this," he said. "Butterworth is gonna sell you three sections of land on credit, with no collateral whatsoever, then he's gonna furnish you with five hundred head of breeders and twenty bulls. And all he expects out of it is a third of the calf crop. Have I got that right?"

Houston nodded.

Fowler laughed again. "I won't ask you what you've got on that man, Camp, but it sure must be something bad. Either that or you're a better bargainer than anybody else I know."

"I didn't do any bargaining at all," Camp said, getting to his feet. "It was all John's idea. The man's well-off, Runt, and he's getting on in years. He knows he can't take it with him, and I guess he just took a liking to me. That must be the case, 'cause he's done about everything an older fellow can do to help a younger man get a place of his own." He headed for the kitchen. "Nope," he said over his shoulder, "I didn't make a single suggestion. John thought up the whole deal himself." He walked to the stove and added wood to the firebox, then began to prepare himself a bacon-and-egg breakfast.

A few minutes later, Fowler poured himself a cup of coffee and took a seat at the table. Camp dumped half a dozen scrambled eggs into a bowl. "You want to help me eat these?"

"Nope. Ate about a pound of that smoked ham over there when I first got up." He blew into his cup, then took a sip of coffee. "I wanted to talk to you about the barn. Guess I'll be starting on it within the next day or two."

Camp folded his hands on the table. "All right, let's talk."

"Well, I first intended to put it down there about where the shed is now, but I'm beginning to think a whole lot less of that idea. Maybe we should put the barn and the corral both on that slope across the road. Just those few showers we had last week washed most of that horse manure right down the hill and into the creek. Now, I don't know that it's gonna hurt the creek any, but right there in that deep pool below the big tree is where we all bathe ourselves. I don't care to do my bathing in a creek full of horse shit, so I think we oughta move the whole shebang across the road." He pointed to the east side of the house, then down the hill. "When the heavy rains come this winter, all the fertilizer'll wash right down into that field yonder. It'll just be lying there waiting when we get ready to plant a garden next spring."

Houston had unfolded his hands, and was busy eating now. He washed down a mouthful of food, then chuckled. "You've convinced me, Runt. Build the barn wherever you think is best. And I guess we should have a bigger corral, 'cause we're eventually gonna need more horseflesh."

"Done thought of that, too," Fowler said, getting to his feet and dropping his empty cup into the dishpan. "Gonna make it a lot bigger. Fact is, I'm gonna start marking off the whole layout right now. Later on, I'll dig a ditch to send the spring's runoff through the new corral." He headed for the door. "You want to come along?"

Camp shook his head. "Nope. You just go ahead and do things your own way. I've got some business in Menardville, and I want to visit a few people. I'll be gone for two or three days, maybe longer." Half an hour later, he saddled the roan and rode off the hill.

13

Houston arrived at the Rocking A Ranch two hours before sunset. Even as he rode up the hill, he could see that Bama Angleton was on her knees beside the porch tending her rosebushes. Hearing the horse's footfalls and the creak of saddle leather, she quickly became aware of Camp's presence. She placed one hand on the doorstep and pulled herself to her feet as he rode into the yard. "Camp Houston!" she said loudly, laying the trimming shears aside. "I do declare."

He dismounted and tied the roan. "It's good to see you, Bama."

Her big smile and dancing eyes made it obvious that she was delighted with his visit. She crossed the yard to meet him, placing both of her hands in his. "You're one of our very favorite people, Camp. Thank you for coming. George and I have both been concerned, and we sit right here on this porch talking about you almost every night."

He released her hands and hugged her tightly. "No reason for you to worry about me, Bama. I'm not gonna fall in a hole. I know this country too well."

She nodded, and began to lead the way toward the house. "Yeah," she said, "I guess you do. But we've both been worried ever since you went after those men, afraid that maybe things wouldn't . . . uh . . . turn out right."

"Well, you can stop worrying. I'm doing great, and I never felt better." Camp seated himself in one of the porch chairs as Bama disappeared inside the house.

When she returned, she handed him a large glass of lemonade. "George is in Menardville today," she said. "Left about an hour after sunup." She pulled up a chair and took a sip from her own glass. "He probably couldn't make it back today even if he wanted to," she added, giving Camp a knowing wink. "Of course, I don't think he wants to. I believe he likes things just fine right there at the great Menardville Hotel."

Camp sipped at his drink, deciding that he would say nothing on the matter. Not in a million years. He changed the subject. "I bought some more property up on Calf Creek, Bama; got six sections now."

"I'm so proud for you, Camp. You got the place stocked already?"

He shook his head. "Won't have my cattle till next spring. Runt Fowler's already built the house, though, and he's working on a barn right now."

"Then I suppose you'll have a good house and barn both," she said. "George knows him well, and he's told me more than once that Mr. Fowler's mighty handy with hammer and saw. Sounds like you've got the right man up there."

He nodded. "I believe so. I've certainly been pleased with everything he's done so far." He drained his glass, and set it on a nearby table. "I was actually headed to Menardville myself," he said, "but I decided that I couldn't get there before midnight. I hate traveling in the dark, so I rode by here to see if you'd let me sleep in the bunkhouse tonight."

She shook her head emphatically. "No, sir, Camp Houston. There'll be none of that sleeping in the bunkhouse. Nobody's slept in that back bedroom for years, and it's a good bed. It's yours for the night, or for however long you want it."

Camp chuckled, and got to his feet. "Well, I guess by gosh I know when I'm well off, so I'm not gonna argue with you." He stepped into the yard and headed for the barn. When he had watered and curried the roan, he stabled the animal and poured a bucketful of oats in the trough. He would leave the horse in the stable overnight. The Rocking A corral was larger than most, and, being close to an expert at dodging a rope, the roan was not always easy to catch. Camp tossed a forkful of hay into the stable, then hooked the latch. When he opened the door with the bridle in his hand in the morning, the horse would have nowhere to run.

He spent the next hour sitting on the porch alone. The familiar sounds that he could hear from the kitchen told him that he would soon be eating a good supper. He had eaten numerous meals in this house in the past, and enjoyed all of them more than anything he had ever been served in a restaurant.

He was still sitting in his chair when the ranch hands began to ride in from several different directions. When they had taken care of their horses, some of them walked to the cookshack, while others headed for the bunkhouse. And though all of them looked the house over, and surely noticed him sitting on the porch, Camp offered no greeting, for he saw no one that he knew. He sat quietly watching the men till they entered the other buildings.

Then he was on his feet, playing a game that he had played many times before: he was trying to identify the aroma that was coming from the kitchen, so that he would know what was on the table long before he was called to supper. He sniffed a while longer, then nodded as he became convinced that he had identified the smell. He took a seat on the doorstep, looking forward to eating the meal of beefsteak, corn bread and fried Irish potatoes.

The lady called him to supper a few minutes later, and Camp was more than ready. He walked first to the back porch to wash his hands, then on through the kitchen to the dining room. He seated himself at the end of the table and eyed the food hungrily: pork chops, thick gravy, candied sweet potatoes, cabbage, black-eyed peas, hot buttered biscuits, and a pie made from dried apples.

He was quick to notice that none of the things he had expected to see was on the table, and decided that maybe his sense of smell was not so keen after all. He would remember that, for he might someday be in a situation where following his nose could get him in trouble.

He sat with his hands in his lap while the lady continued to move around the table. Finally, she poured two cups of coffee, then pulled out a chair for herself. She thanked the Lord for providing the food and asked Him to bless it, then spoke to her visitor. "I want you to eat everything in sight, Camp. Looks to me like you've fell off a lot since the last time you were here."

Camp was busy loading up his plate. "You're probably right," he said. "Of course, I've been traveling for most of that time, and good food is not always easy to come by." He smiled, then began to cut into a pork chop. "I've never yet known of anybody getting fat on the trail," he added.

Night came on before the meal was over, and they finished eating by the light of a coal-oil lamp. Then they sat on the porch in the darkness, listening to the entertaining sounds of countless nocturnal insects and animals that would never be seen in the light of day.

When the mosquitoes finally chased them inside an hour later, Camp headed for the bedroom he was shown. Even after he blew out the lamp and stretched out on the bed, he could still hear Bama moving around in the kitchen. He smiled at the sound. The saintly lady was no doubt cleaning up her kitchen, getting ready to prepare him another big meal in the morning. He turned over once, then went to sleep.

It seemed that he had just closed his eyes when he heard her knock on the bedroom door. "It's daylight already," she said softly. "Breakfast'll be ready by the time you are."

He dressed himself quickly, then left the house through the rear door. After a trip to the outhouse, he stopped on the back porch and washed his face and hands in the ever-present pan of water, then used the towel that hung from a nail driven into a post. He combed his hair with his fingers, then walked to the dining room, where he took a seat in the same chair he had occupied for supper.

The beefsteak he thought he had smelled cooking the night before was now on a platter beside his plate, which held a stack of flapjacks and several scrambled eggs. Another platter in the center of the table held a sliced cantaloupe, and a smaller dish contained garden-fresh tomatoes. He sat quietly as Bama talked to the Lord about the food, then seated herself at his elbow. He buttered his flapjacks, then poured on a river of syrup, saying, "If I ever marry, I sure hope I get a woman who can cook like you, Bama."

She chuckled softly. "I don't reckon they're terribly hard to find, Camp. Not if a handsome man like you lets them know he's looking. As soon as the word got out, I'd say that a lot of them would be going out of their way to strike up a conversation with you. Young girls are usually just waiting for a man like you to come along, and most of them know how to cook. The ones who don't can learn."

He washed a mouthful of food down with coffee. "I can't be thinking about a wife right now. I've got too many things to do." He sat quietly for a few moments, then added, "As for getting the word out, I wouldn't have the slightest idea of how to go about that." He laughed aloud. "Should I just put an ad in the newspaper?"

"You don't have to put an ad anywhere," she answered quickly. "You see, a young girl wants whatever she thinks all the other girls want. All you have to do is escort one or two of them around town a little, then stand back and take your pick when the rest come running."

He pushed his chair away from the table and got to his feet, shaking his head and laughing. "I never heard it put quite like that, Bama, but I suppose you should know. Maybe I'll try it sometime."

He walked to the bedroom and buckled on his gun belt, then returned to the dining room, hat in hand. "Thanks for putting me up, Bama, and I appreciate all the trouble you went to."

"No trouble at all," she said, "and I enjoyed your company." She followed him to the door.

He stepped onto the porch, then put on his hat. "I'm headed for Menardville, so I might meet George on the road. Is there anything in particular that you want me to tell him?"

"There sure is," she said, chuckling loudly. "Tell him that I've done run off with a younger man."

A few minutes later, he put the roan to a trot down River Road. Both the road and the San Saba River ran west from the Rocking A Ranch to Menardville in almost a straight line. Camp always enjoyed the ride, especially during the early morning. The air was always cool, and the sparkling dew on the wildflowers created a scene that was pleasing to the eye.

Grass was plentiful on both sides of the river, and wild game was so abundant that even a greenhorn would have no problem filling his bag. Though Camp had ridden no farther than a mile this morning, he had already seen a large number of animals, including three deer that had trotted across the road in front of him, well within rifle range. Indeed, Camp knew of no location that offered better hunting.

And though there had been reports of antelope sightings in Menard County over the years, Houston was more than a little skeptical. He knew that the speedy animals would not long remain in a brushy area, but would seek out more level country where they could depend on their keen vision and fleetness of foot to defeat predators.

He could not recall the name of any man claiming to have seen an antelope, but had heard the tale many times. He shook his head at the thought. He himself had not only been scouting and hunting in the area for several years, but he also knew something about the habits and preferences of the animals in question. To any group of men he heard discussing the claim, he was always quick to offer his own firm opinion: there were no antelope in Menard County.

Camp stopped once to relieve himself, then continued at a steady trot. The road crossed the river at John's Ford, and he arrived there three hours later. Looking toward the west bank, he could see that George Angleton was also there, about to ford the river on his way home. Camp moved to the side of the road and sat waiting. The rancher's horses waded the shallow water, then leaned into their collars, straining to pull an overloaded wagon to the top of the sloping east bank.

When Houston kneed the roan into the road, Angleton yanked on the reins, bringing the team to a halt. "Who in the world is that I see?" the rancher said loudly, wrapping the reins around the brake and stepping to the ground. "I sure can't think of anybody I'd rather see this morning. How've you been, Camp?"

Houston was on the ground now, extending his right hand. "Things just keep getting better as I go along, George. I can't think of a single thing that I'd have the gall to complain about."

Angleton grasped the hand and pumped the arm for a long time. "Me either," he said. "I ain't gonna be doing no complaining this year." He finally released the hand. "What're you doing traveling on River Road? Did you go by my house?"

Camp nodded. "Slept there last night," he said. "Ate up most of your grub."

The rancher's skinny body began to shake, and he made a sound that was somewhere between a giggle and a snort. "Well, by gosh I'm happy to hear that," he said. "Bama's always liked you, so I bet she fed you good."

"She did that, all right. She also asked me to tell you that she's done run off with a younger man."

Angleton guffawed and slapped his leg. "Funny woman, Camp. Funny, funny."

Camp led the rancher's team to the side of the road, then pointed to the wagon, which was loaded with gunny sacks stacked high above its sideboards. "I never knew you to load a wagon that heavy, George. Must be gold in those sacks."

"Aw, I knew it would be a big drag on the team, but I've been taking it easy on them. I just got a bargain on some shelled corn that I couldn't pass up. It ain't every day that you find it for twenty cents a bushel."

Camp nodded, satisfied with the answer. "I don't suppose you could even grow it that cheap," he said.

"That's the truth," Angleton agreed. "The corn's been in Bill Williams's barn for three years, and he finally had to damn near give it away in order to move it out. He's got a big crop in the fields right now, and it's almost harvest time."

"Sounds like Williams might be needing another barn," Camp said, chuckling. "Maybe I should inform Runt Fowler of that fact when he gets done at my place."

They stood at the roadside talking for more than an hour. Then Camp shook the rancher's hand and bade him good-bye.

He trotted his animal for the remainder of the morning, and at one o'clock in the afternoon rode into Menardville. At the livery stable, he dismounted and handed the reins to his longtime friend, Sid Blankenship. "I'll be staying in town tonight," he said. "Might be around for two or three days."

Blankenship led the roan forward and loosened the cinch. He was a dark-haired, barrel-chested six-footer who was about forty years old, and had been the town's busiest black-

smith as well as its most popular liveryman for at least a dozen
years. "Glad to hear that you're gonna be around a while," he
said. "All of us people who worry about you don't get to see
you very often." He stripped the saddle from the roan and
placed it on a nearby sawhorse. "Maybe we can have a drink
together after I close up here. You gonna be at the hotel?"

Camp nodded. "Come on up," he said. "I'll probably be in
the hotel bar about dark." He walked through the wide doorway and up the street, stopping at Riley's Restaurant. He had
eaten in the establishment many times, and was not only acquainted with both the owner and his wife, he also knew
everyone else who worked there. Or thought he did.

As he seated himself at a table against the wall, he noticed
that everything in the building had been rearranged since the
last time he was here. And though he could see several em-
ployees moving around, he recognized none of them. No
doubt about it, he was thinking, all the signs suggested that
the restaurant was under new management.

His suspicion was confirmed when a young woman appeared at his table, pad and pencil in hand. Her pink lips
parted on perfect white teeth as she went into her well-
rehearsed spiel: "Hi, and welcome to Riley's," she began
stiffly. "My name is Ellen Bice, and I'll be your waitress. My
uncle, Henry Trout, is the new owner, but he has elected not
to change the name of the restaurant. Nor will the motto
change. We remain committed to serving the same good food
at the same reasonable prices." She paused for a breath of air,
then asked, "May I have your order, sir?"

Camp took his time about answering. That the young lady
was new at this line of work was obvious, and he was thinking that he might very well be her first customer—ever. He
had been impressed with her lovely voice, however, a little
lower in pitch than that of most girls, but nevertheless totally
feminine. Even so, he knew that the long-winded spiel that
someone had written for her should be discarded, for people

in this town already knew all there was to know about Riley's Restaurant. When they walked through the door they would be expecting food, not conversation.

He had noticed right away that the girl wore no wedding band. "I'll have a T-bone steak," he said, smiling flirtatiously, "and a platter of fried potatoes."

She smiled and fluttered her long eyelashes, then headed for the kitchen. Camp followed her with his eyes till she disappeared behind the batwing doors. She was a well-proportioned brunette with sky-blue eyes, and appeared to be eighteen or twenty years old. The fact that she was not a local girl was obvious, for her accent suggested that she had come from someplace north of Texas.

The girl was still on Houston's mind when he paid for his food and stepped out onto the street an hour later. When she delivered his food to the table he had introduced himself by name, and, to satisfy his curiosity, asked her from whence she had come. "I grew up in Lincoln, Nebraska," she said, "and I came here two weeks ago to live with Uncle Henry and Aunt Mary." She smiled and headed elsewhere, and Camp did not see her again. He did leave a twenty-cent gratuity on his table, however, making sure that Ellen Bice would not forget him or his name.

He walked west till he reached the Menardville Hotel, where he rented a room on the second floor.

14

Just before sunset, Camp seated himself on a stool at the hotel bar. "Nice to see you again, Wes," he said, offering a handshake to the middle-aged bartender, who was a former heavyweight prizefighter named Wesley Hawks. "I'll have a beer."

Hawks grasped the hand. "Good to see you, too, Camp. I just opened a new keg, and the first mug's always free." He delivered the beer, then added, "I sure ain't seen much of you lately. Where've you been keeping yourself?"

Camp had been about to take a sip of his beer. He stopped his arm and held the mug in midair till after he answered the question. "Oh, I've been in town several times within the past few months," he said. "I guess the reason you didn't see me is because the urge to have a drink didn't hit me. I slept right here at the hotel, though."

Hawks nodded. "I don't ever really know who's in town. About the only people I see are the ones who come in the bar.

Hell, I come to work at ten o'clock in the morning, and everybody's done gone to bed by the time I get off at night." He poured himself a drink of whiskey, which he drank in one gulp, then dropped the empty glass in a pan of water. "Things have been slow in this place all year, and I ain't had no trouble that I couldn't talk my way out of." He laid his hands on the bar as if to invite Houston's inspection. "First time my damn knuckles have had a chance to completely heal in several years."

Camp shifted his eyes from one of the man's scarred hands to the other, then took a sip of his beer and nodded. "Your knuckles look good to me, Wes," he said with a chuckle. "I'd almost bet that they'd hold up for at least another hundred rounds."

"A hundred rounds, my ass." Hawks said as he refilled Camp's mug. "Don't wish nothing like that on me, 'cause I'm getting too old for that shit."

Camp continued to sit at the bar till Sid Blankenship arrived a short while later. The liveryman bought a bottle of whiskey, then he and Camp moved to a table in the far corner of the room. Blankenship poured drinks for both, then held his own glass aloft, proposing a toast. "Here's to your success next time you go hunting."

They touched glasses, and Camp nodded. "It'll be a while yet," he said, "but I appreciate the thought." He wet his lips with the whiskey. "Meanwhile, if you need that packhorse, just holler. I can get him back to you in one day."

Blankenship set his glass on the table noisily. "There you go again, Camp. How many times do I have to tell you that I don't need that horse? I don't need him today, tomorrow or next week."

Camp was quiet for a while, then said, "I just thought maybe somebody might be wanting to rent a horse, that not having him might be costing you money."

"No. Of course, everything does actually boil down to a matter of supply and demand, but my supply is always considerably bigger than the demand. Besides, the way I happened to come by that horse, I don't have but ten dollars in him."

Camp raised his eyebrows. "Ten dollars? Surely you don't mean that. He's a damn good horse, Sid."

Blankenship smiled. "Of course he is," he said, then laughed aloud. "But I'm a horse trader, remember?"

Camp sat thinking for a few moments. "Maybe I should hire you to do my horse buying," he said finally. "I expect to be needing several cow ponies next year." He told Blankenship about the additional property he had acquired, and that he would stock the place with longhorns in the spring.

The liveryman listened attentively, nodding all the while. "Just let me know how many head you want," he said, "so I can put out the word. Probably won't take long."

They were quietly sipping their drinks when Wesley Hawks approached their table a short time later. "I forgot to mention it earlier, Camp," he said, pulling up a chair, "but there's a fellow been hanging around town asking about you. Did he find you?"

Houston shook his head and set his glass on the table. "I don't believe he did, Wes. What does he look like, and where is he now?"

"I don't have any idea where he is," the bartender said, seating himself at the table, "but he's been in here three or four times during the past few days, buying drinks for some of the customers and asking questions about you. I guess I can give you a pretty good description, though: he's a skinny fellow with coal-black hair, probably not more'n twenty years old. Not very tall, either. I guess if you took him out of them high-heel boots and that high-crown Stetson, he wouldn't measure no more'n five-seven. Five-eight at the most. Probably weighs about a hundred forty pounds, if you count that Peacemaker on his left leg. Wears it hanging halfway to his knee in a tied-down holster, like he might need to get at it in a hurry some-time."

As Houston sat listening and thinking, his facial expression slowly turned to granite. He had been through it all before, and had no doubt as to why the young man had decided to seek him out. He spoke to the bartender: "Of course, he didn't say anything about why he wants to see me. Right?"

"Right. I don't reckon he ever told anybody whether he was friend or foe, but I guess we all just figured that he was probably a friend. Don't reckon he made no threats, or nothing like that."

Blankenship, who had been silently listening to the exchange, spoke now. "A fellow fitting that description was in my place two days ago, but he didn't ask me any questions. Bought a feed of oats for his bay, then had me trim the animal's hooves and nail on four new shoes. Flashed a good-size roll of money when he paid his bill, then mounted and headed east. I haven't seen him before or since."

Camp turned to the liveryman. "Any markings on that horse, Sid?"

Blankenship shook his head. "Just a bay," he said. "Bay all over. No stockings, no blaze. I'd say the horse weighs about nine-fifty."

Camp pushed his glass aside. The last thing he wanted right now was another drink of whiskey. He motioned toward the few drinkers who were scattered about the barroom, then spoke to Hawks. "Is there anybody in here right now who talked with the man, Wes?"

"Don't think so," Hawks said, looking over his shoulder. Then he turned his body halfway around, so that he could see every man in the building. "Nope. I sure didn't see any of this bunch talking with him. " He was getting to his feet now, about to return to his position behind the bar. "I just thought it was a little bit strange, this fellow going around asking questions about Camp Houston, then refusing to give out his own name when somebody gets curious. One of the men asked him who he was, but he said it didn't matter, said he didn't need no name." Continuing to shake his head, Hawks returned his chair to the adjoining table, then walked away.

Houston and Blankenship sat quietly for a while. They well understood the implications of what they had been hearing, and each man waited for the other to speak first. Blankenship finally broke the silence. "You're gonna be a sitting duck in that hotel room, Camp. I think you ought to spend the night at my house."

Camp sat quietly for a moment, then asked, "You got room?"

The man nodded. "Sure do. My cellar is actually a fortress, and it's got a good bed. My wife and kids slept down there during the Hoo Doo War, when a lot of crazy bastards were sneaking around taking potshots at people."

"All right," Houston said, "I'll be sleeping in your cellar." He sat staring at the wall for a while. "I've been wondering about something else, Sid," he said finally. "Did that fellow have a bedroll behind his saddle?"

"Yep. Had a tarp, too, and both of his saddlebags were stuffed. I don't believe he was out riding just for the hell of it, old buddy; the shoes on his horse weren't much thicker'n a dime. He's been on the move, all right."

Blankenship returned the half-full bottle to the bartender and Hawks gave him back half of his money, allowing him to pay for only as many ounces of the whiskey as they had drunk.

Camp joined the liveryman at the front door, and the two walked out into the night together. Avoiding the street, they walked down a little-used trail till they reached the livery stable, then turned south. The road leading up the steep hill to Blankenship's house was no more than three hundred yards long, and ended in his front yard.

Both smooth and wide, the well-drained stretch of road had been built by the same contractor who built the house. Camp had heard Blankenship discuss that very thing in the past. "I could have built the house and the road myself," the man had once said to Houston, "but it might have taken me two or three years. Hell, I needed a place to roost right then, 'cause my wife had done started having babies. I was tied up ten or twelve hours a day down at the stable, so I just hired the Wicker brothers to do my building. I never have been sorry, either. They not only know exactly what they're doing, they've got the right equipment to get it done."

When they reached the house, Blankenship unlocked the door and touched the wick of a coal-oil lamp with a burning match. Then he lighted a second lamp and handed it to Camp, pointing wordlessly to the staircase that led to the cellar.

Camp accepted the lamp and crossed the room. Knowing that Blankenship's wife and children were by now sound asleep, he descended the stairway as light-footedly as possible, surprised that none of the steps creaked in protest to his two hundred thirty pounds. Sid had been right about the building contractors, he was thinking. Anything they built was likely to stand for several generations, according to Runt Fowler, who readily admitted that most of what he knew about building he had learned by studying the methods of the Wicker brothers. They were the master builders of west Texas, he declared, and their services did not come cheap.

A short time later, Camp blew out the lamp and stretched out, his Peacemaker close at hand. Sid had not overstated the quality of the bed, he decided. Springy yet firm, the wide mattress was actually longer than his body, which was seldom the case. He tossed and turned as he relived the night's events, recalling the words spoken by Wesley Hawks as he described the young man who had been asking questions.

Houston racked his brain for a long time, but could think of no left-handed acquaintance who fit the description. The man was obviously seeking a showdown, he decided; another youngster hoping to gain a reputation by outdrawing and gunning down Camp Houston. The same thing had happened so many times that Camp was no longer unnerved by it. He shrugged, and fluffed up his pillow. After a while he managed to push all thoughts of the inquisitive stranger out of his mind, and began to think about how well things had gone for him lately. His eyes eventually closed of their own accord, and he slept soundly.

It was long after sunup when he was awakened by Blankenship calling from the top of the stairway. "You're gonna have to come on up here if you're going with me, Camp. I've got to get down to the stable."

Houston got to his feet and dressed himself quickly. At the top of the stairs, he spoke to his host: "I'll visit your outhouse, then meet you in the front yard. And you can tell your wife to forget about feeding me. I'll eat breakfast at Riley's."

A few minutes later, they walked down the hill together. They parted company at the stable, then Camp walked up the street toward Riley's, his eyes constantly darting from one place to another, sweeping the entire area for anything that did not look right. When he reached the restaurant he stepped inside quickly, staking out a table along the rear wall.

Accepting the cup of coffee delivered by a Mexican waiter, he ordered a ham-and-egg breakfast, then sat sipping the steaming liquid as he awaited the preparation of his food. The first of his two reasons for choosing Riley's was the restaurant's reputation for serving the best victuals in town. The second reason was nowhere to be seen. He shrugged, and continued to sip his coffee, supposing that Ellen Bice only worked during the afternoon and early evening.

He sat thinking for a while, and decided that he would pay a visit to the town marshal, even though his heart would not be in it. It was not that Marshal Paley and he had ever been on opposite sides of any particular issue, but for some reason that had never been discussed, each of the men simply acted as if the other did not exist.

Joe Paley had been Menardville's chief lawman for more than three years now. He had been appointed town marshal at the height of the Hoo Doo War, simply because he was the only man who applied for the position when the former marshal gave it up voluntarily. Marshal Manley Kincaid had resigned shortly after all of the unexplained shooting and killing started, proclaiming the job too dangerous for a family man.

Since becoming town marshal, Joe Paley had not spoken to Camp except on the few occasions when they had almost run over each other on the street. Even then he had always looked over Houston's shoulder while mumbling something inaudible. Of course, Camp was not the only person Paley ignored; the man never spoke to anybody unless it was absolutely necessary.

Though his dark-complected face was far from homely, the marshal wore a perpetual scowl, and from all appearances had few close friends. Several men with Menard County interests had even privately questioned Paley's activities during the Hoo Doo War, though it seemed that those expressing doubt of his honesty usually spoke in low tones.

Occasionally, however, some brave soul would speak openly and loudly about the fact that, while practically everyone else in the county had lost property to roving bands of thieves, nothing the marshal owned had ever been stolen. And though senseless vandalism had occurred on almost a daily basis throughout Mason and Menard Counties, Joe Paley's property had not even suffered as much as a torched haystack. The same thoughts had crossed Houston's mind more than once, but had immediately been discarded. He had long ago made a firm decision not to spend one second of his life worrying about something over which he had no control. As was usually the case, it would all come out in the wash. If Joe Paley was a dishonest lawman, his day of reckoning would come.

Houston took his time with his breakfast, and sipped several cups of coffee afterward. When he finally left the restaurant, he very casually walked up one side of the street and down the other, then headed for the marshal's office.

15

★

The marshal's office and the jail were located in the county courthouse, two hundred yards west of the town's main commercial area. The large building also provided office space for the circuit judge, county prosecutor, tax collector and at least two criminal defense lawyers. Paley's office faced the street on the east side of the building, and had a small porch with two rocking chairs.

The front door of the office was open wide, and even as Houston walked into the yard he could see the man sitting at his desk, his attention on some kind of printed material that he held in his hands. Camp stopped at the porch and knocked on a post. "Have you got a minute, Marshal?"

Paley continued to concentrate on whatever he was reading for a moment, then raised his eyes. "Guess so," he said gruffly. "The door's open."

Houston walked into the office and stood before the oversized desk, for he had not been invited to sit down. The marshal laid his magazine aside, and spoke again. "You got a problem of some kind?"

Camp crossed his arms and stood staring at the man for a while. Though Paley was not a tall man, five-ten at the most, he was solidly built, and appeared to be in good physical condition. Though not yet out of his thirties, it was obvious when he was hatless, as he was now, that his thinning dark hair was rapidly turning to gray. His walrus mustache also contained more salt than pepper.

After receiving no answer to his question, he began to shift about nervously under Camp's constant stare. Finally, he tried again, speaking in a much softer tone. "Is there something I can help you with?"

Camp continued to stand, looking Paley in the eye. "There's a man traveling around asking questions about me. He's been here in Menardville several times, and I seriously doubt that he's looking for me because he wants to shake my hand. I was just wondering if you've seen him, or know who he is."

Paley shook his head. "I doubt that it's anybody I'd know, and I haven't seen any strangers recently. Of course, I haven't been on the street lately, don't ever go down there unless somebody sends for me. I don't know if it's because the merchants don't like lawmen in general, or me in particular, but judging from their attitude, I'd say that most of them like it better when I don't come around."

"I don't know about that," Houston said. He took a few steps toward the door, then stopped, adding, "I came by because I thought you ought to be told about this fellow, not because I expected you to do something about him. If he's really hunting me, he'll find me." He stepped into the yard and headed toward town.

Paley, who was standing on the porch now, called after him, "If you happen to run into that fellow anywhere within the town limits, just be sure that you're not the first one to start shooting!"

Houston stopped in his tracks. He stood still for several seconds, then turned quickly and spoke loudly. "Are you suggesting that I give some sonofabitch a free shot at me, Marshal?"

"Well, not . . . I mean . . . just don't . . ."

Camp turned his back to the stammering lawman and walked away.

He drank another cup of coffee at Riley's, then continued on down the hill. Long before he reached the livery, he could see a bay saddler standing in the stable's wide doorway. Sid Blankenship was holding the animal's bridle while carrying on an animated conversation with a man much shorter than he. Believing that he was now looking at the man who had been asking the questions, Camp stepped between two buildings and stood watching.

Though he had a clear view of the stable, he could not get a good look at the shorter man, for he was standing on the far side of the bay. Nevertheless, enough of the man's head towered above the horse for Camp to see that it was crammed as deeply as possible into a high-crown Stetson.

The two men continued to talk for several minutes, and Camp got the idea that maybe Blankenship was using some kind of stalling tactic, keeping the man in the doorway as long as possible in case Houston should happen by. The liveryman finally led the bay into the stable, and the shorter man followed, offering Camp a broad view of his back. The gun belt around the man's waist was easy to see, and the Peacemaker hanging low on his left leg told Houston all he needed to know.

He waited till both men had disappeared down the stable's dark hall, then went into action. Moving as fast as he could without running, he turned north through an alley and continued in that direction till he reached the woods. Then he turned east again, and did not stop till he was slightly behind and north of the stable. He watched from behind a clump of bushes till he was convinced that both men were still inside the building, then crossed the road quickly and quietly.

Now against the north wall of the stable, he began to make his way noiselessly toward the front of the building, where he would simply wait. He had no intention of going inside, for once he stepped in front of that wide-open doorway he would be a perfect target, while the man inside would be almost totally concealed by the dim lighting. Moments later, he stood at the front corner of the building, waiting.

He was still standing in the same position several minutes later when a wagon rattled down the road, headed into town. A farmer and his wife were sitting on the seat, and two small boys rode behind them, their bare feet dangling from the rear of the wagon. The farmer nodded as his vehicle passed within a few feet of the stable. Camp ignored the greeting, for every single one of his senses was attuned to the business at hand.

Standing against the wall, he could hear a conversation going on inside the stable, but could understand none of the words. Blankenship's deep voice was easy to identify, however, and Camp could tell that it was getting closer to the front of the building. Then he began to hear a different voice, even closer now.

Continuing to talk as he walked, the young man was suddenly through the doorway and into the yard. He took a few steps in the direction of town, then turned halfway around to offer a few parting words to Blankenship. "I guess I'll be back about—"

His voice cracked and he froze in his tracks as he saw that Houston, his legs spread apart and his body leaning forward in a slight crouch, was now standing where the liveryman had stood only a moment before. Camp spoke quickly: "I hear that you've been looking for Camp Houston. You've found him."

The man did not speak. He stared sideways at Camp for only a moment, then made a decision that bordered on stupidity: even as he attempted to complete his turn, with his body essentially off balance, he made his play. And though his gun was in his fist very quickly, he died before he could line it up, taking a shot in the mouth from Camp's Peacemaker. A second shot hit him in the throat and knocked him over a wooden sawhorse, where he collapsed and lay still.

Houston stood in the doorway for several moments, his eyes on the fallen man. Though Camp had been through it all before, he had nevertheless been somewhat surprised at the way the showdown came about. He had expected the man to go for his gun, but not before he had completed his turn, planted his feet, and regained his balance. He had obviously convinced himself that he was the fastest draw around, and that he could do it from any position.

Camp stood reliving the past few seconds in his mind. The young gunman had been fast, all right, but he had clearly put himself at a disadvantage by moving too soon. Indeed, the lifeless bundle that now lay on the ground beside the sawhorse had only a few moments ago been nothing short of a quick-draw artist, but he had also been a young man, and young men made mistakes.

Camp holstered his weapon, then walked forward. He turned the body over and decided quickly that he had never seen the gunman before. When he went through the man's pockets he found forty dollars, a watch, a sack of Durham, several matches and a letter addressed to Ben Gillam, in Corpus Christi, Texas.

Camp stood holding the letter for a moment, having no doubt that he was now looking at the remains of one Ben Gillam. Finally, he extracted the single sheet of paper from the envelope. The message consisted of only two lines, but the words jumped out at him instantly: *"STOP CAMP HOUSTON!"* it commanded, then went on to suggest that the Menardville area would likely be the most fertile hunting ground. And though there was no signature, the writer had initialed it. The *W.T.* at the bottom of the page told Camp the name of the sender. He folded the letter and slipped it into his pocket, already anticipating the day when he would wave it in front of Walt Turner's nose.

Blankenship was beside him now. "We're about to have company," he said, pointing up the hill, "and I believe Marshal Paley's leading the pack."

Knowing that the sound of gunfire never failed to bring people out, Camp had expected no less. Looking up the street, he could see several men headed toward the stable. He could even hear them now, speculating back and forth on the reason for the gunshots. As Blankenship had said, the marshal was the point man.

Paley arrived in the stable yard first, and bent over to inspect the body. Wesley Hawks took a quick look, then walked on past the lawman and spoke to Houston: "That's the man who's been asking all the questions, Camp. I see he found you."

Houston nodded curtly, and said nothing.

The young gunman's Peacemaker still lay in the dirt, where he had dropped it when he took the first shot. Paley now walked to the opposite side of the sawhorse and picked up the weapon, sniffing its barrel. "Everybody said they heard two shots, mister!" he said to Camp sarcastically, much louder than was necessary. He held the gun in his right hand and pointed to it with his left. "This gun ain't been fired since no telling when!"

"That very well may be one of the reasons I'm still standing!" Camp said just as loudly, making a conscious effort to match Paley's tone. "You're exactly right, Marshal, the gun hasn't been fired this morning." He pointed to the corpse, speaking even louder now. "But it damn sure ain't his fault!"

Sid Blankenship, who had so far stood in the background and remained quiet, stepped forward now. "It was clearly a case of self-defense, Joe." Though the liveryman's comment had been directed to the marshal, his deep voice carried to every man in the crowd. "He's been hunting Camp for more than a week," Blankenship continued, "and just happened to find him here at my stable. I stood right over there in that doorway and watched it all." He motioned toward the body. "That man tried his damnedest to kill Camp Houston."

Paley sniffed the barrel again, then shoved the Colt behind his waistband. He spoke to the liveryman: "Did you hear every word of it, Sid? Did you hear him threaten Houston? Exactly what did he say?"

Blankenship stared at Paley for a while. "The man didn't say a goddam word," he said finally. "The second he laid eyes on Camp, he just went for his gun." He pointed to the body again, adding, "As you can see, it cost him dearly."

Paley shrugged, then dropped his hands to his sides. The sullen expression on his face made it obvious that he was less than pleased with the liveryman's testimony, but he also knew that there was nothing he could do to change it. He was well aware of the fact that Blankenship's popularity exceeded his own by a wide margin, and that the men of Menardville would accept any statement the stable owner made as gospel. The lawman fidgeted for a moment, exhaled loudly, then turned to Camp. "Did you know the man, Houston?"

"His name was Ben Gillam," Camp said softly. "He lived down at Corpus."

Paley nodded. "Well, you're gonna have to pay for his burial," he said, his own voice softer now. "The town of Menardville sure ain't gonna do it."

Camp's reaction was immediate. "I don't think so, Marshal. I'll let him buy his own funeral. He's got the money right there in his pocket."

"In his pocket? How do you know what he's got?"

Houston ignored the marshal's question, and spoke to Wesley Hawks. "I'd take it as a favor if you'd get hold of the undertaker and tell him to take care of this, Wes. Tell him the dead man's name and where he came from, and that he's got forty dollars in his pocket to pay for his burial."

Hawks nodded. "I'm on my way," he said, then headed up the hill.

Camp stood watching the departing bartender for a few moments, then turned to Blankenship, speaking loudly enough to be heard by every man in the crowd. "I'd appreciate it if you'd catch up my roan, Sid. I've got a home to go to nowadays."

Five minutes later, the liveryman led the big horse through the doorway, the saddle already in place. Without another word to anyone, Houston tightened the cinch, mounted and guided the roan to the road. Then he turned east and kicked the animal to a canter. He was out of sight in less than a minute.

16

★

It was long after dark when Camp rode into his yard and helloed the house. He sat his saddle patiently till Fowler had acknowledged his greeting, then rode to the shed and fed his horse by the light of a full moon. A few minutes later, he entered the house and poked around in the dark till he found his bed. He was asleep quickly.

At the breakfast table, he showed Fowler the letter that he had taken from Ben Gillam's body, and announced that he himself was about to take a trip to Fort Worth.

"I don't know of anything else you can do, Camp," Fowler said. He handed the letter back. "Hell, this thing makes it pretty plain what Walt Turner's up to. If the sonofabitch sent one man after you, how do we know that there ain't a whole bunch of them out there dogging your trail?"

Camp shook his head. "No way of knowing for sure. It would be my guess, though, that he would only send one man at a time. I believe he'll wait till he finds out what kind of luck

Gillam had before he dispatches another gunman. What I'm hoping to do is reach Walt Turner before the news of Gillam's demise does."

He ate a large breakfast, then wrapped up some leftover ham and biscuits for later. He put his bedroll, razor and a change of clothing together, then headed for the corral. No need to worry about cooking and eating utensils; they were still in his pack from the last trip, along with his coffeepot and a good supply of coffee and sugar.

He had already saddled the roan and had just caught up the packhorse when Fowler walked under the shed, carrying a sack in his hand that he laid on a stack of lumber. "I came down to help you fasten the packsaddle on that horse and balance the load," the big man said, taking the harness from a peg on the wall.

Camp backed the horse under the shed. "I appreciate it, Runt. It's a lot easier to do with a man on each side."

Fowler threw the contraption across the horse's back. "At least your old buddy, Sid Blankenship, lent you a good packsaddle," he said.

Camp reached for a strap to buckle. "There's none better. Not at any price."

The packsaddle was a Grimsley, which, to men who were knowledgeable about such things, was enough said. Made by the T. Grimsley Company of St. Louis, Missouri, it was open at the top, with a light, compact, strong tree, whose rawhide covering was put on green and drawn tight by the contraction of drying. It had a leather breast strap, breeching and lash strap, with a broad hair girth.

Several different types of packsaddles were in use, many of which were mere instruments of torture on the backs of the pack animals, lacerating them cruelly and causing them continuous pain. Not so with the Grimsley, which could easily be fitted to the back of an animal of any size. At the outset, these packsaddles had been designed with the comfort of the beast of burden receiving top priority. Indeed, both mules and horses that were equipped with Grimsleys had been known to carry heavy burdens all the way across the country, all of them arriving in California with backs that were unblemished. Without exception, Houston considered the Grimsley the best packsaddle ever devised by anyone.

Just as Camp thought he had the pack loaded, Fowler presented him with the sack he had brought from the house. "Some sweet potatoes in here," he said. "You can bake one of them in the hot ashes of your campfire every night. They're good, and they're good for you, and you don't have no pots or dishes to wash. I'll guarantee you, Camp, that a big bowl of beans and a big sweet potato will stick to a fellow's ribs just as long as beefsteak."

"You might be right," Camp said, accepting the sack. "I've eaten them before, and I'll eat these. I like the taste, and they're sure easy to fix."

He put the potatoes in the pack, then stood looking at the site that Fowler had chosen for the new barn and corral. He fished around in his pocket for a while, then handed the man a hundred dollars. "Get hold of Cornell Wooten," he said. "Hire him and all three of his sons to help you with that barn, if you can. It's too damn much work for one man."

Fowler folded the money and shoved it into his pocket. "I could have done all of it by myself eventually, Camp, but I can sure use the help. With two men cutting and hauling logs, and three men peeling them, notching them and putting them were they belong, that barn's gonna start taking shape in a hurry. A damn sight quicker'n you'd think."

Camp shook his head. "Not quicker than I would think, Runt. I've seen you in action before." He mounted the roan and took up the slack in the packhorse's lead rope. "You take care, now, and don't strain yourself. Let your hired hands do some of the work." He checked his pockets to make sure he had his watch and his pocket compass, then rode off the hill.

When he reached the valley floor, he turned in his saddle and lifted his hat to Fowler, who was now standing at the top of the hill waving. Then he kicked the roan to a fast trot and headed for the town of Brady. There he would buy some bologna, cheese, crackers and several tins of sardines, then head for Comanche, a town that was almost exactly halfway between his home and Fort Worth.

With the exception of a short stop in Brady, he traveled steadily. He even rode a few hours after nightfall on the first day, for the full moon provided as much light as he needed. He finally made a dry camp and slept six hours, but was in the saddle again well before sunup.

At midafternoon of the second day, he halted at the big Colorado. And though the sun was still three hours high, he forded the river and selected a campsite, for he knew that both he and his animals needed a good night's rest. Though that in itself was a good enough excuse, his main reasons for deciding on an early camp had been that, even from the opposite side of the river, he could see that the grass was good on the north bank, and deadwood was plentiful. Of course, such an ideal campsite had not gone unnoticed by other travelers.

Two covered wagons were parked a hundred yards to the west, and their teams grazed in a small meadow nearby. Two additional horses that Houston took to be saddlers were also picketed on the lush, green grass. Closer to the wagons, several people sat around on the ground, probably all members of the same large family, Camp was thinking.

Between the wagons and the riverbank was a campfire that was far too big for cooking purposes, with flames sometimes shooting several feet into the air. A woman whose head and face were mostly hidden by a large bonnet stirred the fire occasionally, obviously waiting for it to burn down some before she began to prepare supper for her family.

Houston unburdened, watered and picketed his animals, then began to gather fuel for his own fire. When he had placed several small sticks of deadwood on a pile of dead grass, leaves and bark, he touched it all with a burning match, then walked to the river and returned with his coffeepot full of water. He threw in a handful of grounds, then set the pot on the fire. A few minutes later, he poured himself a cup of strong coffee.

He had finished eating his supper of bologna, cheese and crackers and was sitting on his bedroll sipping a second cup of coffee when he had a visitor: a skinny young man who was almost as tall as Houston himself approached the campfire, his right hand extended. "Howdy," he said, his wide smile revealing two rows of perfect teeth. "I just saw you over here by yourself, and thought maybe you might like some company. My name's Bo Patton, and I'm from Ringgold, Georgia. I've been on the move ever since I left there, nearly two months ago."

Houston was on his feet now. He introduced himself as he pumped the man's hand, returning its firm grip. He turned to his pack and dug out an extra cup. "The coffee's still hot," he said, pointing, "and there's plenty of cold stuff here to eat. Just help yourself, if you're hungry."

The young man did not hesitate. "I am a little bit hungry," he said. He filled his cup, then took a seat on the ground. As he tore into the bologna and cheese, and began to stuff crackers into his mouth by the handful, it became obvious that he had been more than a little bit hungry. Camp dug into his pack again and added two tins of sardines to the offering. "Eat all you want," he said. "I'm not short on anything."

Camp sat sipping his coffee and watching as the young man continued to eat everything in sight. Sometimes, when he turned his head a certain way, Bo Patton appeared to be a little older than he probably was. Even so, he couldn't be more than eighteen years old, Houston decided; and his long blond hair, dimpled chin and beardless, freckled face made him look even younger.

Camp believed that the young man stood at least six foot two in his socks, and very well might shoot up a few more inches before he stopped growing. He had big hands, long arms and legs, and his shoulders were unusually broad. All of which suggested that, when he finally stopped growing and filled out his frame, he would be a hard man to push off whatever ground he decided to stand.

Camp motioned toward the wagons with his thumb, and spoke to Patton, who was still busy eating. "Is that your family you're traveling with?".

"No, no," the young man said around a mouthful of food. "That's the Joneses over there. I just met up with them a few days ago, and I've been traveling with them. I've been eating supper with them every night, too. Now, there ain't none of them mentioned it to me, but I believe they might be running a little short. Anyway, they eat the same thing every day: corn pone and fried potatoes, and the portions are kinda small, like maybe they ain't got very much." He swallowed the last of his food and sat quietly for a moment. Then his cheeks suddenly turned red, and he began to speak softly and self-consciously: "I guess I ought to just tell you the truth: the only reason I walked over here was because I was hoping you'd offer me something to eat."

Houston nodded. He had suspected as much. "How old are you, Bob?" he asked.

"Twenty-one." Patton pulled the coffeepot off the fire and refilled his cup, then turned to face Camp. "That ain't the truth either," he said, his face flushing again. "I've been telling that lie for so long that I've just about started believing it myself, but it ain't done me a damn bit of good. I ain't but seventeen years old; be eighteen next March."

Camp nodded again. "Where are you headed, and what are you gonna do?"

"Don't know for sure. Mr. Jones said that when he finds some work, I might be able to get a job helping him." He picked his teeth with a splinter for a moment, then looked at Camp sheepishly, adding, "He said I could marry one of his daughters if I wanted to, but I told him I didn't know so much about that."

Houston was smiling now. "What do you know how to do?" he asked.

"I grew up farming, but I hated every minute of it. I'd sure be willing to do it now, though. As broke as I am, I'd take on any kind of job that's honest."

During the next hour, Camp learned a great deal more about the young man, who actually seemed eager to talk about his past. Houston put on a fresh pot of coffee, then leaned back on his elbows, ever the willing listener. Sensing that he had Camp's undivided attention, the youngster also relaxed, and began to speak freely:

Patton had never known his father, who had died on a Tennessee battlefield during the Civil War. After his mother's death, when the boy was ten years old, he had been shifted back and forth between two of his maternal uncles. It had been one of the uncles who had bestowed the nickname Bo on young Julian Patton, and the boy had rarely been addressed by his given name since.

When young Patton reached the age of sixteen, he said good-bye to both of his uncles and took a job on a nearby cotton farm. The living conditions on the new job were a big improvement over anything he had experienced before, especially the food. And though the wage was pitifully small, he nevertheless managed to save enough money to buy a reasonably good saddle and the ten-year-old bay that was at this moment picketed in the meadow beside the wagon teams.

Several weeks ago, after months of reading magazine articles extolling the innumerable virtues of living in the West, assuring the reader that year-round jobs on Texas ranches could be had for the asking, Bo Patton made his move: with one blanket, two changes of clothing and nine dollars in his pocket, he saddled the bay and headed west. Now, after seven weeks of traveling and job hunting, he sat at Houston's campfire.

"What little money I had's been gone for nearly a month

now," Patton said, as he filled both coffee cups and handed one to Camp. He blew air into his cup and sipped at the coffee, then sat staring across the river for a long time, as if in deep thought. "It ought to be against the law for them damn magazines to put out a bunch of lies," he said finally. "Just about every one you pick up back home's got at least one story about how easy it is to get a job on a Texas ranch. I've been asking for work at one ranch after another, but most of them are laying men off, not hiring. All the rest said they only hire men with experience, and I don't know much about cows. My horse don't either."

Camp had listened to Patton's story with interest, and by sunset had taken a liking to the young man. "I suppose there's room for one more down at my place," he said. "One of my friends is in the process of finishing the house, putting up some outbuildings and shaping up the place in general. Since you have nothing else to do, maybe you could help him out."

Patton nodded, and his whole face seemed to break into a smile. "Never have built anything on my own," he said, "but I sure know how to do what I'm told."

Camp chuckled. "Well, my friend's a good builder and a good man; he'll show you what needs doing."

"You got a ranch?"

"I've got thirty-eight hundred acres and a house on Calf Creek, and—"

"Thirty-eight hundred acres?" the boy interrupted. Clearly impressed, he began to shake his head. "Thirty-eight hundred acres!" he repeated loudly.

Camp was quiet for a while, then spoke softly: "I know that sounds like a lot of land to you, and back where you came from it would be. But in Texas, a six-section ranch is considered small. Very small. I don't have any cattle yet, but I expect to stock the place with longhorns next spring. If you happen to be on hand then, you'll get a chance to learn all you need to know about cattle." Houston yawned and stretched his arms over his head, suggesting that the conversation was about over. "The ranch is producing nothing right now, Bo, so I can't pay you much. But if you stay on through the winter, you'll have a few dollars in your pocket, plenty to eat and a warm place to sleep. Then, after I bring in the cattle next spring, you'll be paid full wages."

Patton did not have to think about the proposition for long. "All of that sounds mighty good to me," he said quickly, "and I'd sure be beholden to you."

Camp pointed across the river. "If you'll get an early start in the morning and stay with that road yonder, you'll be in the town of Brady before nightfall." He handed the youngster five dollars. "This'll be enough money to put you up at the hotel and feed you, and to pay for stabling your horse.

"When you leave Brady the day after tomorrow, you'll be headed due south. The road's pretty good, and it passes almost within a stone's throw of my place. You'll know when you reach Calf Creek, 'cause your horse'll either have to wade it or turn around. That's where you leave the main road and turn west. The new log house at the top of the hill is mine, and the man you need to see is Mr. Fowler. If for some reason he happens not to be there at the time, just make yourself at home. He'll be back."

Patton had listened to his instructions closely, nodding occasionally. He put the money in his pocket. "I guess all that means that you ain't gonna be around, huh?"

Camp nodded. "I've got business in Fort Worth, and I have no way of knowing when I'll be home. You'll be in good hands down there, though. Just watch what Mr. Fowler does and listen to what he says. You'll learn plenty."

When Camp yawned again, the young man got the message. "I guess I'll go on over and crawl into my bedroll, Mr. Houston." He got to his feet and offered a parting handshake. "I intend to be on that road before sunup, and like I said, I'm mighty beholden to you."

Camp shook the boy's hand. "Just take care of yourself, and eat a big beefsteak before you leave Brady. It'll stick with you a lot longer than flapjacks."

"Yessir," Patton said, then walked toward the wagons.

As the young man's image faded into the darkness, Houston kicked dirt over the campfire and dragged his bedroll between two bushes. Then he pulled off his boots and stretched out, his Peacemaker close to hand. A few minutes later, he was sleeping soundly.

He awoke once during the night to relieve himself, but soon dozed off again. When he next opened his eyes it was after daybreak, and the eastern horizon had already turned pink. What had awakened him had been a loud splashing sound close by. When he sat up and looked across the river, he could see a rider headed down the road in a southwesterly direction. He was pleased. Bo Patton had just forded the river, and was on his way to Calf Creek.

Houston rekindled the fire, and a short while later sat eating another meal of bologna, cheese, sardines and crackers, and washing it all down with several cups of freshly made coffee.

When Camp had first awakened, the Joneses had been busy harnessing and hitching their teams to the wagons. Now, with that chore completed, the vehicles rolled right in front of him before fording the river and taking the road to Brady. And though three people rode in each of the wagons, and all of them took a good look at Houston, no one offered so much as a nod, or otherwise acknowledged his existence.

Camp was somewhat amused. He believed that the slight had been deliberate, and the direct result of his having hired Bo Patton. The old man had no doubt viewed the youngster as a prospective son-in-law who might eventually gain employment and help him feed the pack, while the girls had had ample time to fall in love. The three young ladies, each of whom appeared to be in her teens, had all given Camp a malevolent stare as they passed.

He watched till the wagons disappeared down the road, then dashed his coffee grounds into the fire and got to his feet. He washed his coffeepot in the river, then rolled up his bedroll and put his pack together. He retrieved his horses from the meadow, and a short time later mounted and headed northeast.

Even though the bright sunlight in his eyes hampered his vision, it was a good day for traveling. And because he wanted to put as much of the crooked road behind him as he could during the cool of the morning, he pushed his horses to a mile-eating canter. Unless they began to show signs of overheating, he would maintain the same pace for much of the day. He expected to arrive in Comanche before nightfall, where good accommodations for both man and animals could be obtained at reasonable prices.

17

The town of Comanche had been established as a trade center for surrounding ranches in 1858. And although severe Indian raids inhibited its growth right from the start, the town's well-armed residents and the cattlemen of the area eventually decided to band together for their mutual defense. Within a matter of weeks they had collectively produced a body count that was totally unacceptable to the marauding Indians. Their depredations then came to a sudden halt, and it soon became obvious that they were no longer in the area. Nobody seemed to know where they had gone, but most believed they had headed for Mexico, hoping to find more plunder and less resistance.

With the threat of renegade Indians now a thing of the past, the area began to prosper, and when Comanche County was partitioned in 1859, the town of the same name became its seat. And though no population boom followed, the town held its own, and even attracted a few additional residents each year.

While most of the new faces belonged to people who would be productive citizens and good neighbors, the area also proved to be a magnet for a different element: as had been the case with many other Texas towns, Comanche had suffered an invasion of cutthroats and gunslingers early on, and gunfights, at one time or another, had taken place in practically every location in town, often in broad daylight.

And although more than a dozen men had died in shootouts during the early years of Comanche County, no one had ever been brought to account. Even during the Reconstruction period, the Union soldiers had rarely interfered with the combatants, seeming to find the idea of Texas killing Texans highly acceptable.

Years later, when Texas Rangers served notice on the rowdy element that their shenanigans would no longer be tolerated, the town took on a different look almost overnight. Most of the thieves and hustlers quickly found reasons to be somewhere else, while the few who remained curtailed their criminal activities and became almost law-abiding.

These days, the streets of Comanche were as safe as those of any other Texas town, and kept so by a thirty-year-old former trail boss named Bill Pennington, who had been town marshal for the past five years. Most outlaws made a special effort to bypass his town, for it was widely known that he was extremely fast with a six-gun and had the guts of a wolverine. He had little tolerance for thieves, and none whatsoever for ruffians who would run roughshod over those least able to defend themselves. Both facts could easily be confirmed by a short walk through the local cemetery: Bill Pennington had provided occupants for at least five of those graves at the top of the hill, one of them so fresh that the grass had not yet grown over it.

Camp Houston rode into Comanche from the west, when

the sun was still two hours high. He halted at the edge of town to take in the familiar view for a few moments, then kneed the roan down the street, his eyes scanning everything in sight. With the exception of several new buildings on the north side of the street, he could see few changes since his last visit, more than four years earlier.

One of the changes he could see, however, even from a distance, was that the town marshal now had his own office and jail, right in the middle of town. Long before Camp reached the building he could see a familiar figure sitting on the small porch beside the office door. Moments later, he brought his animals to a halt at the hitching rail. "Hello, Bill," he said loudly.

The marshal, who had been paying attention to something across the street, turned his head instantly, seeming to recognize the voice. He was on his feet in a second, his face breaking into a broad smile. "Well, I'll be damned, Camp," he said, walking into the street and offering a handshake. "Ain't been more'n three days since I heard a bunch of fellows talking about you, and here you come riding in outta nowhere."

Camp dismounted and shook the marshal's hand. "I'm on my way up to Fort Worth, and decided to stop off here for the night." He tied the roan to the hitching rail, then added, "Cooking on a campfire and sleeping on the ground gets a whole lot less agreeable as I get older."

Pennington laughed. "It never was agreeable to me, even though I just about lived outdoors for several years. I've been sleeping in a good bed ever since I got this job, so I guess the ground would feel even harder nowadays."

The marshal motioned toward his office, and led the way. "I've got just about anything you'd like to drink," he said over his shoulder. "I bought a little of it myself, but I took most of it away from drunks bent on raising hell." He opened a wall cabinet to reveal a shelf lined with bottles. "Name your poison," he said.

Camp shrugged. "I'll drink whatever you're having."

Moments later, Pennington was busy pouring. "I got this bottle without even having to argue about it," he said as he filled two tin cups with expensive rum. "The fellow I took it from didn't even remember having it when I turned him out of jail next morning." After reading a question in Houston's eyes, the lawman added quickly, "That's not exactly like it sounds, now. I don't mean that I steal their whiskey. You see, even though they almost always aggravate the hell out of me and give me a hard time, I don't fine them one cent for getting drunk unless they tear up something. They actually come out ahead, Camp. Where else could they get a night's lodging and a hot breakfast for the price of a bottle of whiskey?"

Camp smiled, took a sip from the cup and did not answer the question.

They had first met in Kansas almost ten years earlier. Pennington had been a trail boss from the San Antonio area at the time, and Houston was a green cowhand who had just completed his first cattle drive up the trail to Abilene. And though a wide gulf separated their respective ranks as far as the other drovers and cowboys were concerned, the two had nevertheless struck up a lasting friendship, no doubt due to the similarity of their ages and backgrounds.

Because of a holdup in getting bank drafts converted to gold or acceptable currency, both men had remained in Abilene for several days. They walked the streets together at all hours of the day and night, taking in one bawdy house or saloon after another. Then, almost a week later, when the bank solved its problem and began to trade bags of cash for bank drafts, both Pennington and Houston were paid in full, and each went his own way.

Although they had never worked together, they had remained friends, and for the next several years had run into each other frequently. Then Pennington had taken his current job, which had brought his traveling to a halt. Today was only the second time Camp had seen him in five years.

Now the marshal sat with one elbow on his desk, his chin

resting in the palm of his hand. "How long has it been since you've been in this town, Camp? For the life of me, I can't remember."

"Four years." Camp finished off his drink and handed the lawman the empty cup. "The fellow you took that bottle away from had good taste, Bill. I believe I could stand a refill."

Pennington poured both cups half full, then returned the bottle to the cabinet, saying, "I don't suppose a week ever goes by that I don't think of you." He reseated himself behind his desk, and chuckled. "The number of men on Earth that I truly like is pretty small, Camp. You're one of the chosen few." He sipped his drink, then wiped his mouth on his sleeve. "You say you're headed for Fort Worth, so I guess you're traveling on business, huh?"

"I've got business there, all right. At least, I think I do." Camp set his cup on the desk and got to his feet. He walked back and forth across the room while he told Pennington the whole story, raising his voice occasionally to emphasize a point.

When Camp finally stopped talking and reseated himself, the marshal set his own cup down and exhaled loudly, as if he had listened to the story without breathing. "I knew about the bushwhacking in Kansas," he said, "and I knew John Calloway. We weren't big buddies or anything like that, but I talked with him once in Abilene, then a few times in Dodge City. I guess one of the reasons I remembered him was because he never would have a drink with the rest of us. More than once I saw him belly up to the bar and buy whiskey for everybody else, but he sure wouldn't drink it himself."

"I never knew John to take a drink, Bill, and I knew him well." Camp sat quietly for a few moments, then handed Pennington the letter he had taken from Ben Gillam's pocket. "Read this, then tell me if you think Walt Turner wrote it."

The marshal walked to the window and stood reading. "Hell, yes!" he said, almost shouting. He handed the letter back. "Hell, yes, Walt Turner wrote it. Who else wants you dead bad enough to hire some punk to kill you?" He stood looking through the window for a few moments, then continued. "You've been killing off his partners, Camp. Just a little common sense is enough to tell him that his own number's gonna be coming up. I'll tell you something else: I'd bet a bundle that Sam Lott's real reason for killing Bill Wiggins down in Brackettville was to avoid giving him his share of the booty. I'd bet that Turner ordered Lott to eliminate Wiggins, so the two of them could keep his share for themselves." He turned to face Camp again. "And I'd also bet that the damn split between Lott and Turner was far from even."

"That's the way I've got it figured, Bill, and I think you're right about Turner. I believe he knows that I'm coming."

"Hell, yes, he knows, and you're gonna get your ass killed if you go riding into his den." He walked around the room once, then stood in the doorway for a while. When he turned back to face Houston, he spoke more softly. "Put your horses up at the livery, Camp, then get yourself a room at the hotel. I'll turn the office over to my deputy as soon as he comes in, then join you at the hotel. We need to talk about this some more. I might be able to get Walt Turner to ride right down that street out there, if I go about it right."

Camp was smiling now. "The hell you say!" he said loudly, then immediately softened his voice. "You think he'd come alone?"

"No," the marshal said firmly. "But I don't think he'd bring a pack of wolves, either. Might bring along a bodyguard or two, but—" Pennington shrugged, rolled his eyes toward the ceiling and left the sentence unfinished.

Camp had heard enough. "I'll go to the hotel and register right now," he said, "then come by here and tell you the room number. After I put up my horses and eat supper at the hotel restaurant, I'll go to my room and wait for you." He took a few steps toward the door, then stopped and turned halfway around. "Bring the rest of that fellow's rum, if you think of it." Then he was gone.

The marshal wrapped the bottle in a newspaper and laid it on his desk. He would eat his own supper at the boarding-house, then join Houston at the hotel.

Bill Pennington had been born and raised on a dairy farm in Ohio, and had come to Texas the year he turned seventeen. He found work on a ranch in the San Antonio area right away, and immediately set about learning the complexities of producing longhorns. The knowledge he had gained while tending dairy cattle back home had helped him immensely on the new job, for to a certain extent, a cow was a cow. He learned fast and continually, and at the age of twenty bossed his first trail drive to Kansas.

Dark-complected, with brown hair and eyes, Pennington was neither big nor tall. He stood about five-ten, and weighed no more than one-seventy. He had broad, drooping shoulders and unusually long arms that reached almost to his knees. As he walked the streets of Comanche he appeared to be ready for anything, with his ham-sized hand hanging flush with the holstered Peacemaker that was a constant on his right leg. And although his methods of keeping the peace were scorned by some, most of them female do-gooders, even they felt a sense of security with his presence, for none doubted that, should the occasion arise, he would be quick to use the gun they preached against to defend them.

Camp Houston had chosen a room on the top floor of the three-story hotel. He raised a window on each side of the room and had just taken a seat on the bed when he heard a faint knock. He walked the necessary steps, then drew his Colt and eased the door open.

Marshal Pennington stepped inside quickly, his eyes on the gun Camp held in his fist. "Turner's not here yet," he said, chuckling.

Houston holstered the weapon. "It's just a habit that I picked up several years ago, and I'm not likely to drop it. I believe that many a man has gone to an early grave because he opened a door empty-handed when somebody knocked. I'll do all I can to keep it from happening to me. I can't believe that you don't take the same precaution, Bill."

"Of course I do," Pennington said, seating himself in the room's only chair. "I can't remember the last time I opened a door without being loaded for bear." He unwrapped the bottle and discarded the newspaper, then poured rum into two cups, handing one to Houston.

Camp reseated himself on the bed. "You said you might be able to get Turner down here," he said. "How are you gonna do that, and how come you're willing to get involved?"

The marshal answered quickly. "I'm willing because I had a strong liking for John Calloway, and deep down, I'm still a trail boss at heart. Another reason is that I don't like Walt Turner. I never was around him much, but it sure wasn't his fault. The sonofabitch hit me up for a job on at least three occasions, but I never would hire him. I just didn't like the looks of him, Camp; didn't like the way he shifted his eyes around all the time, talking out of one corner of his mouth.

"As to getting him down here, I don't know that I can do it, but if I handle it right, I think he'll come running. You see, Turner's an insurance salesman nowadays, and I've even heard it said that he owns a piece of the company. Now, if you were in his shoes, and the town fathers of Comanche sent you word that they wanted your company to insure everything the town owned, including all of the buildings and their contents, and preferred that you write up the policy personally, what would you do?"

Camp chuckled loudly. "I'd come running," he said.

"And that's exactly what I expect Walt Turner to do." The lawman was on his feet now. "Of course, it'll be several days before we'll know whether he bought it or not." He took a sip of his rum, then set the cup on the table. "I can't go out on a limb with this now. I'll have to do something to cover my tracks. I'm not gonna ask the town council to get involved, but the head councilman owes me a few favors, and I intend to collect one of them tonight. We won't send Turner a written invitation, or do anything else that might point to any particular man down here. What I've been thinking about doing is sending a rider who has no name to tell Turner that the Comanche town council wants to buy a policy from him personally, and that he should get here pronto."

Camp was on his feet. "That'll work," he said. He finished off his drink, but held on to the empty cup. "You've already got it figured out, Bill; why the hell do you need the head councilman?"

"Because he does the thinking for the whole damn board. None of the others is gonna question a single thing he says."

Camp nodded. "I see."

Pennington walked to the door and stood with his hand on the knob. "This is the last time I'll visit you here," he said. "I'll get a rider off early in the morning, and it's possible that we'll see the result in about four days."

They shook hands, then the marshal was gone down the hall. Camp closed the door and locked it, then poured a pan of water from the pitcher. He would wash himself and shave his face, then go to bed early.

18

★

Camp was sitting at the marshal's desk at nine o'clock next morning, sipping his third cup of coffee of the day. "Our rider left for Fort Worth three hours ago," Pennington said. "He'll use a name other than his own, and claim to have been dispatched by the town council. He says that, even though he'll stop somewhere and sleep a few hours tonight, he'll be in Fort Worth by late afternoon tomorrow."

Houston nodded, and drained his cup. "You don't think he'll have any trouble finding Turner?"

"Nope, he knows exactly where to go. Even if he don't find him right off, he knows how to ask around. A man ain't all that hard to find, Camp, especially one as well known as a successful insurance salesman would have to be." He pulled the coffeepot off the stove and refilled their cups. "I think Walt Turner will have the message by sundown tomorrow, then he'll spend the night trying to figure out a way to fatten his commission on the big policy he's about to write."

"I guess you've got it figured out, Bill," Camp said, getting to his feet. "I think you figured it right, too." He set his empty cup on a small table beside the desk, then stood quietly for a while, looking through the window thoughtfully. "There's no way in the world that Turner could get here before Monday afternoon," he said finally. "This four-day wait's gonna seem like four months."

Pennington nodded, then began to chuckle. "Of course, you could speed things up by walking over to the saloon and getting yourself a couple more bottles of that rum. Drink enough of that, and four days'll seem like four hours."

"Not a chance, old buddy." Camp walked to the door. "At least I'm gonna have time to get my horses shod. The liveryman looked their hooves over real good when I turned them over to him yesterday. He even picked up my saddler's forefoot and had a look, but he didn't mention the job that both of us knew needed doing. I'll go down there right now and tell him to trim their hooves and nail on some new shoes."

"Russ is good, Camp, but he's not pushy. If you want something done, you'll have to tell him."

Houston opened the door and stepped onto the porch, then spoke over his shoulder. "Tomorrow being Saturday, I guess the town'll be full of people, huh?"

"Always is," Pennington answered. "If you walk around among 'em for a while you might run into somebody you know."

"I guess it's possible," Camp said. "I've always heard that it's a small world." He stepped off the porch and headed for the livery.

Holmes's livery stable, which also served as a blacksmith shop, was located at the east end of Main Street, and was the largest building in town. Russel Holmes, the stable's owner and operator, had brought his young family and all of his tools to Comanche in two covered wagons twelve years before. He bought four lots, hired a helper and immediately set about building the large barn and adjoining corral. He, his young wife and two small children lived in the wagons till the barn was completed, then lived in the barn till he could build a house a quarter mile from town. Nowadays, the muscular thirty-five-year-old Holmes was known and respected throughout the county, and his establishment did more business than both of the town's other stables combined.

When Houston reached the barn, the liveryman was standing in the doorway, wiping his brow. He smiled, and laid the towel aside. "You gonna be leaving us already?" he asked.

Camp shook his head. "Not for a few days yet. I came down to ask you to shoe my horses."

"Be glad to," Holmes said. "I noticed 'em yesterday. The packhorse's hooves need trimming pretty bad."

"They've covered a lot of miles this summer," Camp said. "I hope to leave 'em in the corral this winter; I've got a lot of things to do besides travel."

The liveryman reached for a leather apron that hung from a hook on the wall, and tied it around his waist. "Guess I'd better hop to it," he said. "The later it gets, the hotter it gets." Obviously a man who put business ahead of small talk, he grabbed a rope and headed for the corral, leaving Camp standing alone in the doorway.

Houston walked the streets for the next hour, occasionally stopping in front of a store to gaze at the merchandise in its window: boots, hats, coats, rings, watches and a wide assortment of other things, all showcased for the prospective buyer's inspection. And although he walked past numerous buildings, and peered into dozens of windows, the one thing that caught and held his attention was a large apple pie, sliced into wedges and displayed in the window of a small restaurant. He stepped inside, and found that he was the establishment's only customer.

A dark-haired woman about his own age stood behind the counter. "Thank you for coming in, sir," she said sweetly, her smile revealing two rows of perfect teeth. "May I help you?"

Camp had so far made no move toward a chair. Standing

just inside the door, he pointed to the window. "I think I'd like a slice or two of that pie."

"Certainly, sir." She pointed over her shoulder toward the kitchen. "I've got two more exactly like it that I just took out of the oven. In fact, I believe they're still warm."

"That'll be fine," he said, then seated himself at the nearest table.

A short while later, the lady delivered a platter containing two large slices of apple pie. "Will you be having coffee, sir?"

"Yes," he said. He glanced at her ringless left hand, then added, "Just call me Camp, if you will."

"All right," she said, then headed for the kitchen. Moments later, she set a mug of steaming coffee in front of him, saying, "My name is Bess Bullard, but most of the local people just call me Idaho." Then she was gone through the batwing doors again, no doubt to continue her preparation of the noonday special.

What Camp had in front of him amounted to half of a large pie, for the lady had simply quartered it and served him two slices. He picked up his fork and dug in, although he doubted that he would clean the platter. That doubt disappeared very quickly, however, for the pie was delicious. Though it contained enough sugar to make it sweet, it also had a tart aftertaste that was very pleasing, somewhat like green apples. Stopping only occasionally to take a sip of coffee, he continued to eat until the pie was gone.

A few minutes later, he stood at the counter waiting to pay. "Just leave the money on the counter," the lady called through the open window separating the kitchen from the dining area. "The pie and the coffee'll be fifteen cents."

Camp counted out twenty cents, then left the building. The fact that she had not come to the counter to accept his money had disappointed him, for she was a beautiful woman, and he wanted to know her better. He continued to think on the matter for a moment, then headed for the marshal's office.

Bill Pennington could answer any questions Camp had about Bess Bullard. He would go talk to Bill.

"Bess Bullard, huh?" the marshal asked, when Camp mentioned the dark-haired beauty. "Is that the name she's using this week?" Pennington began to chuckle loudly. "Did she also tell you that she grew up a poor little orphan, that she had to beg on the street and eat out of garbage cans?"

Houston shook his head, and said nothing.

The lawman moved away from his desk and opened the door. He stood in the doorway looking down the street toward the little restaurant for a while, then turned. "Let me tell you a few things about that woman: she's a good cook, and a lot of us like to eat at her restaurant. She's a good-looking bitch that a lot more of us would like to take to bed. But she's bad news, Camp. Avoid her like the plague.

"She's been here about three years, and nobody knows what her real name is. She's even changed it two or three times since she's been here. About two years ago a fellow passing through Comanche said he knew her up in Idaho Territory, and all of us started calling her Idaho after that. Now, that fellow claimed to know her well, but of course he didn't know what her true name is. He said he first met her in a gold camp on the Clearwater River, where she was living under the name of Ruth Meadows. What she did on the Clearwater was the same thing she's doing now, cooking and selling good food to hardworking men. Of course, she eventually sold her restaurant and started marrying lovesick miners.

"That fellow swore that she'd killed at least one husband, and most likely two. At any rate, she married two miners within a period of six months, and neither man lived over it. Both died under mysterious circumstances. According to him, every man in the camp had a suspicious feeling, but none acted on it, for they were simply too busy to take the time off to investigate. He said that gold seekers go at it like ants and won't let up for anything, 'cause most of them are convinced that the next big strike lies only one more shovelful of dirt away.

"Now, if she didn't get around to handing you that orphan bullshit, I guess it means that she has a different story in mind for you. You see, she'll tell one man that she was a poor little orphan who had to eat garbage, then the next fellow gets told that she was the daughter of a wealthy New Orleans banker, and that she got cheated out of her rightful inheritance by greedy relatives. Then occasionally some lucky diner gets to hear the story about—"

"Hell, Bill," Camp interrupted, laughing loudly, "you've made your point. You can let up now. I've already decided to do my eating somewhere else."

Pennington returned to his desk and seated himself. "I don't see any reason why you shouldn't eat up there. Hell, she's the best cook in this town, and I eat there myself when her special of the day happens to be something I like. I just told you all of this because you asked, and because I want to make sure you don't fall for whatever line of shit she decides to feed you."

"Well, you can relax now. Anything she says to me will go in one ear and out the other." He stepped out the door and onto the porch, continuing to talk through the open doorway: "I'm gonna buy something to read, then go back to the hotel. Might even take a nap if I get sleepy." He walked across the street and bought a three-day-old copy of the *Fort Worth Democrat*, then headed for his room. He stretched out on his bed with the newspaper, and fell asleep before he had finished reading the front page.

19

Houston did not visit Idaho's restaurant again. He also avoided the marshal's office for the next few days. He took several two-hour walks during the weekend, and spent many of the daytime hours reading a book about cattle breeding. He spent the early part of each evening in the hotel saloon, having a few drinks and trading stories with a bartender who liked to talk about fishing.

He was sitting on the side of his bed at daybreak Monday morning, alternately staring through the window and reading the last chapter of his book, waiting for the town to come to life. When the sun finally topped the horizon and he began to see people moving about on the street, he closed the book and laid it on the table for the next man to read. Half an hour later, he was having breakfast in the hotel dining room. He ate his food slowly and sipped two cups of coffee afterward, for he doubted that the marshal was in his office yet.

When he finally stepped out on the street he saw that there

had been no reason for his waiting around, for he could already see Pennington sitting in the doorway of his office. He pointed his boots in that direction, and began to step lively.

"Our rider woke me up about an hour before daylight," Pennington said, not waiting for Houston to come to a complete stop.

Camp leaned against a post. "Well, what's the verdict?"

"Turner bought it. Said he'd head for Comanche Sunday morning, which was, of course, yesterday. If he goes about traveling anything like I do, I'd say he'll be here this afternoon or early in the morning."

"He'll be here today," Camp said. "A man'll hurry his horse along quite a bit to avoid having to spend an extra night on the trail." He stepped onto the porch and took the seat beside Pennington. "Did your man figure out anything else about Turner, like whether or not he intends to bring a small army along?"

"He didn't have any way of knowing. He said Turner was alone when he talked with him, and he saw no sign that anybody else was hanging around. Sounds to me like Turner don't have room for anybody else. My man says his office is just a hole in the wall with a desk and two chairs."

Camp sat staring down the street at nothing in particular. "Are you saying you think he might come down here alone, Bill?"

"No," the lawman said quickly. "But like I said at the start, I don't think he'll bring a bunch. One man, maybe two, but they'll be the sorriest sonsofbitches Fort Worth has to offer, conscienceless bastards who'd cut their own mothers' throats for a few dollars."

"You're probably right, Bill." Camp pointed to the dusty street. "Do you think Turner'll ride right into town?"

Pennington shook his head. "I don't think you should let him. Hell, he'll be hunting some of the members of the town council, and they've never even heard of him. I never could find the head councilman, so he don't know anything about it either." He pointed down the street with his thumb. "I believe you ought to intercept Turner at the livery stable."

Camp was thoughtful for a moment. "That was my first thought," he said, "but I had no idea how Russel Holmes would feel about it."

"I'll talk to Russ," Pennington said, getting to his feet. "Fact is, I'll do it right now." He stepped off the porch, then spoke over his shoulder: "You just sit where you are. I won't be long." Then he walked toward the stable.

Houston sat on the porch for what seemed like a long time. The town was wide awake now, with people of all ages, shapes and sizes scurrying from one place to another. Dozens of men rode up and down the street in wagons or on horseback, and Camp could see more women on the sidewalks than was usual for such a small town.

Of the many men who passed directly in front of the marshal's office, all were quick to notice the stranger sitting on the porch. Houston nodded a greeting to those with friendly faces, and attempted to outstare the others. He was still playing the game when Marshal Pennington returned from the stable, more than half an hour later.

"Russ don't give a damn what you do," Pennington said, ignoring the step and taking hold of a post to pull himself to the porch. "I told him about Turner and his bunch slaughtering the drovers up in Kansas, and that one of his hired gunmen had already tried to kill you. Holmes says he can't find any fault with what you're doing. All he asks is that you be careful not to shoot any of his livestock."

Houston nodded. "That goes without saying." He got to his feet and looked at his watch. "It's already past ten o'clock, Bill. I think I'll saddle up and ride a couple miles east of town. I'll hunt myself a good, comfortable seat at the top of the hill and stay there, 'cause I'll be able to see nearly halfway to Fort Worth."

"That's a good idea," Pennington said. "You'll see him an hour or two before he gets to town, so that'll give you plenty of time to beat it back here and get me. I intend to be in the barn with you."

Camp had already taken one step toward the stable. He hesitated now. "The fight's mine, Bill. I appreciate everything you've done, but there's no reason for you to be involved in the showdown."

"Well, now," Pennington said, stepping to the edge of the porch. "You may be right, and you may be wrong." He stood with his thumbs hooked behind his belt. "If Turner comes alone, you're right. If he brings some help, you're wrong. I won't hold still for you facing more than one man at a time, Camp. As soon as you spot Turner, I want you to ride like hell to this office and tell me. We'll walk down to the stable together, because I intend to at least be a bystander." He stood quietly for a moment, then added, "Will you do that?"

"Yes, Bill," Camp said, heading for the stable. "I'll do that."

Less than an hour later, Houston was at the top of the hill, sitting in the shade of a large mesquite tree. He had picketed his horse on the west side of the hill, a hundred yards below the skyline. His view of the road to Fort Worth, while not entirely unobstructed, was at least as good as he had expected. There were several long stretches where no growth at all occurred, and probably an equal number of shorter ones where he could not see the road at all for a quarter mile or more.

He was paying all of his attention to the bare stretches in the distance now, however, for if anyone had been traveling in one of the obstructed areas when he first sat down, they had already had more than enough time to come back into view. He doffed his hat and leaned against the rough bark of the mesquite tree, his eyes glued to an open quarter-mile section of road far ahead. He took a sip of water from his canteen and relaxed, convinced that he could see a man on horseback from a distance of at least five miles.

Two hours later, he was feeling uncomfortably warm in the heat of the early afternoon. The sun had already moved to the opposite side of the hill, and the sparse leaves of the mesquite now provided no shade whatsoever. Looking north, then south, he could see no place where he might escape the hot sun and still maintain a good view of the road.

He had just taken another sip from his canteen when he spotted two specks in the road several miles to the northeast. He wiped the sweat from his eyes and continued to stare. Were the specks moving? He could not tell. After a while he picked out a third speck that he believed to be stationary, a little closer and well off the road, most likely a large bush or small tree. Then he sat watching, minute after minute, as the distance between the specks diminished. When the two specks were finally even with the third, Camp had his answer: he was no doubt looking at two mounted men. He picked up his canteen and his hat, and crawled to the other side of the hill. Moments later, he pointed the roan toward town and kicked the big beast to a hard run.

Marshal Pennington was standing in the doorway of his office when Camp slid the roan to a halt and dismounted. Houston tied the animal to the hitching rail, then held up two fingers. "Two riders coming," he said. "I'd guess them to be no more than five miles away."

Pennington nodded. "Just about what I expected," he said. Then the two men obviously had the same thought at the same time, for each of them stepped inside the office and began to move his gun up and down in its holster, making sure it was riding loosely. Neither man spoke again. They simply nodded to each other, then headed for the street.

They were at the livery in less than three minutes. Holmes greeted them at the front of the building, and Pennington spoke to him: "Two men coming from the east, Russ, and there's liable to be some trouble. I'd appreciate it if you'd go up to the restaurant and have a cup of coffee." Holmes nodded, and said nothing. He headed up the street at a fast clip.

The barn had large doors on opposite sides, and a hall that was wide enough for two wagons to pass each other. The door on the west side, facing the town, stayed open most of the time, but today both were open, flooding the building with light.

Houston took up a position inside the doorway of a stable on the north side, while the marshal stood behind a large stack of baled hay across the hall. "People coming in from the east usually use the back door if it happens to be open," Pennington said. He pointed to the hitching rails behind the building. "I expect them to tie up out there, then walk right in here and say hello."

Each man's position offered a good view of the road to the east, and both stood watching quietly. Ten minutes later, the riders came into view. When they were within two hundred yards of the barn, they brought their horses to a halt and held a short conversation, gesticulating back and forth with their hands. Then they kneed their animals and came on at a fast walk. Houston caught Pennington's eye, and both men nodded curtly.

Both of the riders rode black horses, and neither led a pack animal. And just as the marshal had predicted, they dismounted at the hitching rail on the east side of the building.

Pennington turned his head toward Houston, a slight smile on his face. He nodded again, then winked, for he now recognized both riders.

Hooty Folsom was the man's name who now stood beside Walt Turner at the hitching rail. A dark-haired six-footer who weighed about one-eighty, he was a gunman of some renown, but his reputation as a cattle thief and bushwhacking murderer was more widely known. He had twice been tried for murder in Tarrant County, but had walked out of the courtroom a free man each time. He had gained a self-defense rul-

ing for killing a seventy-year-old man, and an outright ac-
quittal on a charge that he had raped and murdered a young
woman from Fort Worth.

Every time he had a few drinks he was likely to stand at
the bar boasting to any man who would listen, bragging about
his fast gun and all of the shootouts he had survived. Not all
of his braggadocio was fiction, however, for although he only
did so when he was thoroughly convinced that he had the
upper hand, he had indeed initiated a few gunfights. Even
now a Colt Peacemaker hung on his right leg, halfway between his hip and his knee.

The fact that Walt Turner appeared to be unarmed surprised neither of the men waiting in the barn. He considered
himself a big businessman nowadays, and businessmen did
not wear guns; they hired their shooting done. Besides, he had
a meeting scheduled with the town council, and the chances of
any council buying an insurance policy from a man wearing
a gun in a quick-draw holster were somewhere in the neighborhood of zero.

The riders tied their horses and walked to the barn. They
stopped just inside the doorway and looked around for an at-
tendant, then walked on down the hall. "Is anybody home?"
Turner called loudly.

Houston and Pennington stepped into the hall simultane-
ously. "Of course we're home," the lawman said.

Both Turner and Folsom froze in their tracks. Pennington
stepped closer, then pointed to the gun on Folsom's hip. "I'm
kinda surprised that you'd wear that thing into my town,
Hooty. You see, it just might give me the wrong impression."

"Naw, I didn't mean nothing at all, Marshal, I—"

"Let me introduce you to my friend here," Pennington interrupted. "His name is Camp Houston, and he's got a little
business to conduct with Walt Turner." His eyes were locked
onto those of Folsom. "Is that all right with you, Hooty, or did
you sign on to stick with Turner through hell and high
water?"

Folsom shook his head several times. "I . . . I'm just along for the ride. I don't aim to do nothing at all to put myself in your cross hairs, Marshal, and I damn sure don't want no truck with Camp Houston."

"Unbuckle the gun belt, Folsom," Pennington ordered. "Let it fall to the ground, then move away from it." Folsom complied quickly, then took a seat on a bale of hay several feet from his weapon. The marshal was smiling when he turned to Houston and waved his arm in a sweeping motion, no doubt mimicking some entertainer that he had seen somewhere. "The stage is all yours, Camp."

Houston had been watching Turner like a hawk. He took two steps toward the man. "I've been wanting to meet you for a long time, Turner, but I don't suppose I'll be buying a policy from you today. What I had in mind was you and me discussing a trail boss named John Calloway and two of his hired hands named Bill Fisher and Joe Plenty. You remember them, don't you, Walt?"

Turner stared over Camp's shoulder, and did not answer.

"Oh, come on now, Walt," Camp continued. "Jog your memory a little bit. You remember yourself and four other nogood sonsofbitches riding into their camp in a Kansas gully, don't you? Don't you remember the five of you pumping all three of them full of lead, then stealing the money Calloway got for the herd? I'll bet you even remember that you yourself were the first man to draw a gun, and that your first shot went through Joe Plenty's chest.

"Well, Joe Plenty didn't die, Turner, although he lost an arm and a leg. He's very much alive nowadays, and he put the finger on the whole damn bunch. He knew all of you well, 'cause you were the sonsofbitches who helped drive the herd to Dodge City. The fact that the drovers knew all of you didn't bother you one bit, though, because you didn't intend for any of them to be alive to identify you."

Camp reached into his vest pocket. "I have a picture here of the entire crew, Turner." He held it high so the man could easily see it. "Remember the day all of you posed for the picture in San Antonio? Well, this is it, old buddy." He pointed to the picture. "Five of these people are dead now. Of course, you know about Calloway and Fisher, because you killed them. But three members of your bunch are no longer with us, either. You remember Bill Wiggins, Jack Little, and Red Bentley, don't you?"

He took the envelope from his pocket, extracted the single page and waved it in front of the man's face. "Remember this?" he asked. "I took it off the body of a man you sent to kill me. You remember your old friend Ben Gillam, don't you?" Turner continued to stare over Camp's shoulder silently.

Houston folded the letter and returned it to his pocket, then spoke to the man again. "Get your gun out of your saddlebag and strap it on, Turner."

Turner spoke now. "I never carry a gun."

Houston stared at the man contemptuously for a long time. "You don't carry a gun? You spend half of your life using a gun to rob, bushwhack and shoot people in the back, then all at once you don't carry a gun?" Houston was talking louder now. He raised the volume of his voice still another notch, and pointed. "Pick up Folsom's gun and strap it on. Right now!"

Turner shook his head very slowly. "No," he said. "I've given up guns completely, and I refuse to be pushed into a gunfight."

Though Houston was seething inside, he fought to maintain an outward calm. "Just like your bushwhacking partner, Jack Little," he said, looking Turner in the eye. "That murdering sonofabitch wouldn't fight either, but it didn't save his ass." He turned to face the marshal. "Walk over there and search him, Bill. See how many hidden guns and knives he's got on him." Pennington nodded, and moved to comply. "Look in his boots, too," Houston added.

Pennington stepped behind the man and searched him thoroughly, then moved away. "No weapon," he said.

Camp spoke to Turner again: "How many men did you send after me besides Ben Gillam, fellow?"

He received no answer.

Houston unbuckled his own gun belt and handed it to the marshal. He glared at Turner fiercely for several seconds, then spoke again: "You've been doing your damnedest to have me killed, old buddy. Here's your chance to do the job yourself." He began to walk toward the man. "Put up your hands, Turner. This is a fight to the death."

Turner stepped out to meet Houston and they collided noisily, each man blocking and swinging violently. And although Turner put up a defense that under most circumstances would have served him well, it was woefully inadequate protection against Houston's battering fists. The struggle lasted less than five seconds, for Houston landed a smashing blow to the jaw that turned Turner's eyes to glass. The man collapsed instantly, and now lay in the dusty hallway.

Camp hesitated for only a moment, then he was astride the unconscious man, his knees pinning Turner's arms to the ground. Then, seemingly of their own accord, Houston's big hands locked themselves around Turner's throat in a death squeeze, and held on until all signs of life had vanished.

Camp stood up for a moment, then knelt again, turning the man's head from side to side. After confirming that his fists had left no visible marks on Turner's face, he turned to Hooty Folsom. "Let me tell you how we're gonna handle this, Mr. Folsom: we're gonna tie Turner's body on his own horse, and you're gonna take it back to Fort Worth. Now, whatever story you put out when you get back up there is gonna reach my ears, and it damn sure better be the kind of story I want to hear." He pointed to the corpse. "Walt Turner took a fall from his horse and broke his neck, and when I start inquiring about a week from now, I'd better hear that you saw it happen. Have you got that, Folsom?"

The man nodded several times.

Houston gave Folsom a hard look that he believed the

man would remember. "All right," he said finally. "Go get Turner's horse."

They lashed the body to the saddle, then Folsom took the road to Fort Worth. One hour later, astride his roan and leading his pack animal, Camp Houston took the same road, although he was headed in the opposite direction.

20

Houston was back on his own property on Wednesday afternoon. He brought the roan to a halt a hundred yards above the house, and sat looking down the hill at the men building the barn. Cornell Wooten and both of his youngest sons were sitting on top of the building hammering, while Bo Patton was busy helping Fowler sink corral posts in the ground. Houston sat watching for at least half an hour. Things were shaping up nicely, and he was convinced that within a few short years he would own one of the better spreads in the area.

He had decided to call his place the Three County Ranch, for the simple reason that it was partially located in three different counties. He would register his 3C brand within the next few days, then hire Sid Blankenship to make up several branding irons.

He watched his young hired hand pound the earth with a post hole digger for a few minutes longer, then rode down the hill to the barn. He dismounted and spoke to Patton. "I see you found the place all right."

The youngster laid the digger aside. "I came straight to it, 'cause you gave me good directions. I appreciate you putting me on, Mr. Houston, and I'm glad you're home now." He walked to a water bucket and drank from a gourd dipper.

Camp waved to the Wootens, who were busy fitting another log into place. "It looks mighty good, Cornell," he called to the father, "and I certainly appreciate you fellows coming over to help." The Wootens acknowledged the greeting by waving their arms and nodding, then continued with their work.

Runt Fowler was beside Houston now. "I was expecting you back just about now," the big man said. "Did you find your man all right? Did you settle up with him once and for all?"

Camp nodded to both questions, then turned to lead his animals to the corral. Fowler walked along beside him. The big man stripped the saddle from the back of the roan, placing it on a sawhorse in the shed. Then he began to unburden the packhorse. "I'm kinda surprised that you don't use a mule for packing, Camp." He stowed the packsaddle in the far corner of the shed, then added, "A mule's the best damn watchdog in the world. Anytime a man wants to know what the hell's going on around him, all he has to do is look at that mule."

Houston knew from experience that fowler spoke the truth. Although mules had a reputation for stubbornness, and often refused to be hurried, they were far more sensitive to their surroundings than were horses. A horse could see fairly well, hear even better, and possessed a sense of smell approaching that of a dog. All of his senses paled, however, when compared with those of his floppy-eared cousin. The mule was one of the most observant creatures on Earth, day after day after day. Nothing escaped the attention of a mule.

"You're right, Runt," Camp said, "and I used to use one.

The benefit of using a mule is that they can stand more heat, they eat and drink less, and they're usually cheaper to buy. The bad side is that, if a man happens to be in a hurry, they can be a mighty big hindrance." He patted the packhorse on the rump. "Of course, this horse here belongs to Sid Blankenship. All things considered, though, if I had to buy a pack animal today, you can rest assured that I would choose a mule."

Fowler grunted, then returned to his work on the new corral. When Houston walked inside the house, he was pleased to see several thick mats scattered around the floor of the main living room. At least the workers were not sleeping on the ground.

He dropped his pack off in his bedroom, then walked to the kitchen. When he touched an oversized iron pot on the stove and found that it was still lukewarm, he lifted the lid, then stirred the contents with a wooden ladle. At least two gallons of stew, he decided, and whoever cooked it had been more than generous with the beef. He used the same ladle to fill a large bowl, then grabbed a piece of leftover corn bread and headed for the porch.

He was sitting on the doorstep eating when all five of the workers approached. "I decided we'd done enough for today," Fowler said. "All of us have been at it since before sunup."

Houston swallowed a mouthful of stew, then shook his head. "There's no reason for you to kill yourself or anybody else, Runt. The world won't end if it takes a little longer than we expected to build that barn. I think you should cut down to eight hours a day, ten at the most."

"That ain't an easy thing to do, Camp," Fowler said. "There are fifteen, maybe sixteen hours of daylight at this time of the year. It's hard to knock off early, then sit there on the porch for six or seven hours looking at all the things you need to be doing."

Camp chuckled. "I see your point, Runt. Just don't push yourself and your help too hard." He wiped his mouth with the heel of his hand, then set the bowl aside. "Whoever made that stew did it right," he said. "That stuff's plenty good."

Fowler pointed to Patton. "Your young hired hand from Georgia is the man responsible for the stew, Camp, both the fetching and the cooking. He shot the deer just before dark yesterday, then had the stew done before nine this morning. He tells me that all of his family and kinfolk cook venison the same way."

Camp turned to Patton, who appeared to be embarrassed. "I believe that's the best stew I ever ate, Bo. Hell, I thought I was eating beef." He chuckled softly. "You sure you didn't line up your sights on somebody's calf?"

Patton smiled, and shook his head. "Young buck," he said.

Houston spent the remainder of the day simply walking around and looking, impressed with all the progress that had been made on the house, barn and corral, and making a mental note of the things yet to be done. He could see with one eye, however, that the workers would soon be running short of building material. He mentioned that fact to Fowler just before sunset.

"We're gonna be needing some half-inch boards to deck that barn," Fowler began, "and we ain't got near enough tin to roof it. We'll be needing some more nails, and I broke a handsaw yesterday. And I reckon we need—"

"Just make a list, Runt," Camp interrupted. "I'll hitch up the team at daybreak and head for Menardville." He motioned toward Patton. "I'll take him with me and introduce him to the people we do business with, especially Spike Nettleton at the hardware store. Then, whenever you need something from town, you can send Bo after it. He'll be able to get it whether he has the cash money or not."

"Makes sense," Fowler said. He got to his feet, adding, "I'll make the list while I've still got some daylight left." Then he was gone inside the house.

Patton, eager to be off to see new places, woke Camp before daybreak, as he had been instructed. Houston was in the kitchen three minutes later, for all he had to do was follow the beam of light to the burning lamp. Bo had already built a fire in the stove, and had a pot of coffee boiling. He offered to fry some eggs and heat some smoked ham. "None for me," Camp said. "I just get sick of eggs sometimes, especially during hot weather. I'd rather have a bowl of that stew, if there's some of it left."

"Plenty," Patton said, pulling the pot over the stove's firebox.

They were off the hill before sunup, with Patton driving the team. Camp had put all of the tinned food from his pack into the wagon, so they were carrying at least as much as they would need to eat before reaching Menardville. He had busied himself with that, and pretended to be busy with several other things, while Patton hitched up the team.

Camp had kept a close eye on the harnessing and hitching process, wanting to find out if the youngster knew what he was doing. He did. Houston leaned against a front wheel watching as Patton backed a harnessed animal up to the wagon, omitted a corresponding number of links in each of the trace chains, hooked them to the whiffletree, then hooked the whiffletree to one end of the doubletree. He repeated the process with the second animal, then walked in front of the team and hooked up the tongue and connecting reins. "I guess we're ready," he said.

Camp nodded, and climbed to the seat. "You drive."

Workhorses were seldom eager to run, and almost never did so of their own accord. Houston's team, however, on this particular morning, refused to travel at a walking gait. Each time Patton pulled the animals down they would walk for only a short distance. Two minutes later, they'd be moving at a fast trot.

The team had just begun to move out again when Camp spoke to Patton: "Let 'em choose their own pace, Bo. I don't know what the hell their problem is, unless they're just in a hurry to get home. They were both raised right over here where we're going, but I wouldn't think they know it."

"I'll bet by gosh they do," Patton said quickly. "And mules know it better than horses. I remember an old stripe-legged mare mule we used to have. Her name was Ida, and you couldn't ride her away from where she was raised no matter how much you whipped her. You could make her pull a wagon away, but you weren't gonna ride her nowhere. She'd just go around in circles. Around and around."

Camp chuckled. "I know a little bit about stubborn mules, Bo. When he makes up his mind not to do something, he'll dig his heels in mighty deep. I once saw a farmer shoot one dead in its tracks when it refused to pull a plow."

Patton sat thoughtfully for a few moments, as if trying to remember something from the past. "I don't reckon I ever saw one actually balk in the field," he said finally, "but I've sure felt like shooting one a time or two. I guess they have days when they don't feel like working, just like people do, but it still makes you madder'n hell when they won't mind a word you say."

They rode quietly now, each man taking in the passing scenery. "This sure is pretty country," Patton said after a while. "Ain't nothing like it in Georgia."

Camp smiled, and said nothing. He himself had spoken almost the same words on his first visit to the region several years before. He had decided early on that he would eventually put down roots in the three-county area, for, although he had done his share of looking, he had found no place that was more suitable for ranching. The weather was usually agreeable to humans and animals alike; the summers were warm, but the temperature seldom reached a hundred degrees.

Both spring and fall were mild, and the winters were comfortable, with no more than a few days of below-freezing temperatures. It snowed only once every few years, then only a few inches that would be gone a day later. The scenery of the area was easy on the eyes at any time of the year, but spring offered an added bonus with its profusion of wildflowers, especially the colorful bluebonnets that covered the hills and meadows and lined both sides of the road.

Autumn brought the brilliant colors of fall foliage: the crimson leaves of the sumac and red oak; the gold of the cottonwood, sycamore and wild chinaberry; and, lining many of the crystal-clear streams, the golden needles of the bald cypress. And if a man was lucky, he might occasionally come upon an isolated group of maple trees, their tops ablaze with their distinctively radiant red.

And there was absolutely no excuse for any man with a rifle going hungry in this country, for game was abundant. Five deer had already crossed the road in front of the wagon this morning, and so many rabbits that Camp had not even bothered to count them. Indeed, any man who could force himself to stand still in the woods could get meat for his pot quite easily.

A good example was the buck Patton had shot two days before. Bo said that he had been sitting on a log for no more than ten minutes when he scored. He shot the animal less than two hundred yards from the house, and said that even as he fired, he could hear the other men talking on the porch. The deer had no doubt heard the conversation also, but had not been alarmed.

Though they stopped to make coffee and eat their tinned goods at midday, they held to a steady pace during the afternoon, and arrived in Menardville two hours before sunset. Camp delivered Fowler's list to the hardware store immediately, then made the introductions between Spike Nettleton and Bo Patton. They left the wagon parked directly in front of the warehouse at the back of the store, so the man could load the material as he selected it.

Then, with Patton leading the team, they walked down the street toward the livery stable. They met several of Camp's acquaintances moving in the opposite direction, and he waved or nodded a greeting to all of them. They came abreast of Riley's Restaurant just as Ellen Bice was arriving for work. She had been about to open the door, but took a step backward when she saw Houston. "Hi," she said, waving to him and moving away from the door. "We haven't seen you lately. Have you found a better restaurant?"

Camp stopped for a moment. "I haven't been looking for a better restaurant," he said. He looked her up and down admiringly, then added, "And staying away hasn't been easy." He pointed down the hill. "We're headed to the stable to put up the team, then we'll eat supper with you."

The girl disappeared inside the restaurant, and the men continued on down the hill. "I think she's pretty," Patton said. "What do you think?"

"The same thing you do," Camp said. He paused for a few seconds, then added jokingly, "I'm liable to get around to marrying her one of these days."

"Oh," Patton said, then dropped the subject.

They turned the team over to Sid Blankenship, who went about caring for the tired animals immediately. Meanwhile, Camp seated himself on a bale of hay near the front of the building, and spoke to Patton: "I need to talk with Sid for a few minutes when he gets done there, Bo. Why don't you go back up to the restaurant and wait for me? Order up anything you like, and tell the waitress that I'll be eating whatever's on special."

"I'll do that," Patton said. He moved off at a fast clip, and did not look back.

Houston walked deeper into the building, stopping at the stables. Blankenship had already grained the horses, and was busy tearing apart a fresh bale of hay. "I'm certainly relieved to see you again," he said to Camp. "Just a little common sense told me that you'd gone hunting Walt Turner. Did you have any luck?"

Houston nodded. "I found him."

Blankenship grasped a currycomb and began to drag it

along a horse's back. "I suppose the fact that you're standing there tells the rest of the story," he said.

Houston made no other comment concerning Walt Turner. As the liveryman curried both horses, animals that he himself had bred and raised, Camp stood by watching quietly. When he finally spoke, it was to ask a question. "Has most of the talk about that thing with Ben Gillam died down, Sid?"

"When Joe Paley lets it," Blankenship answered quickly. "Nobody in this town gives a shit about Ben Gillam, and they all know that you did exactly what you had to do. Paley won't let it go at that, though. He's always running his mouth about how you're trying to turn the town of Menardville into a shooting range."

Camp made a motion to leave. "I don't know what Paley's problem is," he said, "but if he keeps trying to poison me, I'll probably discuss it with him eventually." He took a few steps, then stopped. "I'm going up to Riley's and eat supper, then get a room at the hotel. I'll be in the hotel bar later tonight, and I'll have a bottle of decent whiskey on the table."

"That last remark settles it," the liveryman said, laughing. "I'll be there."

Camp joined Patton at the restaurant, and both men ate a supper of baked beef ribs covered with some kind of spicy sauce. "One of the best-tasting things I've ever eaten," Houston said to Ellen Bice as she retrieved his empty platter. "I'll be back at this same table for breakfast."

"Thank you," she said. "I won't be here, but I'm sure my uncle appreciates your business."

Camp glanced at her with raised eyebrows, then began to stare at the table, a childish look of dejection on his face. "All right, then," he said jokingly. "I refuse to eat breakfast if you're not gonna be here."

She finished clearing the table, then smiled flirtatiously. "You'll survive," she said. She disappeared into the kitchen, and did not return.

Camp rented a separate hotel room for Bo Patton, for he

was not sure that he himself would be sleeping alone. He had been without a woman much longer than usual, and intended to at least look over the possibilities in the hotel saloon. He remembered that the last time he was in town he had decided to do the same thing, but the only two sporting women he encountered during the night were old enough to be his mother, and both were disgustingly drunk.

Sid Blankenship arrived at the saloon shortly after dark, and just as Camp had promised, he had a bottle of the good stuff on the table. Houston motioned to the bartender for another glass. Hawks was there quickly, shaking hands with the liveryman. "Good to see you, Sid," he said, pouring whiskey from Camp's bottle. "Thank you for stopping in." He pushed the glass across the table to Blankenship, then returned to his position behind the bar.

They had been sitting at the table drinking for more than an hour when Patton excused himself and headed for the outhouse. Blankenship took this opportunity to pass on some additional information to Houston. He leaned across the table and spoke softly: "If I were you I wouldn't trust Joe Paley any farther than I could throw him, Camp."

Houston smiled. "I don't," he said.

"Well, what I told you earlier ain't the only things he's said. He said that one of these days you were gonna make the mistake of crossing him, then he'd show the whole town just how overrated your shooting arm is. Now, I didn't hear him say that, but Mark Harvey swears that he did. You and I both know that Mark don't shoot no shit."

Camp nodded. He knew Mark Harvey well, and knew him to be an honorable man whose spoken word would be doubted by few. Houston sat thoughtfully for some time. "I know Mark," he said finally, "but he'd be the last man I'd expect to hear repeating something that was obviously told to him in confidence. I wonder why he decided to go spreading it around."

"He didn't do it voluntarily," Blankenship said, then

hoisted his whiskey glass. He wiped his mouth with his hand, then added, "I fished it all out of him after I saw him and Paley having a long talk. They stood at the hitching rail in front of the dry goods store for damn near an hour. Now, there ain't no way in hell that they've got that much in common, Camp. Neither can Paley talk that long without shooting off his mouth. Next time I saw Mark I just asked him what the hell the marshal was talking about, and he told me."

Camp accepted everything he had just heard as gospel. "Well, that's something I'll be keeping in mind," he said.

They spent another hour in the saloon, then called it a night. Blankenship went home, while Houston and Patton returned to the hotel. Camp said good night to his young hired hand, then once again went to bed alone. The pickings in the saloon had been dreadfully slim, and besides, hearing all the things that Paley had been saying had dulled Houston's desire for female companionship. He tossed and turned a few times, then he was sound asleep.

They had breakfast in Riley's Restaurant at sunup, then walked to the livery stable. Half an hour later, they hitched the team to the loaded wagon in front of Nettleton's warehouse, then headed for Calf Creek. The animals showed no inclination to trot this morning, for the wagon weighed three times as much as it had when empty.

21

November brought unusually high winds and below-freezing temperatures to the Calf Creek area. Most of the hardwood trees gave up their leaves very quickly, and the perennial grasses turned a golden brown, cured on the stem by a week of heavy frosts. Then, just as suddenly, the weather turned mild again, and the days and nights were almost like summer.

On the twentieth day of the month, Houston decided it was time for another trip to Waco. He left his bed early next morning, and was at the new corral at sunup. Runt Fowler followed, and caught up the packhorse while Camp saddled the roan. Then, working together, they lashed the packsaddle to the back of the black.

"Shouldn't take no more'n five days for you to get to Waco," Fowler said as he added a sack of grain to the animal's burden.

"More like four," Camp said, "unless I get delayed." He

mounted and pulled on the packhorse's lead rope. "Take care of yourself, Runt. Teach Bo as much as you can, and don't look for me back here till you see me coming." Then he was off the hill. He would be traveling in a northeasterly direction beside the San Saba River, and expected to be in the town of the same name by noon the next day.

He traveled about thirty miles the first day, and made camp at the point where Brady Creek emptied into the river. He dropped off his saddle and packsaddle at the spot where he intended to build his campfire, then picketed the horses in the nearby meadow. There was plenty of grass, and though it was no longer green, the animals took to it eagerly.

He found deadwood easily enough, and was soon eating warmed-over food and sipping strong coffee. At sunset, he kicked dirt over the fire and pulled his bedroll away from the smoking remains. He was no longer averse to sleeping near the water, for the recent freezing weather had played havoc with the pesky gnats and blood-sucking mosquitoes. Of course, both would be back tenfold in the spring, when the eggs left behind by this year's crop began to hatch.

As darkness closed in, he gathered up twigs, small pieces of bark and several handfuls of dry grass and placed it all under his pack. He had learned tricks like this the hard way, by waking up to find his kindling so wet with dew that it was difficult or impossible to start his morning fire.

A few minutes later, he stretched out on his bedroll, and, after tossing and turning for close to an hour, finally went to sleep.

He rode into Waco three days later in a steady drizzle. The rain had started to fall shortly after daybreak, and continued all day. The upper portion of his body was dry because he was wearing his slicker, but both legs were wet and he had water in one of his boots. He headed straight for the livery stable.

The middle-aged hostler accepted the horses eagerly, and thanked Houston at least twice for bringing them by. Maybe there were more stables in Waco than there used to be, Camp was thinking. Maybe the man had lots of competition. "I wonder if I could use your office for a few minutes," Camp said, taking clean, dry clothing out of his pack.

The hostler understood Houston's predicament very well. "Why, o' course, young fellow," he said, pointing to the small room. "You just help yourself there. I'll be busy with these horses for a while."

"Thank you," Camp said, and headed for the office. He changed his clothing and was back in the stable before the hostler was. He took a seat on an upended nail keg and waited. He felt like a different man now that his legs and feet were dry. He had also slipped on a new waistcoat that he was wearing for the first time. He had bought it the month before for no other reason than that it had a small pocket on each side. Of course, he also liked the fact that it was made from light material that could be worn comfortably at any time of the year. And since there were no sleeves, he had free movement of his arms, and the garment stopped well short of his gun belt.

"You figure to be staying in town for a while?" the hostler asked when he had taken care of the horses.

"I don't have any way of knowing, sir," Camp answered, "but just as soon as I can take care of my business, I'll be gone. Should I give you some money for my horses now, or pay when I leave?"

"You pay when you leave," the man said. "I'm just glad I could be of service."

Camp nodded. "Good day to you," he said. He walked out the door to find that it had stopped raining, and the sky was growing lighter in the east. He stepped around a mudhole, then made a beeline for the Bryan Hotel.

A young man who appeared to be in his late teens greeted Camp at the desk. "May I help you, sir?"

"You got a vacancy on the top floor?"

"Yes, sir, eighty-five cents a night. Dollar and a dime, if you want a bath."

Camp smiled. "I've been riding in the rain all day, so I feel like I've already had a bath. Maybe tomorrow, if I'm still around." He laid a dollar on the counter.

"No, no," the youngster said, pushing the money away. "Just sign the register. You don't pay till you get ready to leave."

Houston wrote the name "Bo Granger" in the book, and the kid handed him a key. "Room two-twelve," he said.

Moments later, Camp stepped inside the room and locked the door. He laid his pack on the bed, then walked to the window and raised the shade. He not only had a good view of the street below, but could even see people moving around on the opposite side of the river. The sky was much lighter now, and it appeared that the rain was gone for the day. He stood at the window for a while, then returned to the bed and took his shaving soap and razor out of his pack. He was soon busy scraping off a four-day growth of beard.

A few minutes later, he was standing in the doorway of the hotel, looking up and down the street. He was trying to decide where he was going to eat supper, for he could see at least three restaurants. He glanced at his watch to learn that it was already four o'clock, time for him to put on the feed bag if he intended to beat the suppertime rush. He headed for the Texas Saloon, for he well remembered the good Mexican food he had eaten there so many times.

He stepped inside the establishment a few minutes later, and moved away from the door quickly. He stood with his back to the wall till his eyes adjusted to the dim lighting, then headed for the dining room, which amounted to nothing more than a roped-off area separating the diners from the drinkers. He immediately recognized the bartender as Flint Hastings, the same man who had been behind the bar the last time he had been in Waco.

Houston ignored the bartender and the few drinkers at the bar, and walked to a table along the rear wall. A young Mexican waiter stood at the table waiting for him, bill of fare in hand. "I'll just have the regular enchilada dinner," Camp said. He pulled out a chair and seated himself, then added, "I'd also like a bowl of those peppery Mexican beans."

Still clutching the bill of fare, the waiter nodded and headed for the kitchen. The young man had had no reason to speak. Camp believed that he could surely speak English, however, for very few of the Texas Saloon's patrons were of Mexican descent. The majority of the Mexicans did their drinking along the river several hundred yards to the south, in rickety clapboard buildings owned by other Mexicans.

Twenty minutes later, the waiter was back at the table with Camp's supper. "I hope you enjoy your food, sir," he said in perfect English. "If you need something else, just hold up your hand."

Houston nodded, and dug in. The food was just as good as he had remembered, and he emptied both the plate and the bowl in short order. He was in no hurry to leave the table, however, so he took much longer than was necessary to drink the remainder of his coffee. He could see that he had not been the only one with the idea of beating the rush hour, for several men had come in while he was eating. Four tables were already occupied on the opposite side of the room, and even now, three men who were dressed like lawyers were moving into the dining area.

Camp paid for his food and left the building, for the last thing he wanted at the moment was a conversation with this particular bartender. He walked to the corner and turned north, continuing up the hill until he reached the McLennan County Courthouse. The sheriff's office was on the ground floor, and Sheriff Dave Dubar had just locked the door and stepped onto the sidewalk when Houston arrived. The lawman stopped in his tracks and stood beaming. "Well, I'll be damned!" he said loudly. He stepped forward with his right hand extended. "Camp Houston! Seems like a hundred years since I've seen you."

Camp pumped the hand a few times. "It hasn't been quite

that long, Dave, but I'll admit that I do think of you once in a while."

"Same here," the sheriff said. "You just visiting, or here on business?"

"I'm on business, Sheriff, and that's what I want to talk to you about." He motioned to the office. "Can we go back in?"

"Absolutely." The lawman unlocked the door, and Camp followed him inside. "Sounds kinda funny hearing you call me Sheriff," Dubar said. "Hell, we go back to the days when both of us were punching cows or busting broncs for thirty a month. Just call me Dave, if you will. Especially when we're alone like this."

Camp nodded, and accepted the chair he was offered. It was true that the men had known each other for a long time. Houston had been eighteen years old when they first met, and Dubar about twenty-five. They had both been ranch hands at the time, and although they worked and lived on different ranches, they had nevertheless become close friends, and saw each other often.

Dubar had taken a job as deputy sheriff the same year Houston left the area, and ascended to his present position in 1872, when Sheriff Hampton Pitts died after a fall from a horse. Dubar had been McLennan County's top law officer ever since, and was liked and respected by most.

Camp got right to the point. "Did you ever know a man named John Calloway, Dave?"

"Heard of him, didn't know him. I do know that he's dead now."

"That's right," Camp said, "and one of the sonsofbitches who bushwhacked, robbed and killed him lives right here under your nose." He pointed to the chair behind the lawman's desk. "Just take your seat and listen while I tell you a few things about a bastard named Sam Lott."

Dubar hung his high-crown Stetson on the wall, revealing a healthy crop of dark, curly hair. He pulled out his chair and seated himself. "All right," he said.

Talking nonstop for the next fifteen minutes, Houston laid out the entire story. He exaggerated nothing; the only thing he failed to mention was the exact manner in which Walt Turner had died. He ended the long-winded narrative by adding, "I know you weren't acquainted with John Calloway, Dave, but if you could see what's left of Joe Plenty, and talk with him a few minutes, you'd want to burn Sam Lott at the goddamn stake."

Dubar had listened attentively, and had not interrupted once. He got to his feet and began to walk around the room. "I had already heard part of the story, Camp. Of course, I hadn't heard the part about you going around the country eliminating the participants." He stopped for a drink of water, then dropped the dipper into the bucket noisily. "I've known Sam Lott for most of his life," he continued, "and I've known that he wasn't worth killing for almost that long. I've heard it said that some folks suspect him of being one of the bunch who robbed and killed the drovers, but a man's liable to hear damn near anything. Sure as hell ain't nobody charged him with it. Anyway, there ain't a thing in the world I could do about it even if I wanted to. I'm just a Texas sheriff, and I reckon the crime took place in Kansas."

Camp nodded. "According to Joe Plenty it did, and I believe every word he says. He's been up that trail time after time, and he knows the country. If he says it happened in Kansas, by God it happened in Kansas." He got to his feet and helped himself to a drink of water, then continued. "One more thing, Dave, just so you don't read me wrong. I'm not asking you to do anything about Sam Lott. I'm just asking you not to get in my way." He stared through the window for a moment, then spoke loudly: "I intend to kill the sonofabitch!"

Dubar was quiet for a while, then began to chuckle, sounding much like he often had in the old days. "To tell you the truth, I've got more important things to do than worry about whatever kind of trouble Sam Lott might have gotten himself into." He reseated himself and continued, "The town marshal's name is John Bisco, and he's the exact same type of low-down sonofabitch that Lott is. Bisco ain't gonna give you no shit about killing Lott, though. He hates Same Lott's guts."

The sheriff had been busy building a cigarette. He returned the makings to his vest pocket, then struck a match on the sole of his boot. He took a long puff and inhaled deeply, then got to his feet again, blowing a cloud of smoke toward the ceiling.

Dubar was not a big man, weighing in the neighborhood of a hundred fifty pounds. He stood about five-nine, but his stooped shoulders sometimes made him appear to be even shorter. And this was one of those times. As Dubar stood looking through the closed window, puffing on the cigarette, Camp noticed that the lawman's shoulders drooped considerably more than in bygone days. Maybe the problem, whatever it happened to be, was getting worse. The sheriff turned back to his desk and snuffed the cigarette out in an ashtray. "I don't know whether Lott's got back from Dodge City yet or not," he said. "He took a herd up the trail for Albert Wells about three months ago."

"More than four months ago," Camp corrected.

Dubar took his seat again, then smiled. "Whatever you say," he said. He stared at his desk thoughtfully for a full minute, then spoke again: "It ain't gonna do for you to go walking around asking questions, Camp. I can personally guarantee you that Sam Lott ain't a damn bit above putting a dozen gunslingers on you. And neither he nor the bunch he runs around with would be very particular about whether or not they were looking you in the eye when they pulled the trigger. They'd just as soon shoot you from the back as from the front, and creeping on you in the dead of night wouldn't be out of character for a damn one of them."

Camp took a seat on the edge of the sheriff's desk, leaving one foot on the floor. "I've been thinking about that, Dave. I can't just hole up at the hotel, but I'd probably be foolish to think that somebody won't recognize me if I keep walking around. If word gets out that I'm in town, I don't think it'll take Sam Lott long to figure out why."

"Of course, you're assuming that he knows he's your quarry."

Camp nodded. "Yes," he said, "I'm assuming. But it didn't take a whole lot of imagination."

Dubar was on his feet once again, busy with another cigarette. He dumped a small pile of tobacco in a paper and smoothed it out evenly with a forefinger, then licked the edge of the paper and twisted it a few times. After he lighted up again, he continued to talk: "I can find out the things you need to know, but you're gonna have to keep your ass outta sight while I'm doing it."

Houston nodded. "I can handle that."

Dubar pointed to the window. "As you can see, this day is just about over. If you'll stay here till it gets dark, then ease on back to the hotel, I'll either come by or send somebody to talk with you before the night's over. What's your room number?"

"Two-twelve."

Camp was back in his room in less than an hour, lying on his bed and reading by the light of a coal-oil lamp. He had bought the magazine at the drugstore across the street from the sheriff's office, and had stopped nowhere else. He had walked through the dark alleys on his way back to the hotel, and had met no one.

He read a short article about Arizona Territory, then tackled a longer story about the California goldfields. Two hours later, he was still reading the writer's directions on how to strike it rich when the magazine slid from his fingers and fell to the floor. He was sound asleep.

Houston heard the three faint knocks on the door, but the sound failed to bring him out of a hard sleep. As the knocks continued, he began to dream that he himself was knocking on somebody's door, and that what he was hearing was his own knuckles rapping against the wood. When he got no answer, he began to knock harder, till the sound became loud enough to wake the dead. And wake the dead it did, for Camp was suddenly on his feet.

His head cleared instantly, and he knew right away that someone had been knocking on his door. "Hold on," he called softly. "Be there in a minute." He stepped across the room quickly, holding his six-gun behind him as he unlocked the door with his left hand.

A small, dark-haired woman stood in the hall. Her face was heavily painted, and she appeared to be about twenty-one years old. "The sheriff sends you a message," she said, almost whispering. "He wants to meet you for breakfast in the morning at seven o'clock." She pointed south. "He'll be at Kate's Restaurant, right next door to the hotel."

Camp nodded. "Thank you."

Though she had delivered her message, the young woman was in no hurry to leave. She peered into the room, licking her lips and fluttering her eyelashes seductively, then spoke again: "Do you always spend your nights alone?"

He took his time about answering. Although it was not going to be easy, he knew that he must send the woman on her way. She was a pretty thing, all right, but he had seen it all before. He had known more than one man who had hunted for a doctor only a few days after an encounter with a hotel woman. And some of those women were even prettier than the young thing who stood at his door now. He finally answered her question, using the tried-and-true method of discouraging aggressive women. "No," he said, "I don't always spend my nights alone. I usually sleep with my wife."

"Oh," she said. She spun on her heel and headed for the stairway.

Houston closed and locked the door, then undressed. Believing that his earlier nap would make going back to sleep difficult, he left the lamp burning and picked up his magazine. He stretched out on the bed and once again began to read about some of the get-rich-quick schemes for finding gold in

California, most of them written by men whose knowledge of the West had been gained by traveling all the way to western Pennsylvania.

He read for an hour, then blew out the lamp. He tossed and turned for another hour, then went to sleep.

He walked into Kate's Restaurant at ten minutes to seven next morning. Sheriff Dubar was already there, sitting at a table in the far corner. Looking neither left nor right, Camp pulled his hat low over his eyes and made a beeline for the table.

"I see you got my message," Dubar said, pushing out a chair with his boot.

Houston nodded, and seated himself.

The waiter was there immediately. He delivered two cups of hot coffee, then both men ordered ham and eggs. When they were alone again, the lawman got down to business. "Your boy's out at the Flying W," he said. "Got home two days ago. I guess he's resting up from his trip to Dodge City and back."

Camp blew air into the steaming cup, then took a sip. "I appreciate you getting the information, Dave. About all I can do now is wait till he comes to town."

Dubar shook his head. "I don't figure that'll be long," he said. "He likes to drink and raise hell on Saturday night, and today is Saturday. He'll be in town after the sun goes down, you can just about count on that."

Camp was thoughtful for a while. "Where does he do his drinking?" he asked finally.

"He makes 'em all. He'll be in every saloon in this town before midnight, some of 'em more'n—" Dubar left the sentence hanging, for the waiter was back at the table. He delivered their food and refilled their coffee cups, then disappeared. The sheriff sat quietly for a while, then began again. "I think you should try to catch him at the Texas, Camp, for several reasons: number one, it's his favorite hangout, so he's gonna be there eventually. Number two, I believe that Marshal Bisco is a silent partner in the ownership of the saloon, and like I told you before, he hates Lott's guts. Number three, Al Foster, who claims to be the sole owner of the establishment, hates the man at least as much as Bisco does. In truth, each of them probably hates Lott about as much as the other does.

"Neither of them has ever attempted to put a stop to Sam Lott's overbearing behavior because they're afraid of him. Of course, Foster's an old man, but the marshal's just plain yellow. You just go ahead and do whatever you think you ought to, Camp. I can tell you right now that John Bisco ain't gonna try to arrest you if you shoot Sam Lott, and Al Foster'll probably hunt up some kind of damn medal to hang around your neck."

Both men had finished eating. Camp held up his hand, and the waiter was there quickly. He refilled both coffee cups, then departed. Dubar sipped at the liquid, then spoke again: "One thing's got me puzzled a little bit, Camp. If Lott is such a damn big thief, and if he helped kill those drovers for only a small share of the money they were carrying, why is it that he just now returned from Dodge City carrying all the money Albert Wells had coming? Hell, he could have disappeared with every dollar he got for the whole damn herd, and he wouldn't have had to share it with anybody."

Camp had been listening closely, nodding occasionally. "I've thought about the same thing," he said. "I don't have a good, solid answer, but I do have an idea: what if Lott has something bigger in mind? What if he plans to someday skip the country, change his name and set himself up on his own ranch in grand style? All that would take a lot of money, Dave, much more than was in the poke that he just brought home to the Flying W. You see, there were only two thousand head in the herd he just delivered, so I believe that Sam Lott is setting Albert Wells up for the kill. You and I both know that the Flying W will send two big herds to Kansas next spring, with a total of at least seven thousand head. I daresay that Sam Lott plans on being the man who collects the money for both herds in Dodge City. I also daresay that Albert Wells will never see a dollar of it."

Dubar chuckled, then beat on the table with his fist. "By God that's it, Camp," he said. "I hadn't thought of it that way, but by God that's it. He's just setting the old man up. It was a long time ago, but you've worked out there, so you know that Wells will believe just about anything somebody tells him. Now, he's bound to have heard somebody say that Lott might have been in on that thing with the drovers, but Lott probably told him he wasn't guilty, and the old man took him at his word. Lott must have been mighty convincing, too, 'cause Wells put him in charge of the whole shebang." He hit the table with his fist again. "You've got it figured exactly right, my friend. Lott plans on bossing seven thousand, maybe eight thousand head of cattle up the trail next spring, and when the buyers take 'em off his hands and cough up the money, he intends to be long gone."

Camp nodded. "If he's a thinking thief, I'd say that's what he's got planned."

The sheriff was on his feet now. "I hate to ask you to stay in that hotel room," he said, "but I certainly believe that's the best thing for you to do. When your man hits town I'll know it, and I'll send somebody to tell you. I guess the reason I won't be coming to tell you myself is obvious. I'll also make sure that I'm not in the Texas Saloon when you call Sam Lott's number. It just wouldn't look right."

Camp continued to sit at the table. "Just go ahead, Dave, and I'll wait here for a few minutes. There's no reason for us to even be seen talking to each other. You have to live in this town, but I don't. Fact is, if I'm still in good heath after this thing with Lott is over, I expect to be out of town within three minutes, five at the most." He pointed to the front door. "Go on, now. I'll pay for your breakfast."

The sheriff nodded, and walked toward the front of the building. Camp sat at the table till he heard the front door slam, then got to his feet. He left a coin on the table for the waiter, then headed for the counter with his purse in his hand.

He spent the next several hours in his room, then ate an early dinner in the same restaurant, speaking to no one except a waiter. Then he returned to the hotel. The young desk clerk had been nowhere around earlier, but was now sitting behind the counter. He offered Camp the standard commercial smile. "Will you be staying another night, sir?"

"Not exactly," Houston said. He fished money from his pocket and laid it on the counter. "I expect to be gone before nightfall, but I don't know what time I'll be leaving. Just take enough money for both nights, then it won't matter."

The boy took one dollar and gave Camp fifteen cents change. "I'll just charge you for last night," he said. "You ain't supposed to pay for something you ain't gonna use. If it turns out that you're still here when the sun goes down, then you'll owe me another eighty-five cents."

Houston nodded, then climbed the stairs and stretched out on his bed, intent upon taking a nap. Though it had been said of Camp that he had nerves of steel, he nevertheless felt a fluttering in his stomach, and going to sleep proved to be impossible. He reached for his magazine and began to thumb through it, smiling occasionally at the latest offerings from the political cartoonists. He was still reading when he heard an indefinite sound outside his door. "Who's there?" he asked, swinging his feet to the floor.

He got no answer, but this time there was a definite knock. With his gun in his hand as usual, he opened the door slowly. The same woman who had visited him last night stood in the hall. Her appearance was much more pleasing to his conservative eye on this visit, however, for today she wore no paint whatsoever. Knowing that she was undoubtedly here to deliver another message, he looked at her with raised eyebrows, then stood waiting.

"The sheriff sent you this," she said. She handed him a folded piece of brown paper, then disappeared down the hall.

He relocked the door and took a seat on the bed, then

read the message. With no salutation at the top and no signature at the bottom, the note contained just six words: *"The rabbit is in the box."*

Camp slipped the note into his pocket, then got to his feet. He pulled the shade down on both windows, then spent the next ten minutes practicing his fast draw. His speed was incredible, his actions nothing more than a blur as he slapped his leg and brought the Colt into firing position. He went through the motion more than twenty times, then added a sixth shell to the cylinder and shoved the weapon back in its holster. Then he draped his saddlebag over his shoulder and headed for the stairway.

When he reached the lobby, he spoke to the clerk. "I'm leaving now," he said, continuing to walk toward the street. "You can rent that room to whoever wants it now." He was out the door quickly and headed for the livery stable, moving as fast as he could without running.

The hostler was sitting in front of his office, leaning against the wall with only two of his chair's legs touching the ground. He jumped to his feet quickly. "Looks like you might be about to leave us," he said.

Camp nodded. "Yes," he said. "I'd like my horses just as soon as you can get them out here."

The man said nothing else, just grabbed a rope and headed for the corral at a fast walk. He had both animals up front in less than five minutes, then proceeded to help Camp saddle the roan and lash the packsaddle on the black. Houston paid his bill, mounted the roan and yanked on the packhorse's lead rope. "I appreciate your business," the hostler called as Camp rode through the wide doorway. "If you ever come this way again, you know where I'm at."

Three minutes later, Houston tied his animals to one of the Texas Saloon's three hitching rails. He stood beside the roan for a few moments, taking stock of his surroundings and trying to picture exactly what he would be facing once he was inside the building. He counted five saddled horses at the rails, and noted that only one of the animals, an oversized bay, wore the Flying W brand.

Did this mean that Lott, like a few other foremen Camp had known, had sought out various chores for the ranch hands to perform, while he himself spent the day and night in town drinking? Camp suspected that it did. Four of the five horses now standing at the hitching rails were from other ranches, and he doubted that any of their owners would risk life and limb to side with Sam Lott. There was only one way to find out, he decided. Having no clear idea of what he was walking into, he stepped to the sidewalk and pushed his way through the batwing doors, depending entirely on his quick reflexes to see him through.

Visibility was always better inside the Texas than in most saloons, and today the bartender had all of the shades up and the windows open, letting in even more light than usual. Houston needed no time to adjust his eyes. He recognized his quarry immediately, for the man towered above the two shorter men who stood beside him at the bar. Camp moved quickly to reduce the distance separating him from the three men, who were laughing and talking among themselves and paying little attention to anyone else. Houston stopped thirty feet away, spread his legs slightly and went into a crouch. "Everybody except Sam Lott move away from the bar!" he commanded loudly, almost shouting.

Both of the men standing beside Lott turned to face Camp, but neither moved away from the bar as ordered. Lott looked half around and half over their heads, and caught Houston's eye. "Well," he said sneeringly, tucking a wayward strand of dirty blond hair behind his ear. "I do believe I have company." He emitted a nasal chuckle, then spoke again: "To who and what do I owe this honor?"

Houston's steel-gray eyes bore into those of the skinny foreman. He spoke loudly enough for every man in the room to hear. "I'm here on behalf of John Calloway, Bill Fisher and Joe Plenty, Lott! My name is Camp Houston!"

The two men standing beside Lott moved away from the bar like they had been shot out of a cannon, for they had both heard the name before.

The sneer disappeared from Lott's face quickly. He stepped away from the bar and began to point with his left hand, attempting to divert Camp's attention to something across the room. All the while, his right hand was easing downward. He died in his tracks, for Houston had failed to buy the well-worn ruse. Lott had managed to get his gun in his hand, but had not lived to fire it. He had taken a .45-caliber slug between his eyes just as he cleared his holster. He dropped the weapon to the floor, then fell on top of it. He never moved again.

Houston still held his gun in his hand as he stepped sideways and laid twenty dollars on the bar. "Give this to the undertaker," he said to the bartender. "And tell Al Foster that I'm sorry about the mess I made in here." He walked backward till he reached the front of the building, then holstered the Colt and stepped through the doorway. He mounted quickly and pointed the roan south. He was not headed for Calf Creek just yet. He was on his way to Austin to talk with a friend named Joe Plenty.

22

The residents of the 3C began to eat fresh meat three times a day during the month of December. Bo Patton usually took a rifle or a shotgun into the woods every day, and he seldom returned empty-handed. And the meat would not spoil now. Hanging inside a small enclosure on one end of the back porch, it would be kept fresh by the near-freezing temperatures and the cold wind. And in this area, the wind usually blew day and night during the last few weeks of the year.

"I hate hunting in the wind," Fowler had said to Patton a few days earlier, while watching the young man dress out a doe. "The wind is all I can hear, and if it's cold, it always gives me an earache."

"Not me," Patton said, wielding the skinning knife expertly. "I just put cotton in my ears or tie something around my head, and use that wind to help me find game. If you walk slow enough and quiet enough for long enough, and keep that wind blowing right in your face, you're gonna eat meat for supper. Ain't no animal in the woods gonna know that you're around if you move about quietly, and keep him upwind."

"Well, it's kinda obvious that you know what you're talking about," Runt said, pointing to the carcass. "There hangs the proof." He accepted the deer liver Patton handed him, then headed for the kitchen. It was his turn to cook supper.

Most of the construction at the 3C had been completed, and the Wootens had long since vacated the premises. Fowler had several additional things in mind for the house, however, among them adding another fireplace and chimney. He was constantly touching up one thing or another, or searching out something that had been overlooked in the rush. Only yesterday he had torn down the makeshift outhouse, and replaced it with a sturdy one that would never leak. He also intended to build a small bunkhouse soon, for Bo Patton had repeated Camp's jocular remark that he might marry Ellen Bice.

On the twenty-first day of the month, Houston rode off the hill at daybreak. He had business in both Mason and Menardville, and intended to spend one night in each town. He led the packhorse, but not because he needed it. He was returning the animal to Sid Blankenship.

He traveled at a steady pace, and reached Mason in midafternoon. He turned his horses over to Hamm Harrison at the livery stable, then headed for the bank, which was his only reason for being in town. Roy Holder, whose office door was open, spotted Houston as he entered the building, and was quickly in the lobby pumping Camp's hand. "I've been expecting you," he said. "I figured it was about time you got serious about stocking that ranch, and like always, we'd be delighted to be of assistance." He motioned toward his office. "Yes, sir, that's exactly what we're here for."

Camp shook his head. "I'm not in the mood to take on a large debt right now, Mr. Holder. I've been doing a lot of building at my place, and I'm just here to withdraw some money to pay the people that I already owe."

Undaunted, Holder pointed to his office again. "I understand," he said. "But we need to work out some of the details, so—"

"No," Camp interrupted. "The only thing I'm gonna talk about today is the two hundred dollars I came here to withdraw."

"Very well, sir," the banker said, still smiling broadly. "Just step right over to the window, and Mr. Bradley will take care of it."

Camp was back on the street three minutes later. He walked through town at a fast pace, and did not stop till he reached Ma Franklin's boardinghouse. When he announced his presence with a loud knock at the door, he received an answer from somewhere down the hall: "Just go on into the dining room, Camp. I'll be in there pretty soon."

He recognized the voice, and stepped into the building. "Thank you, Ma," he called. A moment later, he seated himself at the end of the long table.

The lady was there soon after, and walked straight to the stove. She stoked the fire and pulled the coffeepot over the firebox, then walked to the table. "I guess you can drink warmed-over coffee, can't you?"

He nodded. "I do it pretty often, Ma."

She took a seat beside him and offered her usual smile. "Well, if it seems too bitter, just remember that it's not costing you anything." They were both quiet for a few moments, then she spoke again: "I've heard that you've turned that hill above Calf Creek into a show place. Have you stocked it with cattle? Have you got married yet?"

"Whoa, Ma," Camp said, laughing loudly. "Let's talk about these things one at a time. I don't know who you've been talking to, but I certainly don't have a show place. What I've got on Calf Creek is exactly what you'd find on any other ranch: a house and the necessary outbuildings. I must admit that Runt Fowler did an outstanding job on the layout, but it's hardly a show place. As far as stocking the ranch is concerned, I'll be doing that next spring, about April, I suppose.

As for that last question, I'll answer it by asking you one: Married? Me married? Who in the world would want to marry me, Ma?"

She sat staring at him for a while. "Well, I'll be damned," she said finally. She walked to the stove and poured two cups of coffee. "Who'd want to marry you?" She handed him one of the steaming cups, then reclaimed her seat and answered the question herself. "Just about any young girl would want to marry you, Camp Houston. That is, any girl who knows which side her bread's buttered on." She sat thoughtful for a moment, then added, "But I'm sure you know a lot of things about Camp Houston that I don't. Maybe I should be asking you just why it is that none of the girls wants to marry you."

He laughed, then shook his head. "I just said that to be having something to say, Ma. I didn't mean it the way it sounded. But in all honesty, I sure don't recall ever seeing a bunch of pretty young things tripping over themselves trying to get my attention."

"I certainly know at least one of the reasons for that," she said quickly. "It's the expression you carry on your face. I mean, most of the time you look like your mind's a thousand miles away." She sipped at her coffee, then continued. "You just take stock of yourself and think about what I'm telling you, 'cause I know exactly how a female thinks: she might be dying to speak to you, but she won't do it, not with you looking like your mind is in a different world.

"You're one of the best-looking men around, Camp, and if you change your ways a little bit, you'll have more female friends than you can shake a stick at. Whenever you see a woman that you'd like to know better, you've got to give her an encouraging look. Just slow down, look her right in the eye and give her that big old handsome smile of yours. Let her know you're interested, and she'll make the rest of it easier for you. If you want to court her, say so. If you want her to go somewhere with you, ask her. Hell, she won't bite you."

Camp leaned back in his chair. His body shook a little, for

he was laughing inside. "You sound just like Bama Angleton," he said.

"That don't bother me none. Bama Angleton is a smart woman, and I'd almost bet that she told you the same thing I'm telling you."

He sat staring at the table with tight lips for a moment. Then his face slowly broke into a smile. "Well, it was pretty close."

He talked with the lady for another hour. Then, when she informed him that she had work to do, he sought conversation elsewhere. He spent the remainder of the afternoon on the front porch talking with two of her regular boarders, then joined them at the supper table and ate two helpings of everything in sight. A short time later, he was shown to the only unoccupied room on the premises, where he slept in a better bed than he could have found at any hotel in three counties.

He was back at the livery stable early next morning, and rode out of town at sunup. He kicked the roan to a fast trot immediately. The trip to Menardville was a full day's ride, and he had no intention of spending the night on the road. He traveled steadily throughout the morning, and reached Big Rock Spring an hour past noon. The spring was roughly the halfway point between Menardville and Mason, and a common stopover for traffic headed in either direction.

A covered wagon was parked beside the spring's runoff, and a young couple and two children sat beside a campfire eating. Houston waved to them, then dismounted. The man, who appeared to be about Camp's own age, returned the greeting. "We've got more hot coffee here than we're gonna use," he said. "You're welcome to drink it if you want to. All we'll do is just pour it out."

Camp nodded. "That's the best offer I've had today," he said. "After I take care of my horses I'll be right over." He watered the animals and poured grain in their nose bags, then dug his cup out of his pack. A few moments later, he approached the dying campfire. "I appreciate this," he said, offering his cup. "It sure beats washing my biscuits down with water."

The man poured the cup full and handed it back. "I guess you had coffee of your own on that packhorse," he said, "but the hard part is finding wood to heat it. We always carry kindling in the wagon, 'cause campers have already gathered up most of the stuff along the road that'll burn. They ain't overlooked nothing within a quarter mile of this spring."

"I never even think about building a fire here when I'm traveling on horseback," Houston said. "This road is pretty heavily traveled, and almost everybody stops because of the spring. I'd bet that there's been a shortage of deadwood here since the Civil War."

The man looked Houston over closely. Then his face suddenly took on a serious look. He got to his feet quickly and refilled Camp's cup, then dashed the remainder of the coffee into the fire. "All right, Tom and Jane," he said to the children, "get yourselves into the wagon. We've gotta get moving." The children moved instantly, as did both parents. The man removed the nose bags from his horses and watered them again. Then he helped his wife to the seat and climbed up beside her. Without another word or so much as a glance in Camp's direction, he backed his team away from the ditch and headed down the road toward Mason.

Leaning against the big rock from whence the spring's name derived, sipping the coffee and eating ham and biscuits provided by Ma Franklin, Houston stood watching the wagon, still thinking about the man's odd behavior. Though the man seemed friendly enough at first, he had grown quiet seemingly in midsentence, and his wife had never spoken at all. Houston stood shaking his head as the full realization hit him: his own reputation as a gunman had spread far and wide, and the family's quick departure simply meant that he had been recognized.

He swallowed the last of his food, then washed his cup in the spring's runoff. A few minutes later, he was headed for

Menardville. Trying to make up for lost time, he traveled at a canter for several miles, then slowed to a trot.

He arrived in Menardville shortly after dark, and was pleased to find that Sid Blankenship was still at his bellows. By the feeble light of a coal-oil lantern, the muscular blacksmith was busy pounding on a long piece of metal with a heavy hammer. He laid the work aside when he saw Houston. "Hello, Camp," he said, wiping his hands and offering a handshake. "It's good to see you."

They shook hands, then Blankenship pointed to his unfinished work. "I've been hoping to get that damn rim fixed for old man Bouton before I call it a night, but I ain't gonna make it." He motioned toward the rimless wagon wheel leaning in the corner. "He'll be wanting that thing about sunup, but he'll just have to wait a while."

Haley Bouton was a grouchy, white-haired farmer who was past seventy years old, and very well known in the vicinity. "The old man'll wait, all right," Houston said, chuckling, "but only because he has no other choice. He'll probably give you a piece of his mind while he's doing it, too."

"Of course he will. He bitches about everything I do for him. He keeps coming back, though, so I guess I can't complain."

Houston stood quietly for a moment, then pointed over his shoulder. "I brought the horse and the packsaddle back to you, Sid. I don't suppose I'll be needing them anymore."

Blankenship nodded. "Are you saying that Calloway's bushwhackers are in the ground?"

"All of them."

"Well, I'll be damned," the liveryman said. "That news'll be easy to live with." He walked to the hitching rail and untied the black, then led the animal inside the barn. He began to unlash the packsaddle. "I knew you'd get 'em, Camp. I knew it right from the first day you told me that you were going hunting. It's just a good thing that we've got somebody like you around to help rid the country of such riffraff."

Houston changed the subject. "I'll be in the hotel bar later on, if you want to join me for a drink."

Blankenship shook his head. "Not tonight. I appreciate the offer, but I'd better get on home. That oldest girl of mine ain't feeling too good lately, been sick for nearly a week."

"I'm sorry to hear that," Camp said. "Maybe she'll be feeling better tomorrow." He turned to leave. "I guess I'll have to settle for a little conversation with Wesley Hawks, then." He took a few steps toward the doorway, then stopped suddenly. "Oh," he said, "I almost forgot." He fished a piece of paper out of his pocket and handed it over. "I need some Three C branding irons made up. Can you do it?"

Blankenship stood looking at the "3C" Houston had written on the paper. "I sure don't see anything complicated about it," he said. "How many do you want, and when are you gonna need 'em?"

"Just make up six or eight. No hurry about it. I'm not gonna have anything to brand for a long time yet."

Blankenship nodded. "That'll give me something to work on when business is slow. They'll be ready before you need 'em."

Camp lifted his hand in a saluting gesture. "I'll see you sometime tomorrow," he said. Then he was gone up the hill. He stopped at a hole-in-the-wall restaurant and ate a bowl of stew, then registered at the Menardville Hotel half an hour later. Having left his saddlebags at the livery stable, he was empty-handed, and had no reason to head for his room just yet. When he walked into the saloon he saw right away that he was the only customer in the house. He seated himself at the bar, directly in front of the idle bartender. "How's business, Wes?" he asked jokingly.

Hawks placed a glass on the bar and reached for a bottle of good whiskey. "It's just like it's been for the past two weeks," he answered. "It'll pick up Friday, on account of that being Christmas Eve, but it'll just be good for that one day. New Year's Eve'll be along a week later, and you won't even be able to get in the place then. But on the first day of January, she'll die a natural death."

Camp took a sip of whiskey. "A natural death, huh?"

"Absolutely. The hotel carries the saloon in the off-season. This bar don't even do enough business to pay its own way in the wintertime. The people who own it are the same ones who own the hotel, and they just keep it open for the convenience of the guests." He laughed. "From where I stand, it all looks like a losing proposition. I doubt that the hotel has more than five or six rooms rented right now. Maybe seven, if you're gonna be staying overnight."

Houston pushed his glass forward for a refill. "Seven," he said.

By the time Camp left the saloon he had decided that Hawks's complaint about business being slow was valid, for the bartender had had only one other customer during Houston's two-hour stay: a man who bought a bottle of whiskey and walked right back out the door. All of which was no skin off Hawks's nose, Camp was thinking. The man obviously received the same monthly salary no matter how much whiskey he did or did not sell.

In his hotel room, he slid under the covers as quickly as possible, for the night was cold. Once his body was warm, he began to think about the approaching holidays: Saturday would be Christmas Day, and a week later, most people would party in the new year. Christmas. Although he could not get as excited about it as he had when he was a child, he nevertheless still appreciated its meaning.

And tomorrow, he would buy gifts for a few friends. Sid Blankenship already had everything a man was likely to need, so Camp would buy him a bottle of premium whiskey to sip at his pleasure. And he had already spotted knives at Spike Nettleton's hardware store that he would buy for Fowler and Patton: a three-bladed folding knife for Fowler, and a fine hunting knife for Bo Patton. He smiled at the thought, then went to sleep.

He was up early next morning, and walked to the same small restaurant that had fed him a good bowl of stew the night before. He had a breakfast of flapjacks and sausage, then decided to head for the livery stable, where he had left his shaving soap and razor in his saddlebag. He would shave his face in Sid's office, for he was taking no chances that he might accidentally run into Ellen Bice while wearing a two-day growth of beard.

Menard County Sheriff Walter McMichen was just passing the restaurant as Camp walked out the door, and the two almost collided. "Excuse me, Sheriff," Camp said quickly. "I guess I need to watch where I'm going."

"No harm done," the lawman said.

Sheriff McMichen was at least sixty years old, and had openly stated on more than one occasion that he was too old for the job. The county voters had disagreed, and reelected him for another term just the year before. Most of those same voters had now begun to believe that McMichen had known what he was talking about, however, for immediately after the election he began to spend at least ninety percent of his time at his farm, rarely coming to town unless sent for. Today was the first time Camp had seen the man in at least a year.

"I haven't seen you in a while, Sheriff," Camp said, extending his right hand. "You're looking good."

McMichen grasped the hand and pumped it several times. "I don't get around much these days, Mr. Houston. I've sure been hearing a lot of things about you, though. You just keep up the good work." He walked around Camp and continued on up the hill. Houston stood watching till the man turned the corner, then he himself headed down the hill to the stable.

When Spike Nettleton opened his hardware store an hour later, Houston was there with money in his hand. "I want to settle up whatever I owe on that last load of building material," Camp said. "Then I want to buy two of those knives at the end of the counter."

A few minutes later, he left the store with the knives in the saddlebag that he now carried over his shoulder. He walked around town for a while, trying to decide what to do next. He knew that he could make it home before dark if he left now. He also knew that he wanted to see Ellen Bice, and that she only worked at the restaurant during the afternoon and early evening.

He was walking down the hill casually, looking at the merchandise in the window of one store after another, when he suddenly realized that he was abreast of Riley's Restaurant. Maybe he would have a cup of coffee, he thought as he opened the door and stepped inside. Ellen Bice stood behind the counter. When she spotted Houston, her beautiful face broke into the most honest-looking smile he had seen in months. "Hello, Camp," she called sweetly. "Do you want to come and sit at the counter?"

Did he want to sit at the counter? Of course he did. The closer the better. And she had called him by his first name. "Give her that big old handsome smile of yours," Ma Franklin had instructed. He spread his lips and offered the broadest smile he could muster. "Well," he said, beginning to walk across the room. "There stands the prettiest girl in this town." He stood at the counter for a moment watching her blush, then seated himself on a stool. "It's good to see you again, Ellen, and I mean it when I say that you look prettier every time I see you."

She blushed again, and fluttered her eyelashes. "Thank you, Camp. I must say that this is sure something different, coming from you. I really didn't think you'd ever paid much attention to me."

He was getting braver by the moment. "Why, I paid all of my attention to you. Fell in love the first time I ever saw you." He took a sip of the coffee she had set on the counter, then added jokingly, "Made up my mind right on the spot that I was gonna take you to Calf Creek with me one of these days."

She giggled softly, and slapped his arm playfully. "I wonder how many other girls you've said that to."

His facial expression suddenly turned serious. "I've never said that to anybody else, Ellen." Then, almost as if taking an oath, he added, "And that's the truth."

Her own smile faded quickly. "I believe you," she said.

He was not about to stop now. He pointed over his shoulder. "It's entirely too cold to enjoy it anytime soon, but I was wondering if you'd want to take a buggy ride with me when the weather warms up."

She answered quickly. "I'd like that, Camp. Sunday would be the best day for me, because I don't have to work then." She picked up a bill of fare and stood looking across the room, for five people were now busy seating themselves in the dining area. She leaned close to his ear and spoke almost at a whisper: "I'm going to be real busy for the next few hours, and I won't have time to talk. I'll be looking forward to the buggy ride, though." Then she was gone to check on the diners.

He walked out of the restaurant with a feeling of accomplishment. Ma Franklin had known what she was talking about, all right. By doing exactly as Ma had told him, he had broken the ice with the girl from Nebraska. He bought the bottle of whiskey that was to be Blankenship's Christmas gift, then headed down the hill to the livery stable as fast as he could walk. Twenty minutes later, he mounted the roan and took the road to Calf Creek.

23

One afternoon in the last week of March, John Butterworth's buggy rolled into Houston's yard. The rancher jumped to the ground spryly as Runt Fowler hurried from the house to meet him. "Hello, Runt," Butterworth said, his right hand extended. "I'm sure Camp told me that you were down here, but it must have slipped my mind. It's mighty good to see you again."

Fowler grasped the hand. "I'm glad to see you, too, Mr. Butterworth." He motioned toward the barn. "Camp's down there fooling with some new horses he bought from Blankenship, and I doubt that he even knows you're on the premises." He cupped his hands around his mouth and called Houston's name at the top of his lungs.

Camp stepped from a stable, and recognized his visitor immediately. He was in the yard moments later, shaking the rancher's hand. "I've been thinking about you all day, John," he said. "I've even thought about riding up to your place."

"No need for that. My men are busy cutting out five hundred head of old stuff right now, so your breeders'll be here in about ten days. Four of the riders'll stay around to help you for a week or two, or however long it takes for the cows to settle down."

"That's mighty good to hear, John. I guess they'll start dropping calves anytime now, and I've already had some branding irons made up."

"A lot of 'em have done dropped. I'd say that about twenty percent of 'em have got calves following 'em already."

"I like the sound of that, too," Camp said. He pointed up the hill. "Come on up to the house. I don't have any wine to offer you, but I can have a pot of coffee ready in a hurry."

The rancher stepped to his buggy and reached under the seat. "I brought my own wine," he said, coming away with a gallon jug in each hand.

The three men were soon sitting at the kitchen table, sipping the rancher's wine from tin cups. Butterworth handed Houston an official-looking piece of paper. "I registered the whole six sections in your name," he said. "Then I got to thinking that maybe I'd better come down here and show you where the corners are. Ain't no way in the hell you'd ever find 'em all by yourself."

Camp accepted the document, then laughed. "I don't know exactly where any of the corners are," he said. "Thank you for coming."

At that moment, Bo Patton walked into the house, a double-barreled shotgun under his arm. "I've got that big old tom turkey outside," he said as he laid the gun on two wooden pegs that had been driven into the wall for that purpose. "I've been calling him for a month, and he's been answering for a month, but he never would come into shotgun range." He smiled victoriously. "I reckon my calls must have sounded more like a real hen today, 'cause he came running like the woods were on fire." He chuckled aloud. "Damn near ran down my gun barrel."

Camp introduced Patton to Butterworth, and when the handshaking was over, spoke to the youngster: "What do you plan to do with the turkey, Bo?"

"Weather's too warm to keep him overnight. I'm gonna pluck him and singe him, then put him in the oven to bake." He walked to the stove. "I'll start a fire so the oven'll be hot by the time I need it."

"Never mind, Bo," Houston said, getting to his feet. "Just go ahead and work on your turkey. I'll build the fire." Patton nodded, and headed for the backyard.

During the next two days, Butterworth pointed out all four corners of the six-section ranch to Houston, Fowler and Patton. They, in turn, would acquaint the Lazy B riders with the boundaries. As each corner was pointed out, Fowler and Patton cleared all of the vegetation away from the immediate area and drove an iron stake in the ground. A piece of red cloth was then tied around the top of the stake.

The rancher spent one more night on the ranch after his mission had been accomplished, then announced at the breakfast table that he was about to head for the Lazy B.

"I wish you'd stay around a little longer, John," Camp said, making an all-out effort to saw through a chunk of tough venison with a dull knife. "The cows'll probably be here in less than a week."

"Nope, gotta be getting on home." He took a sip of coffee, then frowned as he set his cup on the table noisily. "Besides," he added jokingly, "we've drunk up all of the wine."

Camp lifted his cup. "I can't do anything about that," he said. "All I've got is bitter coffee."

An hour later, after having said his good-byes and shaking hands all around, the rancher climbed to the seat of his buggy. He waved good-bye once more, then slapped the mare's hip with the reins. He was off the hill quickly, and just before he disappeared around the curve, Camp saw him move one of the empty wine jugs to the back of the buggy, as if their rattling against each other had already begun to get on his nerves.

Camp stood in the yard with a lump in his throat long after the buggy was out of sight. He had a special feeling for the driver of that vehicle, for no man had ever treated him so kindly. John Butterworth had bent over backward to help him get started with a place of his own. And though Houston could think of nothing that he himself had ever done to deserve such treatment, he was determined to turn the 3C into a profitable concern. He would bring in some Hereford bulls at the beginning of the third year and begin to upgrade his herd. And the old man would be proud. Camp swallowed hard, then headed for the barn. He wanted to be alone for a while.

He stood outside the corral for a while, looking over the four black horses he had bought the week before. Though he had ridden them before buying and decided that they were sound animals, he had had no way of determining their knowledge of cattle. They would surely be tested when the breeders arrived the following week.

Blankenship himself had known little about the animals. "I got 'em from old man Whitten down in Kimble County," he said, "and he assured me that they're all excellent cow horses. If it turns out that that ain't the case, bring 'em back. I'd nearly bet that they're gonna be all right, though. The old man never has lied to me yet, and he certainly wouldn't have a reason to start now. He knew that I was getting the horses for you, and he knows that you know all of the differences between a cow pony and a jackass." He lifted a front foot of one of the animals and inspected the frog. "Why would he lie when he knows that he's gonna get the horses right back if they don't please you?"

Camp laughed. "All right, Sid, you've got me convinced. I have no doubt that the horses'll work out fine, and I especially like the price. Where else could I have bought cutting horses for forty dollars apiece?"

Blankenship shot him a knowing look. "Aw, I reckon that's about the going rate, Camp. The bottom's out of horse-flesh right now."

Houston nodded. "Good. I might be needing a couple more head before long."

Now, Camp stepped into his own corral and angled toward the larger of the black horses, speaking in low tones as he walked. All of the other animals shied away, but the one he had chosen stood waiting, stiff-legged. Camp rubbed the horse's neck and shoulder for a while, then, taking a firm hold on its lower lip, led the animal to the barn.

A few minutes later, he rode the black through the gate and headed down the hill. He took the Brady road and let the animal run at an easy canter for a couple miles, then turned up the slope and into the woods. Riding through or sometimes around the scrub thickets and underbrush, he began to think about just how fast a fire could devastate the area if somebody got careless.

Of course, it could happen without somebody getting careless. Mother Nature had her own ways of renewing the land, the most obvious of which was to burn everything in sight and start over. And she had her own ways of starting fires. Camp knew that his property would be in better shape right now if a raging fire had swept it a couple years ago. Had that happened, much of the area that was now covered with underbrush would instead be producing graze for animals.

But it was too late to be thinking about that now. With the cattle on the way, the last thing he needed was a fire. He would caution all of the riders to be extra careful with their campfires and cigarettes, for the vegetation was almost as dry as powder, and a careless spark could get out of hand in an instant.

Camp rode the black for another three hours, by which time he had decided that the animal possessed all of the qualities required of a good cow pony: he was quick, surefooted, well balanced, and could turn on a dime. On the way home, Camp ran him all-out for more than a mile, and he was not breathing hard. Good lungs, Camp thought. Which meant

that the horse could cut calves out of a herd all morning without a break. "If," Camp said to himself, "he actually knows
what a damn calf is." He kicked the animal to a canter and
headed home.

He fed and curried the black, then walked to the shed and
seated himself on the wagon tongue. He was thinking of Ellen
Bice and the buggy rides they had taken together. He had
called on her twice driving a rented rig, and expected to do the
same again two days from now. Tomorrow was Saturday. He
would ride the black cutting horse to Menardville and spend
the night at the hotel, then pick her up early Sunday morning
and spend the day in the country.

On each of their previous rides, one in January and the
other in February, they had spent the entire day traveling up
and down the San Saba River, eating dinner from a lunch basket, and talking about Nebraska. On the second occasion,
Camp had suggested riding south to the Leon River, but the
girl had correctly decided that they would probably not be
able to make it back to Menardville before dark. Which, of
course, would not have bothered Houston in the least, except
for the fact that she had asked him a direct question: Could
they make it to the Leon and back before darkness overtook
them? He reluctantly admitted that they could not.

He had held her hand for most of the day on both buggy
rides. He had never kissed her, but she had almost kissed him
once. Or he believed that she had at least been thinking about
it: they had been sitting on a blanket on the bank of the river.
He had been telling her stories about his childhood, and about
how he used to walk up and down the streets of Little Rock
peddling garden produce.

She learned that he had been almost grown before he out-
grew his dislike for shoes, and that when people in Little Rock
sometimes asked why he walked around barefoot, he would
tell them that he was from a poor family and could not afford
to buy shoes. Then the people almost always bought some-

thing from him. Of course, he was not from a poor family, and he had several pairs of shoes in his closet. The real reason he was barefoot was because he hated shoes.

She had been giving him her undivided attention as he talked, and every word brought her face a little closer to his. Her lips were almost touching his cheek when she suddenly jerked her head away. She sat blushing once she realized what she had been about to do, and was probably even more embarrassed because she knew that he had read her actions. She began to fiddle around with the picnic basket and soon laid out their dinner. Camp never mentioned the fact that he knew she had almost kissed him.

He sat on the wagon tongue reminiscing, trying to recall every conversation that had ever passed between them. He usually tried to keep her talking as long as she would, for her soft voice was much like music to his ears. Besides, she was the only person he had ever spent much time around who spoke the English language the same way it was printed in the books he read.

When Camp got to his feet, the blaze-faced black was standing with his head hanging over the top pole of the corral, looking like he was ready to go for another run. "Early in the morning," Camp said, as if the animal could understand. Houston would saddle the black in the morning and be on his way to Menardville at sunup. He must catch up on all of his running around, for by this time next week he would be married to five hundred twenty-five head of longhorns.

He walked into the house to find Fowler standing by the stove stirring the iron pot, and Patton sitting at the table sipping coffee. "Saw you giving one of the blacks a workout," Runt said. "What do you think?"

Camp nodded. "He's a solid animal, Runt. He's quick on his feet, he can spin like a top, and he can run like hell. Got good wind, too." He chuckled. "Now that I've said all of that, I guess we'll have to wait till next week to find out whether he's worth a shit or not."

Fowler laughed, then changed the subject. "We're gonna have some good stew here in a little bit. It's got two fox squirrels and a rabbit in it: a big cane cutter."

Houston filled a coffee cup and took a seat. "Bo, I'm gonna take the blaze-faced black with me tomorrow, but I want you to give all three of the others a good workout every day between now and the time the cows get here."

Patton nodded. "I'll put 'em through their paces," he said. "My pa used to say that if you leave a horse in the corral long enough, he'll finally get the idea that all he has to do to earn a bucket of oats is stand around switching his tail."

Camp got to his feet and dropped his empty cup in the dishpan. "Your pa was right," he said, then left the room.

He was off the hill shortly after breakfast. The cold air was invigorating, and the black wanted to run. Camp allowed the animal to set its own pace, which turned out to be a steady canter. And although the wind finally set Houston's nose and ears to stinging, he continued to let the horse run. Anyway, the colder his face became, the better the morning sun felt on his back.

After about three miles, the animal slowed to a trot, then to a walk, which was pleasing to Camp. He had been riding with the reins wrapped around the horn and both of his hands in the pockets of his heavy coat. He was using the top button of the garment for a change, with the collar turned up around his ears.

As he rode along he was thinking that tomorrow morning would probably be just as cold. If so, he would wait till about midday to call on Ellen Bice. Or, if the afternoon turned out to be too cold for a buggy ride, he would simply visit her at home, for both her uncle and her aunt had treated him with the utmost courtesy.

Indeed, Mary Trout never passed up a chance to praise Ellen's cooking ability whenever Camp was present, and seemed to be overjoyed that her niece might be involved in a budding romance with a local rancher. "Don't reckon she's ever been serious about a man before," the lady had once said to Camp, ignoring the fact that her words might be embarrassing to the girl, who was well within earshot. "She's gonna be twenty years old next May, too." Ellen had given her aunt a polite look of tolerance, then climbed into the buggy.

Houston led the black into Blankenship's stable two hours before sunset. The liveryman accepted the reins with humor. "It hasn't been long since you were bitching about the horses I sold you, then here you come riding one of 'em."

Camp smiled. "Dammit, Sid, I didn't bitch about the horses. I just mentioned the fact that I didn't know anything about 'em." He pointed to the black. "Now, that horse rides good and he handles good, but I'm still not sure that he knows a cow from a damn jackrabbit."

The liveryman led the horse forward a few steps and unbuckled the cinch. "He knows." He laid the saddle and blanket on a wooden rack, then led the animal toward a stable, leaving Camp standing alone. Houston walked into the office and seated himself in a ladder-back chair. Blankenship was there a few minutes later, and took a seat on his desk. "You just come from Calf Creek?" he asked.

Camp nodded.

"Well, I don't guess you've heard the rumor, then."

"I don't hear anything on Calf Creek, Sid. You know that."

The liveryman got to his feet and stood looking through the window for a few moments. "I don't know exactly how much truth there is to it," he said to the windowpane, "but the word is out that the town council is fed up with Joe Paley." He turned to face Houston, adding, "The latest scuttlebutt is that they're gonna fire him at their next meeting."

Camp sat thoughtful for a while. "What's Paley done that pissed 'em all off?" he asked finally. "Who's gonna be their new town marshal?"

"I think it's just his overall attitude that's about to do him in," Blankenship began. "It could be that the council members are just tired of watching his lordship strut around town barking at people. He's overbearing as hell when he runs across somebody that he knows'll put up with it, Camp."

When Blankenship failed to answer the second part of the question, Houston repeated it. "Who's gonna be their new marshal?"

The liveryman reseated himself on his desk, then laughed aloud. "I don't guess they really know yet, but I've heard it said that, before they consider anybody else, they're gonna offer the job to a man named Camp Houston."

Camp was on his feet instantly. "Bullshit!" he said loudly. "That's completely out of the question." He stood quietly for a few moments, then began again: "I want to nip this shit in the bud, Sid. I don't want to have to hurt Ned's feelings, so I'd appreciate it if you'd get word to him that I don't have the slightest interest in being Menardville's town marshal, and that I positively will not accept the job if he offers it. Besides, I don't even live in this county. Part of my ranch runs over into it, but my house is in McCulloch County."

"I'll tell him," Blankenship said, continuing to smile. "But he sure thinks you'd make a good marshal."

"It don't make a shit what he thinks, Sid. It's what I think that counts, and I think the whole idea is ridiculous." He walked around the room for a while, then added, "Even if I wanted the damn job I couldn't accept it. I'm just now getting my place in good shape, and I've got five hundred head of longhorns coming next week."

"I'll tell him," Blankenship repeated, still smiling.

"I appreciate it," Camp said. He walked to the door, then turned. "I'm going up to the restaurant and get something to eat. I'm hungry enough to eat a skunk."

24

★

The supper crowd was already gathering in the restaurant, and Houston seated himself at one of the few vacant tables. With a coffeepot in her hand, Ellen Bice was there quickly, looking even prettier than he remembered. When she was working, she usually wore her dark hair in a ball at the back of her head, held there by several large combs. Today it hung loose on her back and shoulders, and supplied a perfect background for her sparkling, sky-blue eyes. She smiled as she filled his cup. "I was hoping you'd come today," she said softly.

"I wouldn't have missed it for the world, been planning it for nearly a month."

Her smile widened. "Thank you." She waved her arm toward the diners. "As you can see, this is the rush hour, so I won't have any time for conversation." She laid the bill of fare on the table. "If you'll decide what you want for supper as quickly as you can, I'll be able to get on with my work."

He ignored the bill of fare, and sat looking into her eyes. "I think you're smart enough to look at me and tell what I need. I'll eat whatever you bring me." He folded his arms and continued to gaze into her eyes, adding jokingly, "Anyway, after I take you to Calf Creek you're gonna be planning all of my meals."

She stuck out her tongue playfully, then headed for the kitchen.

Half an hour later, he sat eating a juicy, tender beefsteak that weighed at least a pound. There was also a bowl of brown beans and a separate platter containing fried potatoes, pickled beets and buttered biscuits. And off to the side, in a smaller dish, a large wedge of apple pie awaited his attention. He had definitely made the right decision, he was thinking: Ellen Bice had known exactly what he needed.

When he had finished his meal and walked to the counter to pay, Mary Trout was there to accept his money. "Ellen is real busy right now," he said to the lady. "Will you give her a message for me?" Not waiting for an answer, he continued, "Tell her that I'll be over in the morning, that if it's not too cold, I'll be in the buggy."

She nodded. "Early in the morning?"

"About ten."

"I'll tell her." She leaned across the counter, speaking more softly now. "Ellen sure looks forward to your visits, Mr. Houston, and there's never a day goes by that she doesn't bring up your name."

"That's nice to hear," he said. "Good night."

He paid for two consecutive nights' lodging at the hotel, then walked into the saloon to find that the bartender was the only man in the room. Wesley Hawks sat on a stool behind the bar, reading a magazine. Camp offered the man what had become his usual greeting when entering the empty saloon: "How's business?"

Hawks laid the reading material aside. "I wish to hell you'd think of something new to say, Camp. Seems like everybody who walks through that door spits out that same tired joke."

"Well, pardon me all to hell, old buddy. I had no idea that it bothered you."

"Bother me? You know me better'n that, Camp. I was just kidding with you. I don't let anything bother me. I learned a long time ago that there wasn't a single thing in this world that I could change, so I just take it all however it comes. You gonna have a drink?"

"I'll just have a beer, Wes, something that won't cloud up my mind too much."

Hawks soon set a foamy mug in front of Houston, then slid his own stool down the opposite side of the bar. He poured himself a stiff drink of whiskey, then took a seat on the stool. "I hear the town council's gonna can Joe Paley's ass," he said, then took a sip from the glass.

Camp wiped the foam from his lips with his hand. "I heard the same thing," he said. "But I've learned to take most of the things I hear with a grain of salt."

"Me, too, but I think you can sort of count on that happening. Ned Riddle is the head councilman, and he's done said that Paley's got to go." He took another sip, then continued, "Of course, I didn't hear that from Riddle's own mouth, now. I got it secondhand, but the man who told me ain't one to go around spreading a buncha shit."

Camp finished off his beer. "Well, we'll see," he said, pushing his mug forward for a refill.

Two hours later, he climbed the stairs to his room. He crawled into bed and pulled up the covers quickly, for the night was cold. He lay wide awake for a while, thinking. He was hoping for some still air in the morning. The sun would surely shine, for that was almost a given at this time of the year. The wind was what made the difference. If it blew again tomorrow, he would sit by the fire with Ellen Bice. If not, he would show up in the buggy about ten.

Miss Ellen Bice. Since he had come to know her, it sounded like the prettiest name he had ever heard. And the girl herself was no less. She was a true beauty who was a joy to be around, and Camp got a warm feeling every time he thought of her. "There's never a day goes by that she doesn't bring up your name," her aunt Mary had said. Camp smiled into the darkness. He fluffed up his pillow and was soon sleeping soundly.

He left his bed at sunup, and was on the street a short while later. The morning air was still, and from all appearances, a beautiful day lay ahead. He stood around on the corner for a while, then stepped inside the small restaurant next door to the hotel, whose breakfast specialty was pork sausage, gravy and buttermilk biscuits. Once inside, he saw very quickly that he was not the only man who liked the simple things in life, and he had to stand in line for half an hour before he could even get a stool at the counter. Once he managed to get a seat, however, his food was not long in coming.

Once he was done eating, he was up from the stool and out of the building. He had plenty of time to kill and would normally have done it at that counter, but he did not possess the necessary gall to sit nursing a cup of coffee while hungry men stood in line waiting for a seat. Back on the street and looking down the hill to Blankenship's office, he could see smoke coming from the flue. Knowing that Sid always had a coffeepot on in the morning, he headed for the livery stable.

The liveryman sat in his office with a coffee cup in his hand. He got to his feet and filled another cup for Camp, then reseated himself. "I've been sitting right here for the past hour trying to come alive," he said. "I believe this is about my fourth cup of this damn stuff." He set the cup on the small table. "I think after you drink a certain amount of coffee, something happens to you, Camp. I mean, you finally get to where it won't even wake you up."

"I imagine that might be the case with most anything if a

man overdoes it, Sid. I've even heard that a drunkard finally reaches a stage where whiskey don't make him drunk anymore."

"Maybe so," Blankenship said. Then he began to laugh. "Hell, you can get drunk on coffee, Camp. I know that for a fact, 'cause I'm drunk on it right now."

They sat talking for more than an hour. Then, when told that he could use a rig free of charge if he roped and hitched up the animal himself, Camp grabbed a rope and headed for the corral. A short time later, he backed a harnessed mare between the shafts and hitched her to the buggy. Blankenship sat on an upended nail keg, watching. "That cargo you're gonna be hauling this morning is the best-looking thing in this town," he said to Camp. "But I suppose you knew that without being told."

Houston was bent over hooking up a trace chain. He straightened his body and made a show of trying to readjust his back with his hand. "I must admit that I had already noticed that, Sid." He climbed to the buggy seat. "I expect to be back before sunset, so I guess you'll still be here."

The liveryman made no effort to rise. "I don't know of anyplace I'd be going," he said. "I don't feel worth a damn today, Camp; felt bad when I woke up this morning." He pointed down the hall. "I've got to shoe that gray mule sometime this afternoon whether I get to feeling better or not, though. Man's coming by to get him before dark."

Houston nodded, then slapped the mare with the reins and headed up the street. He waved or nodded a greeting to the few acquaintances he passed, and soon left the town behind. Ten minutes later, he reached his destination. The Trouts lived in a small, two-story home a mile west of town and two hundred yards off the main road. The front porch was no more than six feet long, and most of the townfolk probably considered the place to be quite ordinary.

But there was nothing ordinary about it as far as Houston was concerned. He thought it was one of the prettiest places in the county, and kept so by a middle-aged couple who spent at least twelve hours a day, six days a week, at their restaurant. The white house with green trim always had the appearance of being painted yesterday, as did all three of the outbuildings.

And, of course, there was the matter of the lawn, which was two hundred yards long and a hundred yards wide. The grass was always well trimmed during the growing season, and several flower beds dotted the landscape. He doubted that the Trouts had ever employed a yard man, for Camp had often seen both the man and his wife working there on Sunday afternoons.

Henry Trout had spent several years in the United States Navy, which was where he had learned to cook. Upon his return to civilian life he had continued to earn his living as a chef, and had worked in a dozen different restaurants over the years. Then, when Riley's came on the market at a price they could afford, the couple jumped at the chance.

The navy had taught Henry Trout about as much as any man needed to know about food, Houston was thinking as he sat at the end of the long drive admiring the whitewashed trees in the yard. Maybe Trout had acquired his penchant for neatness there, too.

Camp trotted the mare down the drive, circled the tall mesquite and stopped in front of the doorway. The girl was already on the porch, smiling as always. "I saw you coming down the road, and wondered why you stopped."

He jumped to the ground. "I was just sitting there admiring this pretty place, and wondering how they're gonna keep it looking like this after I take you to Calf Creek."

She ignored his words, and reached for the door. "I'll be right back." Moments later, she placed a blanket and a picnic basket in the buggy, then held out her hand. He assisted her to the seat, then walked around the vehicle and joined her. "Where are we going today?" she asked, after they reached the main road.

"Same old place, I guess. The road along the San Saba's the only pretty place that's close enough to visit and still get back before dark." He placed his hand on hers, and could not resist adding, "I don't mind that at all, though, little one. One of these days we won't have to worry about the sun going down. We'll be spending all of our nights together after I take you to Calf Creek."

The girl looked straight ahead and said nothing for several minutes, causing Camp to rethink what he had just said. In fact, he had said almost the same thing to her several times in the past, and had always gotten about the same reaction. It was time for him to think of something different to say, he decided. "I'm sorry, Ellen," he said. "It finally dawned on me that you probably don't see any humor in what I've been saying about me taking you to Calf Creek. I won't say it anymore."

She squeezed his hand and smiled. "Thank you."

Though Camp always spoke in a jocular manner, and made sure that he had a smile on his face when he mentioned taking her to Calf Creek, he had never been joking. He had decided months ago that he would eventually ask her to be his wife. And he believed that she would agree if he gave her enough time and did not scare her off beforehand. Ma Franklin had told him exactly how it was with women. He would try to remember all of the things the lady had said, and be more careful of what came out of his own mouth from now on.

They spread the blanket on the riverbank in the early afternoon, where they ate a dinner of fried chicken and potato salad. "Did you cook this stuff yourself?" he asked, gnawing on a drumstick.

She smiled, then nodded. "Right after I got up and saw that we had a pretty day."

They sat on the blanket for the remainder of the afternoon, holding hands and talking. Houston tried to kiss her on the mouth once, but she moved her head quickly, and his lips barely touched her cheek. "I don't want to get into that," she said, sounding almost apologetic, "because I don't do anything halfway. I know what you want, and I know that I have it, but I'm not ready yet. I've got to have more time."

He continued to hold her hand, and apologized for the second time today.

The sun was still two hours high when he delivered Ellen Bice to her home. He had thoroughly enjoyed the day, despite his slight disagreement with the girl on how much kissing was too much. She had given him another peck on the cheek just before they reached her home, although she was careful to do it before they came in sight of the house.

As Houston turned off the main road he could see that both Henry Trout and his wife were busy working in the yard. He waved to them and continued on down the long drive. When the buggy reached the front door of the house, the mare stopped of her own accord. Then she turned her head and stood looking back at her passengers. Camp chuckled. "Smart mare," he said. The girl smiled at the incident also, but said nothing.

Camp wrapped the reins around the brake and jumped to the ground. He helped her from the buggy, then continued to stand with his hands encircling her small waist. "I'm down now," she said finally, smiling broadly and stepping backward out of his reach.

"I'm sorry," he said for the third time today, "but you just felt so nice and soft that I couldn't let go."

They stood holding hands for a few moments. "Good-bye for now," she said. She kissed his hand lightly, then stepped inside the house and closed the door.

He climbed into the buggy and slapped the mare's hip with the reins. He waved to the Trouts once again as he passed, then turned onto the main road.

25

★

He had traveled no more than halfway through town before he decided that things were not right. He had seen hardly anyone on the street, and as soon as he came within sight of the stable he could see that a crowd of men had gathered there. He urged the mare down the hill at a fast trot. He tied up at the hitching rail, and spoke to Corey Harned, a man he had known for many years. "What's going on here, Corey?"

"It's Sid," Harned answered, sounding as if he had a frog in his throat. "He's dead, Camp." The man's voice cracked and he swallowed hard several times. Corey Harned had been one of Blankenship's longtime friends, and was himself a respected blacksmith. Both Harned and his eldest son had in the past worked for Blankenship on a part-time basis, and Corey had on one occasion drawn a steady paycheck at the stable for three years running.

A brown-haired, muscular man of medium height and ap-

pearing to be about thirty-five years old, Harned had come to
Menardville from somewhere in Florida several years earlier,
traveling with a pregnant wife and a young son. He had
quickly convinced Sid that he needed another man around the
place and that he, Corey Harned, was that man. He had gone
on Blankenship's payroll immediately, and had stayed there
for the next three years. The man was good at what he did,
and Camp had several times stood around watching him shoe
horses, including Camp's own. Now Corey Harned was standing in front of him telling him that Sid Blankenship was dead.

Houston stood in his tracks for a while, dumbfounded.
"Dead?" he asked finally. "Sid? Hell, I just talked with him six
hours ago. He said he wasn't feeling good today, but I sure
didn't think—"

"He didn't just up and die, Camp," Harned interrupted.
"He was killed. That gray mule kicked him right square between the eyes. It was all just as plain as the nose on your face:
that mule tied to the post, and him standing right there beside
Sid's body. Already had three new shoes on, and the other
one was lying in the dirt beside Sid's hammer. If Sid coulda just
managed to nail the shoe on that last hind leg he'd have been
done, and he'd still be alive.

"As I said before, there ain't no question about what happened. The calks on that shoe left imprints on his forehead
just as plain as day." He shook his head a few times, then
continued, "What I'm having trouble understanding is Sid
being careless enough to let it happen. I've known him for a
long time, Camp, and I've never known him to give any animal a chance to do that. Especially one as unpredictable as a
damn mule."

"Who found the body?" Houston asked.

"Me," Harned said. "Me and my boy, Zac. We came
down here to talk about some work, see if he was gonna be
needing us again this spring. When I called his name and he
didn't answer, we walked on down the hall and there he was,
lying there with his eyes wide open."

"Is his body at home now?"

Harned nodded, and pointed to a wooden door leaning against the wall. "Four of us put him on that door right there and carried him up the hill. His wife wanted him put on his own bed, so that's where he is now. Dr. Henson has already been up there to look him over, and he said the same thing the rest of us did: that mule kicked him dead center."

Camp motioned toward the barn. "Is the mule still in there?"

"No. The old man that owned him took him outta here at a run, probably afraid somebody'd shoot him. Wouldn't nobody have bothered that mule, of course. That mule don't know that he's hurt a soul."

Camp was busy untying the mare. "No," he said. "The mule's not at fault." He parked the buggy underneath the shed, then unharnessed the mare and led her to water. Then, when he had dried and curried her coat, he left her in her usual stable with a bucket of oats and two blocks of hay. Moments later, he was walking up the hill to have a talk with Sid Blankenship's widow.

When the tiny, dark-haired woman met him at the door, she was sobbing uncontrollably, and almost fell into his arms. He hugged her shoulders, patted her back and let her cry. "It's awful, Camp," she said finally. "It's just awful."

"I know, Stella," he said softly. "I know." He continued to pat the top of her head, which was well below his own shoulder. "You've always been a strong woman, and you've got to be even stronger now. There's nothing in the world that you can do to change it, so you've got to learn to live with it. You've got children to raise."

"Oh, I know it. I know it."

He led her to the kitchen table and helped her into a chair. "Thank you, Camp," she said, "and thank you for coming." She wiped her eyes on a towel. "I . . . I'll be all right now."

He touched her shoulder. "Stay right here, Stella. I'll be

right back." He headed for the bedroom to view the body. It was not so much that he distrusted anyone; he merely wanted to satisfy himself that the cause of death had been correctly diagnosed.

Although the sun still shone brightly outside, the shades had been drawn on the bedroom windows. A coal-oil lamp on a bedside table provided as much light as Camp needed, however. He stood close to the bed, gazing solemnly at the face of his departed friend. Someone had washed the blood from his head and face, and a coin now lay on each eyelid. When Houston looked closely at the dead man's forehead, he could plainly see the imprints left by the calks on the animal's metal shoe. There was no doubt about it: the gray mule had ended the liveryman's life with one instinctive kick.

Houston returned to the table and took a seat beside the widow. There were other people about the house, for he could hear them talking, but none entered the kitchen. Maybe they sensed that the woman wanted to be alone with a close friend. Except for an occasional sniffle, she was quiet now, and though swollen, her eyes were dry. He reached across the table and covered one of her small hands with his own. "Is there anything I can do, Stella? Anything at all?"

Her answer was slow in coming. She got to her feet unsteadily, stoked the fire in the stove and pulled the coffeepot over the firebox. Then she placed two empty cups on the table and reseated herself. "I can't think of anything anybody can do, Camp. Other than the fact that we're gonna be by ourselves, I guess we'll make out all right. Sidney was always a good hand at putting most of his money by, so I don't reckon any of us'll go hungry."

"How about the livery stable?"

"Oh, I'll keep that," she answered quickly. "Selling that stable would be the last thing in the world Sidney would have wanted me to do. Besides, it provides us with a good, steady income. Corey Harned says he'll run the place for me, and you know yourself that he's a good man. I never mentioned it to my husband, of course, but I've heard that some people thought Corey might actually be a better blacksmith than Sidney."

"I don't know about that, but I've watched Corey work, and it's obvious that he knows what he's doing. He's well liked, so I believe that he can at least hang on to Sid's regular customers. I also believe that he's an honest man, so you'll get every dollar that's coming to you."

She nodded, and said nothing.

He got to his feet and poured their cups full of coffee, then reclaimed his chair. "Have you decided where you're gonna bury Sid?"

"Me and him talked about that very thing last winter," she said. "We both decided that we wanted to be buried over there on the hill above the old Spanish fort, so that's where we'll be taking Sidney tomorrow. I've done sent word to the undertaker, so he'll take care of getting the grave dug and everything. One thing Sidney didn't want is a lot of preaching. He just wanted some of his friends to speak a few words, whatever comes to their minds." She smiled weakly now. "He said the last thing he wants to hear before they cover him up with dirt is somebody singing his favorite song, "Home Sweet Home."* Do you know anybody who can carry a tune? Somebody who might know the right words?"

"Offhand, I can't say that I do. There are no professional singers around here, and talking somebody into singing a solo in public would be more than a little bit difficult. It might be a lot easier if we just ask all of his friends to sing the song together at graveside. I think about everybody knows most of the words."

She was thoughtful for a while. "Yes," she said finally, "I reckon that would be better. Hearing the voices that he rec-

---

*Written by John Howard Payne in 1823, it was one of the most popular songs in the West for the next hundred years.

ognizes would mean more to him anyhow. Somebody's gonna
have to lead 'em in the singing, though."

The funeral procession formed at the livery stable at one
o'clock the following afternoon. Because the deceased had
not been a churchgoer, and had requested that no preaching
take place at his funeral, the religious element was largely
missing. And since a majority of his friends were male, so was
the segment of the population who would be following the
body up the hill to its final resting place. Although he made no
effort to count them, Houston estimated the number of men
in the crowd to be about forty. The widow and her two
daughters were the only females present.

Stella Blankenship had politely refused the undertaker's
offer of a hearse. Her husband would want to ride up the hill
in one of his own wagons, she said, and that wagon should be
drawn by one of his own teams. Town Councilman Ned Riddle, who had largely taken charge of the funeral arrangements,
saw that the lady's wishes were carried out: the pine coffin
now lay in one of Sid's new wagons, with two of his black
horses in the traces.

The widow and her daughters sat on the seat of the
wagon, which would be the only vehicle involved. Everyone
else in the procession would be afoot, including both of the
dead man's young sons. No man in the crowd wore a sidearm,
though Camp's little Remington that sometimes rode in his
boot was now tucked away in his inside coat pocket. For a
man with his reputation and potential enemies to walk around
completely unarmed would have been pure folly, even in a funeral procession.

At a word from Riddle, who would lead the team, the procession began its slow trek up the hill. Camp Houston, accompanied by three other men, led the way, followed by the
wagon, then the remainder of the mourners.

At the top of the hill, two men standing beside mounds of
fresh dirt marked the location of the open grave. Camp saw

one of the men hide the picks and shovels behind a nearby bush as the procession drew near. Riddle parked the wagon a good forty feet away, for the last thing he wanted to see was the family of the deceased gazing down into that hole.

Several wooden benches had been set up, and four men now placed the coffin between the benches and the grave. The Blankenship family was then seated on the bench nearest the coffin. A few of the others seated themselves, but most remained standing.

Ned Riddle did not tarry. "We've all come together to say good-bye to a dear friend," he began, "and to offer our deepest regrets to his family. Sidney Blankenship was an asset to this community, a good-hearted soul who always had his hand out to help his fellow man." He hesitated for a moment, then added sheepishly, "In fact, I owed him eight dollars myself, a debt that I shoulda and coulda paid a long time ago. Of course, he won't need no money where he's at now, but I'll be handing it over to his widow before this day's out." He pointed to the coffin. "Right there lies the remains of one of the best men ever born." He motioned toward the crowd. "I'm sure there's somebody else here who can say it a lot better than I can, so I'll get out of the way."

No man moved or spoke. After enduring several moments of silence, Houston, who sat on the end of the family's bench, got to his feet, hat in hand. "I guess Ned has already described my own feelings for Sid Blankenship," he said. "I'd just like to add that Sid was one of the best men I've ever known, every day of the week, and I feel honored that he called me his friend." Camp returned to his seat, and the crowd was silent again.

After a few moments, Riddle was back on his feet. "The deceased himself chose the song he wanted to hear at his funeral. My own voice ain't much, so I'm asking all of you to join in and help me. I reckon you all know the words." Then he began to sing, waving his arm in an attempt to lead the others. No one else joined in the singing. Riddle rushed on alone, however, arriving at the last line of the song in less than a minute: "Be it ever so humble, there's no place like home." Then he raised both of his arms and shouted loudly, "I declare this funeral over and done! Let's all move back down the hill now. There are men here to inter the coffin after we're gone!"

The crowd dispersed. The wagon disappeared down the hill quickly as Corey Harned drove Stella Blankenship and her children home at a fast trot.

When Harned returned to the livery stable with the empty wagon, Houston was standing out front. "I wish you'd catch up my roan before you bother with the team, Corey," Camp said. "Even if I leave now, it'll be nearly midnight when I get home."

Harned nodded. "Won't be but a few minutes," he said. He tied the team to the hitching rail, then headed for the corral with a rope in his hand. Three minutes later, he was busy helping Houston saddle the roan.

Camp stopped at Riley's a few minutes later, and ordered a bowl of beef stew. Ellen Bice's face was a little longer than usual, probably because she knew that he was mourning the loss of a friend. "I'm real sorry about Mr. Blankenship," she said. "I know that the two of you were real close."

"It was an accident," he said, "and worrying about it is useless." He changed the subject. "I'm gonna empty this bowl as fast as I can, then head home. I've got a herd of cattle coming any day now, and I need to be there."

She laid her hand on his. "I understand, Camp, but please don't stay away any longer than you have to." Then she was gone to the kitchen. He paid his way out of the place a few minutes later, then mounted and headed for Calf Creek.

26

Two miles north of 3C headquarters, there was a plateau that was at least a mile long and half as wide. The area was treeless and almost brushless, and was probably the best graze on the premises. It was here that the cattle would first be driven. They would be allowed to graze on the plateau for the remainder of their first day on the 3C, then bedded down and guarded throughout the night. Next morning, the calves would be branded, then the herd would be allowed to scatter at will. The cows still belonged to John Butterworth, and would continue to wear the Lazy B brand.

On Wednesday morning, Houston and Fowler hauled two wagonloads of wood to the plateau, and off-loaded it in two separate piles. Mostly oak, it would burn slowly and create hot branding fires. Houston dropped off four branding irons at each woodpile. "I expected to hear something from Bo before now," he said. "You think he found that perch we told him about?"

"Oh, yeah," Runt answered. "If he don't find it right off he'll know it, and keep looking around till he does. He may be young, but that Georgia boy don't think near as slow as he talks."

Camp chuckled. "I know that for sure," he said.

At sunup that morning, Patton had been dispatched to a particular ridge four miles northeast of the ranch house. The ridge was the highest elevation within a twenty-mile radius, and would offer the youngster an unobstructed view for at least five miles in the direction of Mills County. When he spotted the cattle, Bo's instructions were to ride to the plateau to inform Houston and Fowler, each of whom had a saddled cow pony tied at the edge of the woods.

At the plateau, Camp sat on the tailgate of the wagon, his long legs resting on the ground. He took a sip of water from his canteen, then wiped his lips with his sleeve. "I'm just wondering if the drovers ran into some kind of problem, Runt. The cows ought to be here by now." When Fowler said nothing, Houston added, "I can't imagine an easier cattle drive. The only body of water they have to cross is Brady Creek, and I've never seen it much more than knee-deep."

"Quit worrying, Camp," fowler said, taking several swallows from his own canteen, then throwing it into the wagon with a loud thump. "The cows are coming."

Fowler had hardly finished speaking when Bo Patton rode out of the woods from the east. He sat his saddle a half mile away waving his hat, which was the agreed-upon signal. "See?" Fowler asked, pointing. "He's spotted the cows."

A few minutes later, Fowler untied their saddle horses at the south edge of the clearing, and Camp tied the wagon team to the same tree. Then both men mounted and headed east, joining Patton at the lower edge of the plateau.

They met the herd an hour later, and sat on a small rise waiting for the point man to reach them. The rider trotted up the slope on a small bay, and stopped almost within touching distance. A small man with sandy hair and a copper-colored beard, he spat a mouthful of tobacco juice, then spoke: "You Camp Houston?"

Camp nodded. "Sure am. What we—"

"Which way?" the man interrupted.

When Houston pointed west, the man motioned for him to get out of the way, then waved the drovers on up the slope. As the herd continued to move up the rise at a steady gait, the point man moved his bay alongside Houston's stirrup. "Didn't mean no disrespect back there. I just wanted to keep these critters moving. It's too damn hard to get 'em lined out again if we let 'em stop and start milling around."

"I understand perfectly," Camp said with a toothy smile. "I've been right where you are more than once." He offered a handshake. "I appreciate you fellows bringing 'em down."

"I'm Dub Hamilton," the drover said, pumping the hand, "and I'm in charge of the drive. I reckon I went to work at the Lazy B just a few days after you quit the job of ranch foreman. Everybody there spoke mighty highly of you."

"Well, that's nice to hear," Camp said, then introduced Runt Fowler and Bo Patton. Even as the men shook hands they continued to walk their horses west, and the cattle followed.

After meeting and sizing up Dub Hamilton, Camp had instructed Fowler and Patton to stay clear of the herd and offer no assistance whatsoever. Nor had he himself approached the cattle. Three hours later, however, when they came to the plateau, Houston made his wishes known. He met Hamilton in front of the herd and rode beside him stirrup to stirrup, pointing north all the while. "Lead 'em on down to the lower end of this plateau," he said, "then circle 'em back uphill and bring 'em to a halt. We'll let 'em graze the rest of the afternoon, then bed 'em down right here. We'll brand the calves tomorrow, then let 'em all scatter and hunt up some water."

Hamilton nodded obediently, and turned his horse downhill.

Then Camp rode at a canter to the top of the clearing,

where Fowler and Patton stood beside the wagon. "What do you think of Hamilton?" Runt asked as Camp dismounted.

"Aw, he's probably all right," Camp said as he tied his horse to a wagon wheel. "He might be a little bit touchy, but I don't guess it's carved in granite that we have to like him. He's already done everything that we needed him for, so as far as we're concerned, he can just head on back home now."

"You tell it while I pat my foot," Fowler said gruffly. "I can tell by his actions that I don't like him, and I ain't likely to the next time I see him."

"Mr. Butterworth said that four men are gonna stay here to help us," Patton said, "and that ain't but half of this bunch. I've already counted eight men, so I guess four of 'em'll be going back home right off. I believe Mr. Hamilton'll be among that four. Might leave this afternoon, if we're lucky."

Patton's prediction proved to be accurate. The herd had no more than been circled back into itself and the cattle begun to graze when Hamilton approached Houston's wagon. "The boss told me to leave four men with you," he said, "so I'll be leaving the Brown brothers, Weed Ellum, and Sim Waltrip. I reckon feeding them's gonna be your problem, so I'll take the cook and the pack animals on back to the Lazy B with me." Although it was considered a breach of western etiquette for a mounted man to attempt to carry on a conversation with a man on the ground, and even worse to offer a handshake to any man who was not also mounted, Hamilton continued to sit his saddle as he extended his right hand. "We'll be leaving now," he said.

Camp walked the few steps and took Hamilton's hand. "Tell John that we're all thinking of him," he said. "Tell him I'll be up to see him some time this summer."

Hamilton nodded, then whirled his bay and went down the hill at a canter. The three men who would accompany him back to the Lazy B waited at the edge of the clearing. All four disappeared toward the northeast a few minutes later, the lead ropes seeming to stretch the necks of the lagging pack mules.

Camp motioned down the hill to the mounted men. "Know any of 'em, Runt?"

Fowler squinted into the late afternoon sun, then shaded his eyes with his hand. "That short one might be Low Boy Brown. Looks like him from here, anyway. And that fellow talking to him right now might be his younger brother, Harmon. Everybody calls Harmon High Boy, 'cause he's at least a foot taller than Low Boy."

Houston chuckled. "High Boy and Low Boy, huh?"

"Yep," Fowler said, untying his horse. "High Boy's about six-two, and Low Boy ain't but five feet. Why there's so much difference in the size of 'em is anybody's guess. Just looking at 'em you'd have to say that they had the same daddy, 'cause they look as much alike as two peas in a pod." He mounted, and turned his horse down the hill. "Big pea and little pea," he added.

Houston and Patton mounted and followed Fowler down the hill, and within minutes, Fowler and Low Boy Brown had introduced every member of both groups. Runt had been correct in his identification of the Brown brothers, both of them lean, wiry, dark-complected men with black beards.

Weed Ellum was the tallest of the bunch, and had no doubt come by his nickname because of the fact that he was so skinny. Camp estimated that the man would weigh about a hundred forty pounds with his boots on. He had blue eyes, a ruddy complexion and blond hair that curled around his ears. He appeared to be about thirty years old, and had the firmest handshake of any man in the group.

A man of medium height and weight, Sim Waltrip was the least talkative of the drovers. His gray hair, badly in need of a trim, hung around his neck and ears loosely, and he appeared to be well past the age when most men hung up their spurs and sought a different line of work. However, the fact that looks can be deceiving was once again brought home to Houston as Waltrip dropped Camp's hand in the middle of a handshake and galloped up the hill like a man half his age. A cow had bolted from the herd and headed for the woods at the top of the plateau. Waltrip beat her to the timber, and lashed her back into the herd with his rope. Houston had sat watching. *Nope, Sim Waltrip's not quite done yet,* he was thinking.

Hamilton had left the bedrolls belonging to Waltrip, Ellum and the Brown brothers, along with a large tarpaulin, in a pile at the eastern edge of the clearing. Pointing in that direction, Houston spoke to Patton: "Take the wagon and move those bedrolls up the hill, Bo. Drop 'em off right there by the woodpiles, where the branding fires are gonna be. Then I suppose you ought to build a campfire and get supper started. This is gonna be a hungry bunch."

Half an hour later, Patton had a campfire going in the levelest place he could find. The two big boxes that Fowler had loaded onto the wagon that morning were now resting on the tailgate, along with two coffeepots. Several jugs of water were also in the wagon. Fowler had brought twelve tin cups, the same number of tin plates, and enough spoons for a small army, for he had had no way of knowing how many men would have to be fed.

There was a big iron pot half full of presoaked beans, and a hindquarter of venison wrapped in oilcloth. One of the boxes contained two cakes of corn bread and twenty biscuits, along with salt, pepper and sugar for coffee. As he peered into the boxes, taking stock of the things on hand, Patton quickly decided that he himself had little to do. He would simply add water to the pot and put the beans on to boil, fry up a dozen slices of venison and make two pots of coffee, then get the hell out of the way. He stoked the fire again, then reached for a jug of water.

Houston and Fowler had both joined the drovers in chasing cows back into the herd. Surprisingly, not a single one of the bulls had attempted to quit the bunch, and even as Camp watched, one of them had found a willing cow and was busy earning his keep. The cow now being bred had a calf beside her that was no more than two months old.

"We call her Old Broke Horn," Weed Ellum said to Camp, pointing. "Mr. Butterworth says she's eleven years old, and has calved like clockwork every eleven months since she was a yearling."

Houston smiled. "Good," he said. "She's exactly the kind of cow I need."

The riders continued to circle the cattle, never crowding them, giving them plenty of room to graze like there was no tomorrow. Finally, with full bellies and the sun about to set, they began to lie down: first one, then two, then ten, then a hundred head. When only one old bull was left standing, Fowler chuckled and pointed. "Makes me want to go up there and kick his legs out from under him."

"He's the boss," Waltrip said. "That sonofabitch would charge you like a tiger if you went up there messing with him or any of his girlfriends. Especially if you happened to be afoot."

Because the moon was already up when the sun went down, there never was a period of total darkness on the plateau, and none of the cows could hope to sneak away from the herd without an alert cow pony being right on her tail. Eventually, the cattle seemed to reach that same conclusion, and simply lay around chewing their cuds.

Two hours after sunset, Patton began to feed the riders two at a time, while the other four continued to hold a circle around the herd. Though the cattle were all lying down now, Houston was taking no chances. "These old cows have been through it all before," he said to Weed Ellum. "They know exactly what's gonna happen in the morning, and they're probably lying there right now trying to figure out some way to hide their calves in the brush."

"Hell, yes, they are," Ellum agreed. "I've seen it a hundred times: about the time you get to thinking you've got 'em under control"—he snapped his fingers—"they're gone." He motioned toward the still herd. "If that bunch right there all of a sudden took it in their little minds to head for the brush, it would happen so damn quick that anybody who ain't seen it wouldn't believe it. Within one minute we wouldn't have the slightest damned idea which way any of them went."

"Well, the fact that they're all old cows makes 'em less likely to run," Houston said. "They don't have as much get-up-and-go as they once did."

When all of the riders had been fed, Camp announced that Fowler and he would take the first watch. "You fellows go ahead and hit your bedrolls," he said to the Lazy B men. "You've all been putting in some long days, and Runt and I haven't been straining ourselves lately. The two of us'll stay with the cows till after midnight, then I'll wake Ellum and Waltrip. Then about three o'clock in the morning they can wake the Brown brothers and let them finish out the night." He stepped into a stirrup and threw his leg over the saddle. "Is that agreeable to everybody?" Several of the men mumbled assents, then headed for their bedrolls.

Houston and Fowler then rode down the hill and began to circle the herd in opposite directions. Though the campfire was allowed to die, two lanterns burned all night. "We ought to keep some kinda light going," Waltrip had said early in the evening. "Cattle associate lanterns with humans. As long as they can see the light from that lantern they know that humans are on guard, and that no predator is gonna come anywhere near the herd."

Houston had never before given any thought to what the man was saying, but it certainly made sense. Besides, Waltrip had been herding cattle longer than most of the others had been alive, and Camp was not about to take the man's advice lightly. He ordered Patton to place one burning lantern next to the wagon and another at the bottom of the hill, on the opposite side of the herd.

The night passed without incident, and Patton rekindled the fire at daybreak. He made two pots of coffee, then put the leftover beans and venison on the fire. Then he called to the sleeping drovers, all of whom rolled out of their blankets and walked to the woods to relieve themselves, then congregated around the fire.

"Ain't got much to offer for breakfast, men," Patton said as he poured each man's coffee cup full. "Just more of what we had for supper. Soon as we get done with the branding, I'll fix a good dinner back at the house." He pointed to the cattle. "Mr. Waltrip says there ain't more'n about fifty of them calves, and that we'll have 'em marked, branded, cut and sent running long before dinnertime."

No man complained as each of the riders picked up a tin plate and lined up for the leftovers. "Hell, this stuff tastes better than what I've been getting at home," one man said after a while.

Camp had been busy building a branding fire. When it was roaring, he joined the men at the campfire. "As soon as that burns down a little, we'll start heating the irons," he said. "I had intended to use two fires, but we don't have as many calves as I expected. With one man holding 'em down and another man branding, cutting and marking them, we should run through this little bunch in two hours or less. We'll need two men roping, and the other two will be responsible for holding the herd together while the branding's taking place." He turned to Patton. "Bo, you'll be the man who keeps the irons hot. I mean red-hot." Patton nodded, and headed for the branding fire.

As Camp filled his coffee cup, Low Boy Brown walked to the fire and stood beside him. "Ain't none of my business to be trying to line things out here," he said, "but I believe it would all move along faster if you let me and my brother do the roping. Of course, Runt is the biggest one here, so he oughta do the holding and let Sim do the branding and castrating. Sim's mighty good at that. That'll leave you and Weed to make sure the herd don't leave the county while we're busy with the calves."

Camp took a sip of coffee, then chuckled. "Hell, Low Boy, I believe you've already got things lined out. Just go over there and tell everybody what they're supposed to be doing. Then as soon as the irons get hot we'll get on with it. You and Harmon just drag 'em up to the fire. Fowler's plenty big enough to hold 'em."

The branding got under way a few minutes later, and was over in less than two hours. Fifty-seven calves now wore the 3C brand, thirty-two of them heifers. Camp stood watching as the drovers headed the herd toward Calf Creek, then allowed them to scatter at will. Thirty-two heifers! he was thinking. Nothing to boast about, but it was a start. They would all calve next year, and their offspring would do the same the next. And the cycle would continue indefinitely. Indeed, a million head of cattle would eventually walk the earth whose bloodlines could be traced right back to the thirty-two head of heifers they had just branded. As the last of the calves disappeared into the underbrush, Houston stood shaking his head at the wonderment of it all.

Patton poured a jug of water on the fire, and a short while later, with the remainder of the wood and all of their bedrolls loaded onto the wagon, they were ready to head for the ranch house. Fowler untied the team, then motioned Patton up to the driver's seat. "I guess we'd better get on home and eat that good meal you promised us, Bo." The youngster climbed to the seat and clucked to the team, and all of the mounted men followed the wagon.

27

Butterworth's riders stayed on the 3C for nine days. On the tenth morning, with a bedroll tied behind each saddle, they rode into the yard to say good-bye to the ranch's three residents. "You've all treated us quite nicely," Waltrip was saying. "If any of you ever come up to the Lazy B, we'll try to return the favor."

"Oh, I'll be up there eventually," Fowler said, "If for no other reason than to see if that barn I built is still standing."

Waltrip sat thoughtful for a while. "Didn't know you built it," he said finally, "but it's sure as hell standing. Best barn in Mills County."

Fowler nodded, and accepted the compliment with a smile.

Bo Patton spoke to no one in particular: "I never have seen a ranch anywhere near as big as the Lazy B. Maybe Camp'll let me ride along with him next time he comes up there."

Although he had heard the youngster's words, Camp stood

by noncommittally. Then he addressed the riders as a group: "I appreciate it all, fellows. Tell John that I'll see him later in the year."

"Will do," Weed Ellum said. He pointed toward the shed, adding, "We left that heavy tarp in your wagon. It's cumbersome as hell without a packhorse, and don't none of us feel like fooling with it. You'll have a need for it sooner or later."

"I'm sure I will," Houston said. He tilted his head skyward, inspecting the clouds. "I don't think it's gonna rain in the near future, so you won't need the tarp when you make camp tonight."

Ellum glanced toward the Brown brothers, and all three began to chuckle. "Make camp?" he asked. "Hell, we ain't gonna be making camp. Today is Friday, and there ain't no way in the world that we're gonna show up at the Lazy B on a weekend. We'll just ride up to Brady and have us a blowout tonight and tomorrow night, then start moping on back home Sunday morning." When all three of his companions nodded their assents, Ellum yanked on his horse's reins. "Hallelujah!" he shouted loudly, and led the way down the hill.

"I like all of them men," Patton said, as the riders disappeared up the road toward Brady. "I reckon they know just about everything there is to know about cattle, and I learned something from every single one of 'em."

Houston nodded. "They know what they're doing," he said. "Otherwise, they wouldn't be working for John Butterworth." He headed for the corral, and motioned for Patton to follow. "Runt's gonna be busy stretching string and driving stakes today, Bo. He's decided to get started on that bunkhouse he's been talking about for months." He pointed to the horses. "Put your saddle on one of them, then fill our canteens with fresh water. Better wrap us up a bite to eat, too. You and I are gonna be riding boundaries today."

With biscuits, venison and a full canteen of water in each of their saddlebags, they mounted two of the black cutting horses a short time later. As Blankenship had predicted, all four of the animals had turned out to be good cow ponies. Camp pointed up the hill to the north. "You know where all of the boundaries are, Bo. Ride north to the northeast corner, then west to the northwest corner, then turn south. You should meet me sometime around noon, 'cause I'll be circling in the opposite direction."

Patton nodded. He kneed his horse, and the animal jumped instantly. "One more thing!" Houston called after him. Patton brought the black to an abrupt halt, and sat listening to his boss. "If you have to chase any cows back onto the 3C," Camp continued, "hit 'em hard enough to hurt 'em. If you lash 'em as hard as you can with the end of that rope, they'll remember it."

Patton turned his horse's head north again. "I'll whip 'em good," he said, "but I sure don't think they'll remember it." He headed north at a canter.

Houston turned his own mount south. "I don't either," he said softly.

He rode south into Mason County till he reached the southeast corner of his property, then turned west. Two hours later, he was at the southwest corner, in Menard County. He took a sip of water from his canteen, then headed north at a slow walk. He had been riding for almost four hours, and had not seen a single cow. All of which could be a good sign, he was thinking. It could mean that the cattle had found suitable graze in the vicinity of Calf Creek, and were content to remain somewhere near the center of the ranch.

He met Patton an hour later. "Have you seen any cattle, Bo?"

"Not a cow," the lanky youngster answered, dismounting. "It's like they all just flew away." He unwrapped his biscuits and venison, and took a seat on a log.

Camp joined him, and also began to eat. "If the cows have bunched up around the creek, which I believe is the case, I'm gonna be real pleased, Bo. Of course, when they eat everything in sight they'll scatter to hell and gone, but they'll be more familiar with the ranch by then. So will we, for that matter."

Patton washed down a mouthful of food. "I stopped once in a while just trying to hear a cow, but I never heard a sound."

"Like I said, I believe they've settled in close to the creek for the time being. The grass is good, and they don't have to hunt water. We'll finish eating, then cut right through the middle of the ranch. If they're on the creek, we'll see 'em."

As they made their way home, they found the cattle easily. Sitting their saddles on a hilltop above the creek, they could see at least a hundred head, some grazing alone, but most in bunches of ten or twenty. "Let's turn south and ride around them," Camp said. "We certainly don't want to upset this good thing we've got going."

Early Saturday morning, Houston saddled the roan and rode off the hill on his way to Menardville. As he had done several times before, he would spend the night at the hotel, then call on Ellen Bice the next day. Though the day was starting out unseasonably warm, and he rode in his shirtsleeves, his fleece-lined coat was tied behind the cantle, for he knew that the area's weather could change drastically from one day to the next.

He allowed the roan to set the pace, and as usual, the animal chose the canter. Always the canter, and the horse would hold the same gait until he began to tire, which was usually about halfway between Calf Creek and Menardville.

He arrived at the livery stable at midafternoon, and Corey Harned was standing out front. Camp dismounted, and immediately noticed the double-barreled, ten-gauge shotgun leaning against the wall just inside the doorway. He pointed to the weapon. "What are you gonna do with that cannon, Corey? Are you expecting somebody to try to rob you?"

Harned pointed up the street. "There's a shitstorm going on uptown, Camp, and I'm just making sure that I don't get caught off-guard. Got me two barrels of double-aught buck there."

Houston handed over his horse's reins. "You say there's a problem uptown?"

Harned dropped the reins to the ground. "You damn well said it. Joe Paley's already killed Ned Riddle, and shot Sheriff McMichen in the leg. I'll tell you right now, he sure as hell better not come down here—"

"Whoa, Corey," Camp interrupted. "Why don't you start all over and tell me what's going on?"

The liveryman related the story as Houston leaned against the wall, listening. The town council had voted to relieve Paley of his duties as town marshal, and, as head councilman, it had been Riddle's job to inform Paley of the decision. Riddle had fired the man late yesterday afternoon, and demanded his badge right on the spot.

Paley had spent the rest of the day hunting up one councilman after another. Cursing and calling them names, he informed every member that, regardless of their votes to the contrary, he was still the marshal of this town. He was the only lawman Menardville needed, he said, and he fully intended to serve out the remainder of his term.

"I reckon Paley must have just seethed on it all night," Harned added, "because about eight o'clock this morning, he put a bullet right between Ned Riddle's eyes."

Camp was still leaning against the wall. "Do you know where Ned was when Paley shot him?"

"Right on the damn street, is what I heard. I ain't been up there myself, but I've been told that he was walking up the hill toward his office, and that Paley just stepped right up to him and blasted him in the face."

Camp stood thoughtful for a while. "Do you know where Paley is now?" he asked finally.

"Locked himself in his office . . . I mean, what used to be

his office. I reckon he's still there. One of the councilmen sent a rider after the sheriff, but hell, Paley ain't scared of him. McMichen walked up there to try to talk Paley into coming out, but Paley put a bullet through his leg and sent him hopping back down the hill. McMichen's deputy ain't around to take a hand, 'cause him and two more men that the sheriff deputized are on their way to the Huntsville penitentiary to deliver a prisoner." Harned exhaled loudly. "I tell you, there ain't no telling what the hell's gonna happen next."

"Where's the sheriff now, Corey?"

"Up there at Riley's, I guess. At least that's where he was a few minutes ago. I heard that his wound ain't bad at all, that the bullet went clean through his leg without hitting anything that's gonna cripple him." He began to laugh loudly. "I'll betcha one damn thing. I'll betcha there ain't nobody having to hold him down to keep him from rushing back up that hill."

Houston smiled, and said nothing.

Twenty minutes later, he stepped into Riley's Restaurant to discover that the place was filled almost to capacity. Though he was well acquainted with most of the men in the room, he spoke to no one as he made his way to a table along the rear wall, where, with a white bandage around his left thigh, Sheriff McMichen was seated with two men Houston had never seen before.

The sheriff used his good leg to push out a chair as Camp drew near. "Mr. Houston!" he said loudly. "Have a seat, and tell me what you think we ought to do."

Camp remained standing. "About what?" he asked.

"Well, uh . . . I just thought you might have some ideas about how to get Paley out of that office. I'm gonna charge him with murder and attempted murder."

"Do you know of any reason he'd have for killing Ned Riddle, Sheriff? I mean, other than the fact that Riddle fired him?"

McMichen shook his head. "Hell, no," he said. "That's it

in a nutshell. Paley thinks he's God's gift to the rest of us poor souls. He's been strutting up and down the street like the cock of the walk for so long that he just couldn't handle it when the council voted him out. That man don't give a damn about nobody, Mr. Houston." He pointed to his bandaged leg. "Hell, you see what he done to me just 'cause I went up there and tried to talk some sense into him."

Houston nodded. "I see."

It was then that he spotted Ellen Bice. Standing next to the kitchen's batwing doors, she was looking directly at him and smiling. He walked to meet her. "I finally got my cattle moved onto the 3C," he said. "Then I just had to see you."

Her hair was down on her shoulders again today, and she had never looked prettier to him. "Thank you," she said. "I'll be up early in the morning."

He pointed across the room. "Will you bring me a cup of coffee and a plate of something good? I'll be sitting over there with the sheriff."

She nodded, and headed for the kitchen.

When he returned to McMichen's table, the lawman introduced his friends, each of whom appeared to be past the age of sixty. Camp shook hands with Bill Hardwick and Manley Jefferson, then accepted the chair and seated himself. "What's wrong with just waiting Paley out, Sheriff? I mean, how long do you think he can stay locked up in that office?"

"Could be a good while. I know he keeps that two-gallon bucket full of water all the time. He's probably got a buncha tinned meat, too."

Hardwick nodded, and wiped his gray beard out of his mouth. "Even if he ain't got nothing to eat he could hold out for a long time. A man can live several weeks without food if he's got plenty of water. Now, if he's got two gallons of that, he ain't likely to come out of there anytime soon."

Houston sat listening as the others talked among themselves. Only when Ellen placed a platter of stuffed pork chops and fried potatoes before him did he speak again. "I'll bet that's just as good as it looks," he said, then dug in.

"I guess a bunch of us could just storm that office and take Paley out of there," Manley Jefferson said. "Probably a dozen men right here in this room who'd be for that."

Houston sat looking around the room for a while, then shook his head. "I don't think you'll find many men in here who are willing to do any storming with you, Mr. Jefferson. They've all seen what happened to Ned Riddle and the sheriff, and they also know that there's no cover whatsoever on the front side of that building. There's not a tree or even a stump within thirty yards of the front door. It would be like shooting fish in a barrel to Paley, and I don't suppose there's anybody left who doubts that he'll shoot."

Jefferson pushed back his chair. "One way to find out," he said. "Let me just talk to a few of—"

"Forget it, Manley," Hardwick interrupted. "This man here's exactly right: that storming idea ain't gonna do nothing but get a bunch of men killed." Jefferson stood quietly for a few moments, then reseated himself.

Hardwick placed his elbows on the table and leaned forward. "That front door ain't the only way into that office, Mr. Houston. You see, I worked on one of the crews that put up that building, twenty years ago. We built the jail, too. There are five of them offices under the same roof, with connecting doors between them." He leaned closer and spoke more softly. "In other words, if you get inside one of 'em, you've got access to all of 'em. The tax assessor's office is on the west side, with three rooms between it and the marshal's office. I remember for sure that we didn't put no locks on them doors, and I don't guess anybody else ever did. Wouldn't have been no reason for it, 'cause there ain't nobody s'posed to have nothing to hide."

Having cleaned his plate, Houston sat for a while without speaking. He was quietly trying to figure out what might be going on in Joe Paley's mind. The man had to know that he would have to come out of the office sooner or later, and that he would eventually have to face a jury. He had killed an unarmed man who was well liked in the community, and put a bullet through the county sheriff's thigh. Had Paley intended to kill McMichen rather than wound him? Houston believed that he had, otherwise he would have shot lower.

Although the conversation at the table continued, Camp scarcely heard a word. He was concentrating on the long building at the top of the hill, for he had decided to try to get Joe Paley out of it. "Any windows between those rooms, Mr. Hardwick?" he asked.

"No. We just put two windows in each office, both of 'em on the front side."

When Camp was quiet for a while, the sheriff spoke: "Are you thinking about trying to get at Paley, Mr. Houston?"

Camp nodded.

"Here," McMichen said, fishing around in his pocket. "Let me give you this, so you'll have some authority." He laid a deputy sheriff's badge in Houston's hand. "I hereby appoint you a deputy sheriff of Menard County, Texas." He looked toward Hardwick and Jefferson. "You men heard me deputize Mr. Houston, now, so you're both witnesses to the fact."

The men nodded. "That we are," Hardwick said.

Houston put the badge in his pocket. "Have you got any prisoners in your jail, Sheriff?"

"Nope. Last one I had is on his way to the Huntsville pen right now."

Houston drummed his fingers on the table for a moment. "Give me the key to that big cell right down the hall from your desk," he said.

McMichen handed him a roll of keys. "It's that square-ended one right—"

"Take it off of the ring, Sheriff," Camp interrupted. "I don't want anything on me that might rattle." He pocketed the single key a moment later, then spoke again: "I'll take it as a favor if all three of you men'll sit right here till you hear from me again. And don't say a word about this to anybody."

"We'll be here," the sheriff said as both of the others nodded.

Camp walked through the front door and turned left. He circled the restaurant on its south side, and headed north. After traveling about two hundred yards, he turned west and walked at a fast clip till he reached the top of the hill. Then he turned south through the woods that grew right up to the rear of the building, with the tops of some of the trees hanging over its roof.

He moved from tree to tree cautiously till he eventually worked his way to the west end of the building. He peered around the southwest corner and saw no one. Nor could he see anyone on the street in the direction of town. He added a sixth shell to the cylinder of his Colt, then shoved the weapon back into its holster. Then he stood looking down the front side of the building to the marshal's office, knowing that Joe Paley could not see him without first stepping outside.

Houston saw little danger to himself in what he was doing, for he had no intention of letting Paley see him. He had climbed the hill counting entirely on the off chance that a door or window had been left unlocked on one of the offices. He pinned the deputy's badge to his shirt, then leaned against the end of the building and took off his boots. Then he stepped onto the porch in his stocking feet, dreading the creak of a board that did not come.

He peeked into a window of the tax assessor's office and saw nothing but a counter and the wall beyond. Paying close attention to its construction, he could see that the window had no locking device, so he believed that he could raise it. How much noise that would make remained to be seen. One long step carried him past the window and to the door. When he tested the knob it turned easily, and the door was suddenly ajar. Whether it had been left unlocked out of carelessness or habit was anybody's guess.

He paused for a few moments, then pushed it open noise-lessly and stepped inside. He noticed immediately that the door connecting this office to the adjoining one was in the middle of the east wall. He could see that it had no locking de-vice, or even a knob. Much like the doors of some saloons, it simply hung there on hinges, and could be opened from either side with a slight push.

He had no more than crossed the room to the connecting door when he heard someone moving in the adjacent office, making no effort whatsoever to muffle the sound of their foot-falls. Houston read the situation instantly: obviously, it had fi-nally dawned on Joe Paley that he might be vulnerable from this end of the building, and he was on his way to check it out.

Knowing that the ex-marshal was about to walk through the doorway, Houston drew his gun and moved to the north side of the door, the side the hinges were on. Camp could hear the man walking around in the adjoining room, no doubt checking the front door and the windows.

Moments later, when Paley pushed his way into the tax as-sessor's office, the door he stood holding open was at the same time hiding Houston. Then, gun in hand, Paley removed his hand from the swinging door and walked across the room, paying all of his attention to the front door. Houston stepped in behind him. "Drop the gun, Paley!" he said loudly. "Don't even think about putting up a fight!"

Paley stood motionless and held on to his gun, no doubt weighing his chances. "Houston?" he asked finally.

"That's right," Houston said. "For the time being I'm Deputy Sheriff Camp Houston, and you're under arrest. Drop the gun! Drop it now!" Though he was slow about it, Paley finally complied with the order. "Move over there and face the wall," Camp commanded. "Put both hands high above your head, palms flat against the wall."

Camp searched the man thoroughly, including his boots, but found no other weapon. He picked up the ex-marshal's

Peacemaker from the floor. "Clasp your hands behind you, Paley," he said with authority. "Then we're gonna walk over to the sheriff's office real slowly. We'll be stopping at that first cell behind the sheriff's desk."

A few moments later, Houston locked Paley in a cell that the ex-marshal knew very well, for he himself had caged dozens of men there in the past. "I suppose somebody'll see about getting you some food and water pretty soon," Camp said, pocketing the heavy key.

"How come you don't do it?" Paley asked sneeringly. "You're the one locking me up."

Houston spoke over his shoulder: "I'm not gonna have time, Paley. I'm on my way right now to resign this deputy sheriff's job." He was quickly out the front door. He retrieved his footwear, then walked down the hill.

When he entered Riley's Restaurant a few minutes later, he saw all of the same faces. Indeed, it appeared that nobody had even moved during his absence. He walked straight to McMichen's table and laid the badge and the key before the aging man. "I'm resigning the deputy's job, Sheriff. Joe Paley's locked in that first cell behind your desk. Maybe you ought to see that he gets something to eat."

With one hand on the table and the other on the back of his chair, the sheriff pushed himself to his good leg. "You hear that, everybody?" he asked loudly. "Listen up, everybody! Camp Houston just yanked Joe Paley out of that office and locked him up in jail, where he belongs!"

The applause was both loud and immediate. "Camp Houston for marshal!" one man yelled. "Camp Houston for sheriff!" shouted another.

Houston began to wave his hands from side to side to discourage the adulation, frowning and shaking his head in an effort to convince them all that he was not the least bit interested in either job. He spun on his heel and headed for the front of the building, only to have Ellen Bice step between him and the door. She had a serious look on her face that he had not seen before. "Do you still want to take me to Calf Creek?" she asked softly.

He stood speechless for a moment as he realized what the beautiful Ellen Bice was saying. "You . . . I . . ." he stammered, then started over: "I've always been serious about that, Ellen. I've always—"

"I'll be waiting at home in the morning," she interrupted. "My bags are already packed." Then she headed for the kitchen.

He stepped through the door and stood in the gathering darkness for a few moments thinking, finding it hard to believe that he was about to get what he wanted most. The lovely Ellen Bice was about to become the mistress of the 3C Ranch. He would rent a team and wagon as soon as the livery stable opened in the morning, and pick her up early. Hell, he knew a preacher who lived right beside the Calf Creek road. He chuckled aloud, shot his fist into the air and headed for the hotel saloon to break the news to Wesley Hawks. This called for a cup of good rum. Two . . . three cups of good rum.

Available by mail from

1812 • David Nevin
The War of 1812 would either make America a global power sweeping to the pacific or break it into small pieces bound to mighty England. Only the courage of James Madison, Andrew Jackson, and their wives could determine the nation's fate.

PRIDE OF LIONS • Morgan Llywelyn
Pride of Lions, the sequel to the immensely popular *Lion of Ireland,* is a stunningly realistic novel of the dreams and bloodshed, passion and treachery, of eleventh-century Ireland and its lusty people.

WALTZING IN RAGTIME • Eileen Charbonneau
The daughter of a lumber baron is struggling to make it as a journalist in turn-of-the-century San Francisco when she meets ranger Matthew Hart, whose passion for nature challenges her deepest held beliefs.

BUFFALO SOLDIERS • Tom Willard
Former slaves had proven they could fight valiantly for their freedom, but in the West they were to fight for the freedom and security of the white settlers who often despised them.

THIN MOON AND COLD MIST • Kathleen O'Neal Gear
Robin Heatherton, a spy for the Confederacy, flees with her son to the Colorado Territory, hoping to escape from Union Army Major Corley, obsessed with her ever since her espionage work led to the death of his brother.

SEMINOLE SONG • Vella Munn
"As the U.S. Army surrounds their reservation in the Florida Everglades, a Seminole warrior chief clings to the slave girl who once saved his life after fleeing from her master, a wife-murderer who is out for blood." —*Hot Picks*

THE OVERLAND TRAIL • Wendi Lee
Based on the authentic diaries of the women who crossed the country in the late 1840s. America, a widowed pioneer, and Dancing Feather, a young Paiute, set out to recover America's kidnapped infant daughter—and to forge a bridge between their two worlds.

Call toll-free 1-800-288-2131 to use your major credit card or clip and send this form below to order by mail

--- ✂ ---

Send to: Publishers Book and Audio Mailing Service
PO Box 120159, Staten Island, NY 10312-0004

☐ 52471-3	1812	$6.99/$8.99	☐ 53657-6	Thin Moon and Cold Mist.	$6.99/$8.99
☐ 53650-9	Pride of Lions . . .	$6.99/$8.99	☐ 53883-8	Seminole Song.	$5.99/$7.99
☐ 54468-4	Waltzing in Ragtime	$6.99/$8.99	☐ 55528-7	The Overland Trail	$5.99/$7.99
☐ 55105-2	Buffalo Soldiers	$5.99/$7.99			

Please send me the following books checked above. I am enclosing $_____. (Please add $1.50 for the first book, and 50¢ for each additional book to cover postage and handling. Send check or money order only—no CODs).

Name _____

Address _____ City _____ State _____ Zip_____

Westerns available from